"Tell me, Lili, did you like that kiss?"

"Yes, I did," she said softly. "It was like nothing I ever knew before. . . ."

She stopped, horrified at what she had almost revealed. She wondered why he continued to stare at her, his gaze so forceful it made it impossible for her to look away, and she was stunned when he took her in his arms and bent his head to kiss her. She closed her eyes. Her heart began to pound. Halpern's lips were insistent and not a bit gentle, but she did not feel threatened. She could feel his hands on her back right through her habit and shirt and shift. She prayed he would not let her go, for she was sure she would collapse in a heap on the ground if he did not support her.

It seemed an age before he lifted his head an inch or so and said in a hoarse voice, "Did you like it better than my kiss, Lili . . . ?"

REGENCY ROMANCE

COMING IN JUNE

A Diamond in the Rough
by Andrea Pickens

A young woman defies convention by posing as a young male caddie on a golf course—only to fall for an English lord and score in the game of love.

0-451-20385-2/$4.99

A Rake's Fiancée by Martha Kirkland

Fate casts a newly titled baron back into the life of the woman who once rejected him. Does he truly desire revenge, or something more passionate?

0-451-20260-0/$4.99

Hide and Seek by Sandra Heath

A beautiful young woman must find her father's will or her half-brother will inherit all, leaving her penniless. Her only chance is to trust a notorious rake with her future—and her heart.

0-451-20345-3/$4.99

To order call: 1-800-788-6262

The Unsuitable
Miss Martingale

Barbara Hazard

A SIGNET BOOK

SIGNET
Published by New American Library, a division of
Penguin Putnam Inc., 375 Hudson Street,
New York, New York 10014, U.S.A.
Penguin Books Ltd, 27 Wrights Lane,
London W8 5TZ, England
Penguin Books Australia Ltd,
Ringwood, Victoria, Australia
Penguin Books Canada Ltd, 10 Alcorn Avenue,
Toronto, Ontario, Canada M4V 3B2
Penguin Books (N.Z.) Ltd, 182–190 Wairau Road,
Auckland 10, New Zealand

Penguin Books Ltd, Registered Offices:
Harmondsworth, Middlesex, England

First published by Signet, an imprint of New American Library,
a division of Penguin Putnam Inc.

First Printing, May 2001
10 9 8 7 6 5 4 3 2 1

To My Readers:

When I finished my last book, *The Wary Widow,* I realized the story was far from over. True, the hero and heroine of that book, Alastair and Cornelia, had fallen in love in Vienna, but what of Lili Martingale, the thirteen-year-old girl they liberated from a French convent? What happened to her?

The Unsuitable Miss Martingale is the answer. I hope you have as much fun reading it as I did writing it. I would like to hear your comments. You can reach me at P.O. Box 672, Hanover, NH 03755.

—Barbara Hazard

Chapter One

While the servant girl was busy arranging the contents of the tea tray, adding coal to the fire, and sweeping the hearth, the two occupants of the room paid her little heed, speaking instead of a recent snowstorm and the state of the roads. But when the girl had curtsied and the door closed behind her, they took seats opposite each other at the table in silence. They ignored the busy inn yard beneath the window. A stage had just rumbled in from London and there was the usual bustle as passengers and baggage were unloaded and the weary team led away to the stables. Not even the commotion some little boys made playing tag around the new team waiting to take its place nor the yelping of a mongrel cur attracted their attention.

"How *is* Lili? And what exactly has she been up to now?" the more fashionably dressed lady inquired as she peered into the depths of the china pot to see if the tea had steeped long enough. "Something, I am sure."

Her companion nodded. The blue gown and bonnet she wore were made of good, quality material, but they were hardly up to the mode. She sat quietly in her place, her hands folded before her on the table. She would never be described as beautiful, nor even passing pretty, until she smiled. Then her face was lit with such warmth and kindness even strangers were hard put not to smile in return.

"I am happy to tell you she is well," she said. "I daresay you would be surprised, she has grown so."

"And she is seventeen now! I hope the gowns I sent for her birthday were acceptable?"

"I assure you, she adores them, 'Nelia. It was only necessary to let out the bodices an inch or so for them to be a perfect fit."

Her companion looked up from the tea she was pouring, her gaze keen. At last she nodded. "I understand, Nancy. I suppose she has been busy captivating every male in the neighborhood in her innocent way. Is that why you wrote and summoned me here so mysteriously? Come now, confess!"

As she spoke she handed her friend a steaming cup of tea and pushed the sugar bowl closer. Nancy Moorland stared at it in an absentminded way before she replied. "Yes, that is the reason indeed. She even practices her wiles on John."

"The curate as well?" Cornelia Russell inquired. She was not concerned with Captain John Moorland's affections. He was devoted to his wife and loved Lili as a daughter.

"Certainly the curate for all he is fifty if he is a day. But what worries me the most, and is the reason I sent for you so urgently is that I caught Lili with one of our farmers' sons in the henhouse. They were lost in a passionate embrace."

The hand that was raising Mrs. Russell's teacup to her lips stilled and she leaned forward. "Ah, lies the wind in that quarter, does it, my dear?" she asked. There was an edge to her voice now, all the gay banter gone.

"No, no, she has no *tendre* for a farmboy, or males in general, 'Nelia. It was he who initiated the embrace. Lili, well . . ."

"Lili what?"

"She said she did not push him away or call for help because she did not want to hurt his feelings, if you can imagine such a thing," Mrs. Moorland added, all her own feelings on full display.

Cornelia Russell looked more cheerful however, and she sipped her tea before she said, "I can indeed. It is just the thing Lili would think of, for she was ever tenderhearted. However, I quite agree we must think of a solution to this problem; decide what to do.

"Drink your tea, Nancy. It grows cold.

"Now, a stolen kiss—in the henhouse, you said? My word—is one thing, but we cannot have her succumbing to, shall we say, anything more serious, simply to spare a gentleman's sensibilities."

"As if most of them have any," Mrs. Moorland said tartly, surprising her companion considerably. It was most unlike her.

"Do have one of the scones, my dear," she said as she passed the plate. "They smell fresh from the oven. I have always enjoyed staying at The Golden Fox. It is a superior establishment."

"John does not understand to this day why you will never come to us at Moorlands, even though I have explained Alastair's aversion to the rooster's crowing at dawn. Such a nicety is beyond him.

"We were sorry you had to miss Lili's birthday celebration this year," she added as she spread butter on her scone.

"I was sorry, too. But Alastair was set on traveling to the Caribbean. I will tell you about it sometime. It is so beautiful there. Beautiful and dangerous both.

"But that will keep for another time. What do you suggest we do about Lili?"

To her surprise, Nancy Moorland reached across the table to take her hand. "Please hear me out, 'Nelia. This is difficult enough for me to say without interruptions."

She waited until Mrs. Russell nodded before she began. "I think the only thing to be done is remove Lili from the farm. If she stays here, I am afraid she will fall in love with some completely unsuitable man. Even now she is becoming the local belle."

She paused for a moment to draw a deep breath before she hurried on. "Indeed, I am afraid John's brother Ben has fallen under her spell. Such a match will not do, 'Nelia. I know that as well as you must."

"You are right. Lili is not for him although I am surprised to hear you say so."

"Oh, I have known from the start that even putting aside the child's background, she would not make a farmer's wife. And

Ben will never be anything but a farmer. It is the life he has chosen, the life he loves. I am glad, for you know he has been my husband's right-hand man ever since John returned from the Penisula wars blind and wounded. Someday soon, much sooner than I can bear to think of, the farm will be Ben's. Even so, I . . ."

She was allowed to say no more, for Mrs. Russell had gathered up her smart merino crepe skirts to come around the table to kneel beside her and hold her tight. "He is worse?" she asked softly.

Nancy Moorland did not reply which was all the answer her friend needed. "I am sorry, my dear," she said, inwardly cursing the inadequacy of those words. "So very sorry."

"There is nothing to be done. All the doctors we have consulted say so. It is only a matter of time.

"But there. Do take your seat again, 'Nelia. You will ruin that very fashionable gown, kneeling in the dust. I meant to tell you how stunning you look. And that hat! Superb!"

"All Alastair's doing," Cornelia Russell said as she stood and shook out her skirts before she took her seat again. She knew Nancy did not care to continue a discussion of her husband's health and so had introduced her gown to safely guide the conversation away from a wound too tender to be probed. Accordingly, she continued to chatter.

"You know how he insists on choosing all my gowns. Was he always so autocratic, even when you knew him as a child? Still, it is a good thing he does, I suppose. I have little interest in style and it would not do for Beau Russell's wife to be a dowd.

"But come, let us repair to Lili's problem again, tiresome child that she is."

"She is not a child anymore. If she were, there would be no problem," came the swift reply.

"You are right. But I seem to recall, even when we brought her here from France when she was only thirteen, she could sometimes appear twice that age in the twinkling of an eye. It never lasted long, but it always brought me up short. I wonder if all girls are like that? Were we? I cannot remember."

"Nor I. But as much as I love Lili, and I do, as if she were truly my own dear daughter, I want her safely away before Ben has a chance to fix her interest. I do not think I am unduly prejudiced when I remind you how handsome a man he is, how capable of attaching her. Nor how mature he is at twenty-five, his advances so polished compared to the hot groping of a boy her own age. Of course now she considers him as an older brother, but who can say what a few kisses might not do to tip the balance? And in the end she would make Ben unhappy."

"Why do you say so?"

"Because she is growing tired of the farm even now. And she will grow tired of him, too, no matter how she might think she loves him if she marries him. He won't be able to hold her. Their love will not last. It cannot. And as you know, marriage is hard enough for equals whose interests are similar."

Cornelia Russell was not surprised at her friend's astuteness. She had always considered Nancy Moorland an intelligent woman with excellent judgment. Her concern for her brother-in-law was thus even more distressing. The situation was serious indeed.

A mental picture of the captain's sturdy younger brother, his handsome face, broad shoulders, and narrow hips came to her mind. Yes, Ben Moorland was a man to turn female heads and cause female hearts to miss beats. But Ben Moorland was a countryman by station and inclination, as Nancy had acknowledged. And Lili Martingale could look much higher than that, orphan though she was. She was related not only to Cornelia Russell, the former Countess of Wyckend, but to other titled persons as well, no matter how distantly. To think of her living out her life here at a farm among the laborers and their families was ludicrous. Cornelia Russell remembered all too well how the girl had fretted to leave the convent, how she had adored Vienna, and she knew how she must be anticipating the Season in London she had been promised when she was older.

But Lili was only seventeen, a year too young for that rite of passage. Or was she?

"What do you suggest we do, Nancy?" she asked her companion.

"I want you to ask Lili to come to Wyckend or to London as soon as possible," came the bald reply. "Oh, I know it is an imposition and far too soon, but I am afraid Ben will declare himself. I am hoping an early departure will nip that proposal in the bud. And even if it does not, that the prospects of such a change might make Lili indifferent to his pleading. She talks incessantly of London and how she is looking forward to seeing it, and to staying with you and Alastair.

"And when she is gone, Ben may well begin to look about and notice other available girls. Girls who have been trying to catch his eye for some time now. Good, suitable girls."

She paused as if unable to continue, and Mrs. Russell said, "I know how you will miss her. And so, I am afraid, will the captain. Does he know this plan? Know you are speaking to me?"

"He knows my concern and shares it. But he does not know I asked you to come here; that we are speaking together."

She looked down at her clasped hands for a moment. "I have discovered men, no matter how practical they might be in everyday matters or strategy, are no more practical than we are when it comes to an affair of the heart. John *hopes* all will be well, that everything will somehow resolve itself satisfactorily. Because he loves Lili so and cannot bear to lose her. I am not so optimistic. By speaking to you alone first, I hope to present him with an accomplished fact."

"I am sure that is wise," Mrs. Russell murmured before she added, "Here, let me pour you another cup of tea. That one has grown cold. Then, while you drink it, we can discuss how we will explain my sudden appearance at the farm when I arrive with you today, and my scheme to whisk Lili away with me to Wyckend tomorrow."

"Tomorrow?" Mrs. Moorland echoed. "You will take her now?"

Her incredulous voice held more than a hint of regret, and her friend put down the teapot to press her hand again. "Oh, yes, best done as soon as possible, don't you agree? It is sure to be less painful for everyone that way, and so much easier than having to arrange for a chaperon and hired carriage."

"I suppose so. Strange. I have wanted Lili away for some time, fretted over it for Ben's sake, and yet now that it is upon me, I find myself most reluctant to accept it. No doubt you think me a widgeon with more hair than wit."

"Drink your tea, dear. I do not think you anything of the sort. You are a woman with a woman's heart, just as I am. Lili has been like a daughter to you for the past four years. Indeed, you are the only mother she has ever known. She will always be your daughter, you know. Now I am only a distant cousin, which is not at all comparable. Still, we are her family, you and I.

"Now then, what shall we say at Moorlands? How explain this sudden urge of mine to have Lili come to Wyckend?"

The two women put their heads together and began to discuss the ways and means they would employ. It was decided that Mrs. Moorland would claim to have seen her friend arrive at the inn as she was passing the yard; that the reason Mrs. Russell had come to Oxfordshire was to surprise Lili and take her away on a visit. She planned to say Alastair Russell was expecting them both at Wyckend as soon as possible, making an early departure on the morrow imperative.

"I do not think it at all necessary to tell Lili—or anyone else for that matter—that this is to be a permanent move," Cornelia Russell continued.

"The less said the better," her friend agreed. "Oh, how I do hate practicing deceit! But I quite see there is no other way. Someday I may tell John what we have done. I doubt I will ever tell Ben."

"Much better not." Mrs. Russell nodded. Ben Moorland would not be pleased to have his plans for a future with Lili upset. Picturing the hard set of his jaw if he should find out, and imagining the eruption of what Nancy had told her was an exceedingly hot temper, made her shiver even though she did not consider herself a timid soul.

As the two rose to gather their things for the journey to the farm, Nancy Moorland put a timid hand on her friend's sleeve. "You will bring her back to us sometime, won't you, 'Nelia?" she pleaded, her blue eyes wet with tears. "When it is safe to do so, that is?"

Cornelia Russell gave her a fervent hug. "Goose!" she said fondly. "I'd like to see anyone try to keep her away."

Chapter Two

The two ladies—Cornelia Russell in her handsome traveling carriage, and Nancy Moorland in a sturdy gig—were soon on their way to the farm. Little did they suspect it was already too late to keep Lili and Ben Moorland apart, for that morning, soon after Mrs. Moorland left for Oxford and some nonexistent shopping, Ben had followed Lili out to the stables. He was not in a very good humor. Indeed, he had not been in good humor since he had learned Lili and Roy Akins had been caught embracing in the henhouse. And to think he had been so careful not to startle her, he told himself in derision as he strode along. So patient to wait until she was a woman grown before he told her of his love and showed her his passion. And now, this . . . this *coupling* with a rough farmhand was the result! Well, he would wait no longer! Miss Lili wanted kisses, did she? Well, kisses she would have! Kisses and a great deal more as soon as the banns could be called. He felt a slight qualm when he thought of her age. Seventeen was not so very old to be marrying after all. Still, considering the alternative, losing her to another, was far too dangerous to contemplate. He decided he could wait until spring but only if he had her promise. That might appease Nancy as well. He suspected he might be in for a battle with her, spoiling the girl as she did, and treating her like a child. Sometimes he thought Nancy's affections must have made her as blind as his brother. Could she not *see* the way Lili tempted men? How she smiled at them and peeked at them from under her lashes? How she teased and laughed and sometimes even grasped their sleeve

or their hand while conversing? All very well if it was *his*
sleeve and hand, he told himself, but Lili was impartial with
her favors.

That will change, he told himself grimly as he strode along.
Really one could hardly blame poor Roy for grabbing her as
he had. In a way, it was the girl's own fault. But he would
keep her safe, when he was her husband.

He had reached the stable door and he paused a moment before he slid it open, startled to find his heart was beating
rapidly. What was this? He was not some lovesick boy! He
was a mature man. As his heart slowed he told himself it must
have been the result of his headlong rush to the stable. Truly,
Lili was driving him crazy, and he didn't like it one little bit.

It was dark in the stable this dreary March morning, and he
had to pause for a moment until his eyes adjusted to the
gloom. Still, he knew where she was. He and his brother had
conspired to give her a new mare for Christmas and she
adored the horse. She had called it Josephine after Napoleon's
empress, much to his brother's disgust. The former captain
had little liking for anything French.

But Lili had prevailed, as she was so apt to do. She claimed
she had secretly adored Josephine from the little she had heard
of her in the convent, and admired her as well. And surely *she*
had had nothing to do with war or battles for she was only
Napoleon's love, and a woman. And perhaps, she had added
eagerly, she had even kept him from some of his more dastardly schemes. Didn't the captain agree that might be the
case? Surely she had more influence with Boney than other
people, didn't he think so?

John Moorland had turned red trying to contain his laughter
at this ingenuous line of reasoning, and said no more about the
mare's name.

She was a beautiful animal, Ben Moorland thought as he
strode toward her stall. As Lili was beautiful.

"Is that you, Ben?" she asked. She sounded apprehensive
and he smiled grimly. He did not know Lili was afraid young
Roy might have followed her here, hoping for another kiss. No

one had told her of the whipping he had received from his father, the tearful lecture he had been subjected to by his mother, the sneers of his older brothers, and the frightened awe of his sisters. Young Akins would not bother Miss Martingale again for any reason, but Lili could not know that.

As Ben drew closer, Lili relaxed. "Have you come out to see if I curried Josephine properly this morning?" she asked pertly as she stroked the mare's velvet nose.

"Nay. I saw to the mare earlier."

"So you still do not trust me to do it right." Lili gave an exaggerated sigh. "Ben, let's go for a ride! It is not that cold today, and for a wonder it is not raining or snowing or sleeting. Please? May we go?"

He did not answer for he was busy organizing his thoughts, trying to choose the best way to introduce the subject he was so determined to have out with her.

"I was so angry when Nancy insisted on going to Oxford alone this morning," she went on as she fed the mare the apple she had brought with her. "I am sure I don't know why I could not go, too. It is too bad! Especially since it is so dull here at the farm. There is nothing to do. Nothing at all."

"What do you mean, nothing to do?" Ben demanded. He could not imagine such a thing; why, he was on the go from dawn to black night. There was always something he could put his hand to, even if it were just a bit of whittling. Like last night, when he had whittled clothespins for Nancy as they all sat in the parlor after supper. True, this was the slow time of year on any farm, but it was hardly dull.

He reminded himself that when he and Lili were married, she would be just as busy as he was, learning to manage the household, overseeing the cooking and preserving, doing all the sewing, and making simples for the stillroom. And when they had children, why then she would say there weren't enough hours in the day.

He smiled, just thinking of it, and surprised a decided mulish expression on her pretty face. "I mean I am tired of practicing my music, I finished my book yesterday, and if I never had to set another stitch in the needlepoint chair cover I am making, I would be delighted."

"Why don't you surprise Nancy and make a dried apple pie for our supper," he suggested. "I'm that fond of dried apple pie."

"I hate baking. And I hate sewing, too. Besides, the maids do it so much better than I can. Please, Ben, do say we can go for a ride? It won't take me long to change."

He looked down and saw the enticing way she was looking at him, her little smile and the way she leaned toward him in her eagerness, and he lost his head. Gone were all his plans to tell her calmly and logically how much he loved her and why they should be wed, gone those careful, measured steps from gentle touch to passionate embrace so as not to frighten her. Instead, he reached out and pulled her close in his arms. Just the feel of her clasped against him made him dizzy, and he bent his head and captured her lips. Her mouth had fallen open a little in astonishment, and he reveled in its soft, pliant contours. She was his! She belonged to him; why, she even felt as if she did. His kiss deepened and he felt her stiffen, felt her hands fight to push him away. For a moment, he held her even tighter, knowing she could not escape him. Then reason returned and he let her go.

She backed away, bumping into the mare, who sidestepped and tossed her head, as if in wonder at these strange doings in her stall.

Ben saw Lili was looking shocked, shocked and frightened, and he was sorry for it. Putting out his hand to her and ignoring the way she flinched, he said, "There now, I am sorry to take you by surprise like that, lass. You may believe it wasn't how I meant to do it. But I love you, Lili. I have loved you truly for a long time. I was going to wait till you were older before I mentioned our marriage, but after Roy, well, I think it best to wait no longer. I'll not have you kissing others, Lili, no, not a bit of it. You're mine, you are."

"I'm not," she whispered, huddled close against the mare's flank.

Ben could tell she was still frightened and he forced himself to step back. He even made himself smile. It was hard to do when all he wanted was to kiss her again, hold her tight, until she agreed to his plans.

"Maybe not yet, you're not, but you will be," he assured her, smiling still to take the sting from his words. "You're not for the likes of Roy Akins. No, someday soon you will be Mrs. Benjamin Moorland, mistress here, my wife and mother to our children."

When she just stared at him, her eyes huge in her pale face, he hurried on. "We can have the banns called starting next Sunday. Or, if you like, we can wait until spring. Yes, Nancy would like that better, I ken, and it will give you some time to get your bride clothes ready."

"But—but I'm going to London this spring or next for the Season," she said. "It is all planned and I have been counting on it."

"You forget all that foolishness right now, Lili! There's nothing in London for you. It's all simpering and dissipation and lechery there. If you want, I will take you to London someday. Oh, not this spring. You know how busy we are on the farm in the spring. Maybe we could go next November or perhaps in the wintertime."

"No," Lili said, easier now he was a little distance away. "No," she repeated, her voice stronger.

"What do you mean, 'no'?" he asked. "Surely you knew I was in love with you, knew I wanted to marry you."

"But I didn't. You are my *brother*, Ben. The brother I never had. Besides, I don't want to get married. I'm not old enough."

"You are if you can be sneaking kisses with Roy Akins in the henhouse, and planning heaven-knows-what-else besides," he retorted.

"I wasn't sneaking them. How many times do I have to explain? He grabbed me when I went to get some eggs for Nancy for supper. I didn't know he was there."

"Ha! So you say," he said, his eyes beginning to smoulder again just thinking about it.

"I don't know why you won't believe me. Nancy does, and so does your brother. Why are you so distrustful? Why must you doubt me?"

He reached for her and she jumped back. Hands dropping to his sides, he said slowly, "I think it is because I love you so. I cannot bear to think of another man touching you—kissing you."

He turned aside then so she would not see the anguish in his eyes. "I want to marry you, lass. I *must* marry you, or go mad.

"But maybe you need time to think about it. Yes, that's it. I startled you. I'm sorry for that. But you think about what I said—how I feel, all my plans for our future. And then tomorrow morning, say you agree. I believe I can survive that long. Will you promise me you will do that? Promise?"

Lili stared at him. She saw there would be no escape until she fell in with his mad scheme, and so she nodded. "I—I would like to be alone now, if you do not mind, sir," she said.

He hesitated for a moment, then spread out his hands in surrender and smiled at her. For some reason she felt like crying. She prayed the tears would not betray her before he left. To her relief, he turned away and a moment later the barn door closed behind him. Nerveless, she slid down to the rough board floor just outside Josephine's stall. The mare neighed at her, hoping for another apple, but Lili did not even hear her.

Marry him, Lili thought. Marry *Ben*.

He had apologized for startling her. Well, he had certainly done that. And stunned her, shocked her, even devastated her. Because she did think of him as a brother. Because he had never been anything but that to her. And she was too young for marriage anyway. Why, she was only seventeen and she had not even had a Season.

She frowned then, absently picking at some pieces of straw that clung to her skirt. Her thoughts were jumbled, jumping from one thing to another with no rhyme or reason to them. She felt trapped, and she resented it. Why had he put her in this position? It was not fair! And there was no one she could go to and ask for advice. Nancy had gone to Oxford—once again resentment at being left at home rose in her throat. If only Nancy had taken her along, none of this would have happened. But that was silly thinking, and she knew it. For if Ben had not confronted her this morning, he would have done so some other time soon. He was not a man to turn from a course, once he had decided on it.

And she could not go to the captain. Ben was his younger brother. For all she knew, he might approve such a union. Suddenly she was sure he would, for it would ensure her remaining here on the farm. John Moorland loved her, she knew it. He would not want her to leave even though he knew she must, someday. Alastair Russell had told her that just before he and 'Nelia had left her here.

"Do not become a rustic, Lili," he had said to her, holding her chin so she was forced to look at him. "This is the best place for you now, but in a few years you will be ready for a wider world. 'Nelia and I intend to see you have it."

If only 'Nelia were here, she thought, absently listening to the homey sounds of the barn, the horses shifting in their stalls, one of them pawing the floor with a restless hoof, the twittering of some birds in the eaves where they huddled together against the cold, even the squeak in the loft that told her the barn cat had found its breakfast. She loved this place, as she loved all of Moorlands, but she admitted she was ready to leave it. And it seemed to her as she sat there musing, that what had happened with Ben showed her it was past time for her to do so. He had said she must give him an answer tomorrow morning. She did not need to consider his proposal. She intended to refuse him. She wished it were possible to avoid a confrontation. But that would not be fair. No, she would be firm, tell him how sorry she was that she could not love him that way, and then she would write to the Russells and beg them to let her come to Wyckend. And until she could escape the farm, she would avoid being alone with Ben.

She knew she would have to do that. Because she had not just been frightened when he kissed her; indeed, if she were to be honest with herself, she had not been frightened at all. Startled, yes. Surprised, certainly. But not frightened.

Instead, she had been amazed at how moved she had been by his kiss. It was nothing at all like the one Roy Akins had stolen. He had grabbed her so hard, it hurt, and their noses had collided before he found her lips. And then he had forced her lips back against her teeth, he had been so fierce about it. But Ben's kiss, ah, there was no comparison. It had been so easy, so right. It seemed as if their lips had been made to fit together just that way. And then he had become more insistent, almost demanding, but not in a way that made her want to escape him. Indeed, for a mad moment she had even pressed closer until she remembered this was Ben, *Ben,* and she began to fight, desperate to get away. Because that kiss had been wrong and she knew it. Girls did not kiss their brothers like that, and Ben was a brother to her. There must never be any repetition of this morning's scene.

As she stood up and shook out her crushed skirts, Lili realized how dangerous that would be. For she had *liked* Ben's kiss too much, wanted more, loved the soft, weak way it made her feel. And that would never do.

It was not necessary for Lili to confront Ben after all, for that same afternoon Nancy returned from Oxford, bringing Cornelia Russell with her. And besides all the news to discuss, there was the excitement of learning she was to go to Wyckend the very next day. Lili only had one bad moment, and that was when she chanced to catch Ben's eye in the parlor after supper. The maids were already packing her belongings; the captain had resigned himself to her departure and was issuing any number of gruff instructions, and Nancy was smiling, her eyes misty with her unshed tears. But Ben had only leaned against the mantel, never taking his eyes from her until at last she glanced his way. What she saw in his face almost made her gasp audibly. He looked as if he were burning inside with all the words he could not say, all the pent-up desire he could not show. She stared at him for a long moment, then as 'Nelia asked her a question about her music, she shook her head and turned away. She did not look at him again.

They went to bed early, for they were to leave at first light. Cornelia Russell intended to cover as many miles as possible the first day. It was how she always traveled, neck or nothing, her husband called it, pretending he did not approve.

In bed at last, with a hot brick at her feet, Lili lay awake staring at the ceiling she could barely see in the last flickering light from her bedroom fire. She was leaving Moorlands and she sensed it would be for good this time, although no one had said so. But somehow her intuition told her if she ever returned, it would only be for a visit. Part of her regretted that, for she loved it here, loved Nancy and the captain and Ben. She pushed Ben from her mind in a hurry, reminding herself instead at least she would not have to miss Josephine. After much discussion, it had been decided she could bring the mare with her.

But as much as she felt regret, a part of her, the larger part, looked forward eagerly to the new world she was to enter. She had had a glimpse of that world in Vienna when she had been there with the Russells for the Congress. Then, at thirteen, she had been only an onlooker. This time she would be a participant, meeting new people and going to parties, seeing wondrous sights. She smiled to herself and cuddled down under her covers. And I shall have dancing lessons and new gowns and perhaps I shall make some friends my own age. How wonderful that would be. She had never known anyone her own age except for her maid in Vienna. Everyone else in her life had been older—the nuns at the convent where she had been raised, as well as 'Nelia and Alastair. And when she came here, these people were older, too. Wonderful and lovable, but . . .

She froze as she heard her door open. She knew it was Ben. Who else could it be? Unnerved, she pretended she was fast asleep.

"Lili? Wake up, Lili!" he said softly but insistently.

She did not speak, only reminded herself to breathe evenly. Go away, she begged silently. Oh, please, *please* go away!

She felt him bend over her, felt his hand caress a curl before he tucked it back in her nightcap. "Lili?" he said again and then he began to cover her cheek with little kisses. Unable to avoid the confrontation, she pretended to stir.

When she opened her eyes, he covered her mouth with his hand.

"It is only me. Don't be alarmed, love," he whispered as he sat down beside her.

"What are you doing here?" she demanded, whispering, too.

"I could not let you go without a word. I had to come and tell you of my love again lest you forget it at Wyckend and in London. Tell you, so you will come back to me. You must come back to me, Lili, just as soon as you have had your fling among the great. Because you belong here—with me."

I don't, I don't, she cried inwardly although she did not say a word.

"I have come to see it would be best for you to observe society yourself," he went on. "That way, you will not be forever regretting what you did not have. But I know you are too fine not to discard it eventually with all its pretension and lies. And then when you come home, we can be married as I planned. I will wait for you, Lili, as I have already waited for four long years. But don't be gone too long, my love. Remember me, and how I will be missing you, loving you, *wanting* you . . . Oh, God, how I want you!"

His voice had deepened and grown a little hoarse, and Lili was suddenly aware that under the covers and her night rail, she was naked.

"You must go," she whispered urgently, as much afraid of her response to him as she was of him. "Please, you must!"

"Tell me you love me then," he ordered.

"Of course I love you," she said quickly. "I will always . . ."

She was not allowed to finish. Perhaps Ben Moorland sensed she intended to qualify her remark, and did not care to hear it. Instead he swept her up in his arms and kissed her.

This time he was not careful, this time she was gasping when he raised his head, his eyes lingering on her face in the dim light, memorizing it for all the lonely nights ahead.

"Come back soon, Lili," he growled as he rose and went to the door. "I will be here. Waiting."

Chapter Three

Lili was glad when they left early the next morning, for the uncertain light made it difficult for her traveling companion to see how upset she was. Nancy had wept copiously and apologized just as copiously for doing so. The captain had stood aloof, but his hug when it came was breathtaking. Only Ben was not there. He had cantered off to Oxford before breakfast. Lili was torn between relief and chagrin that he had chosen this way. But she knew he had said his good-bye in her room last night, and a fervent one it had been. She still seemed able to feel the imprint of his lips on hers, the span of his big hand on her back as he pressed her closer. She wondered if she would ever be able to forget and it was that, almost as much as saying farewell to those who loved her, that made her cry. Suddenly she was nowhere near as certain of the course she had chosen. Perhaps she should marry Ben, she thought. Perhaps they would be happy.

The Russell carriage was well sprung and comfortable; still Cornelia Russell steeled herself. It was a long three days to Wyckend, situated as it was near Denmead in Hampshire, close to the coast. She considered travel a necessary evil although she knew from past experience, Lili would find something to amuse herself.

"You might work on your needlepoint, Lili, as soon as the light improves," she said to the girl at her side. "How fortunate Nancy spied it in the parlor where you had left it. Or was it?" she added.

"I have no secrets from you, 'Nelia darling. I hate needlepoint; indeed, I hate all sewing. I purposely left the bag of work hidden behind a chair."

"I knew it. Your face gave you away when Nancy came running out with it. Never mind. I don't care for piecework myself. I would so much rather read a book."

"I am glad of that. Tell me, will Alastair be at Wyckend when we arrive? It seems an age since I saw him last."

"No, he is in London. An important session with his tailor, I believe."

"Does he still find the country an abomination?" Lili asked next, careful to keep her voice even. When she had no reply, she went on. "I did not make that up. That is what he called it when I was last at Wyckend."

"And he continues to say it," Cornelia admitted. "Still, he seems resigned to spending part of the year there. And I have been amazed, not so much at how he has taken charge, but at how he has managed to turn Sarah up sweet."

Lili turned to stare at her. She could not imagine such a thing, for she was frightened to death by the tiny elderly woman who was Sarah, Dowager Countess of Wyckend. The mother of Cornelia's first husband, who had died young in a hunting accident, she had been unable to accept a diminished role. Her son had allowed her to continue to believe she managed the estate as she had all those years as a young widow herself, until he came of age. His death had been a bitter blow to her, as was the fact he died childless, something she never let Cornelia forget. But there was another blow for her to face. By some strange twist of fate, neither Wyckend nor the estate had been entailed. There would never be another earl, and the estate itself, all eight hundred profitable acres of it, was now the property of Mr. Alastair Russell, Cornelia's second husband and London's premier beau. The late earl had left it entirely to his wife.

"He turned her up sweet? Surely you are not serious, 'Nelia," Lili protested. "How did he do that? I thought she hated him for an interloper."

Her companion chuckled. "Why, by giving her the gravest

courtesy on each and every occasion and treating her as if she
were the queen. And he asks her opinion on every matter. I
found them one morning at the breakfast table, discussing
drains and thatch for the cottages, and I had to leave the room
lest I laugh aloud. Of course, after asking her opinion, Alastair
does exactly as he pleases. Yet somehow, the new manager
and new servants became all Sarah's scheme. You have to
admit it is masterful of him."

"He is very talented, isn't he, Al-as-tair?" Lili asked demurely, giving every syllable of his name separate emphasis,
as she had done when she was only thirteen and fresh from a
French convent.

She turned to surprise a little smile on Mrs. Russell's face.
A secret smile of contentment and happiness, and she wondered if she would ever find a love like that, and prayed she
might.

The travelers were only ten miles or so from Wyckend on
the third afternoon of their journey, when they were stopped
by an accident that was blocking the road. Lili would have
jumped down and run to see what the trouble was, but Cornelia stopped her, sending a groom instead. But before she
could protest, Lili had climbed up on the carriage seat and
stuck her head through the trap in the roof. Of course the
coachman's broad back hid most of the view, but she was able
to see that a small band of men riding cross-country must have
jumped a wall into the road and ridden right into a flock of
sheep. One sheep was down, crying piteously, and the boy
who watched the flock lay ominously still in the road. His dog
hovered over him anxiously, making little yips of distress.

By the time Lili had taken all this in, Cornelia had succeeded in pulling her back inside the carriage again. She was
angry at the girl's hoydenish behavior, but before she could
tell her so, Lili hurried into speech.

"I do not think they know what to do with that poor boy,"
she concluded, her brow furrowed with her concern. "And I
wish they would have the goodness to put that injured sheep
out of its misery."

A gunshot announced the solution to that problem at least.

"Please, 'Nelia, may we not get down and see what we can do to help?" Lili pleaded.

Reluctantly, Cornelia agreed. She was reassured when she saw one of the riding party was none other than Graeme Wilder, Viscount Halpern, a neighbor of hers. She did not know the other two men or their grooms. When she saw Lili running to kneel beside the boy who was lying so still in the road, she hurried forward herself. What would the child do next? she wondered.

"There is no blood I can see," Lili said over her shoulder. "Please, can someone tell us what happened?"

When no one answered, she looked around, her pretty face growing stormy at the expression on the riders' faces. In the months to follow, she would come to call it "The Look." It was partly sneer, partly disgust and indifference, and entirely a display of superiority.

"Ma'am," the viscount said at last, giving Cornelia an elegant bow. "At your service. I beg you not to distress yourself over this unfortunate boy. We shall see to him."

"How?" Lili demanded, rising and confronting him. "By standing about in the road doing the pretty and discussing the problem? He is hurt. He needs a doctor."

Halpern looked her up and down. He was tall, and although of slim build, he had good shoulders. Cornelia was aware Lili's brown cloak and practical bonnet were not at all fashionable. No doubt Halpern thought her some sort of servant. Before she could correct this misapprehension, he addressed her again.

"May I present Percy Ridgeway and Lord Gore, ma'am? Mrs. Alastair Russell, chaps."

As she smiled at them, Cornelia noted their heightened interest in the woman Beau Russell had chosen as wife. She could almost hear them thinking she must have had a sizeable fortune to have tempted that gentleman to matrimony. She did not mind. She was used to this kind of response at first meeting. Beside her, she could tell Lili was seething still, and she prayed the girl would hold her tongue.

"I believe the boy has a broken leg and possibly a broken head as well," Lili announced, her voice challenging. " 'Nelia, do you think we can take him up in our carriage to carry him to the nearest doctor? And we should hurry," she added, sweeping the gentlemen before her with a look as scornful as theirs. "He is unconscious now and so will not feel the pain."

Mrs. Russell nodded. "Certainly that would be the best solution. You gentlemen are riding. You have no way of transporting him."

"You must not trouble yourself, ma'am. I am sure someone will be along soon with a cart or dray," the viscount protested. "I shall leave one of the grooms here to attend him until that happens."

"No, no," Lili insisted. "We can take him."

"Perhaps you do not mind riding in the company of a dirty shepherd boy, miss, but I assure you the former Countess of Wyckend is not at all accustomed to such a thing. It would be most unsuitable."

"As if that mattered," Saint Lili exclaimed. Cornelia knew from experience Lili was relishing the role of saviour that she had assumed, and was amused she had changed so little in four years. She could almost see Lili's imaginary wings, her golden halo.

Fortunately a farm cart rumbled around the corner just then. The two men on the driver's bench stared as they pulled up. They informed the viscount they knew the boy and his family, and they volunteered to see to his care. With a groom's help, and watched by a hovering Lili, they lifted him into the back of the cart, which was happily filled with hay. The dog whined, torn between its desire to accompany its master and the need to round up the sheep as it had been trained to do. One of the men offered to see the flock got home. For all their generosity, the viscount awarded them the dead animal and that was tossed in beside the shepherd.

As Lili marched by him on her way back to the carriage,

Cornelia saw her mutter something and toss her head. She also noted Halpern's reddened cheekbones.

"Obviously that sheep is not his to bestow," Lili said as she climbed to her seat in the carriage again. "I have never met such an arrogant, heedless person in my life. And I would wager anything the boy came to grief because they dashed across that field and jumped the wall without even looking to see if there was any traffic in the road. Insufferable, pompous boors."

"No doubt you are right," Mrs. Russell said as the carriage jerked into motion. She saw Lili refused to look at the men still standing about watching the sheep being herded away. Instead she stared straight ahead, her little chin tilted ominously.

"What did you say to Viscount Halpern just now?" she inquired. "He did not look at all pleased with your remark."

"I am sure I do not care whether he was pleased or not," came the swift reply. "I only said one word. Levite."

For a moment, Mrs. Russell looked confused and then she smiled in spite of herself. "Lili, Lili," she scolded. "What a thing to call him. And he did not pass by on the other side of the road, you know."

"No, but only because it was filled with frightened, milling sheep. You certainly could not consider him a Good Samaritan."

Cornelia Russell shook her head. Then she reached out for her companion's hand. Holding it and looking straight at her, she said, "You would be most unwise, my dear, to make enemies of men in the *ton*. Viscount Halpern is only a courtesy title. Someday that man will be the Marquis of Braybourne. A heady title indeed. His friends are among the cream of society as well, and you were very harsh with all of them."

"But they were rude; indifferent," Lili protested. "They didn't even care the boy was hurt so badly. And did you see the way they looked at me? As if I were a slug. Grrr! I don't care for them or their high position."

"You must remember you will be entering society shortly," Cornelia reminded her, wondering as she did so if it might not be wise to postpone such a debut for another year. "And they have it in their power to make you an anathema if they choose to do so. No one would receive you. You would be scorned and laughed at. And forget Almack's. You would never obtain a voucher."

"He has such power?" Lili asked, sounding awed.

"He will be a marquis. They and the dukes a rank above them are very near royalty, and as such, are accorded much homage. And if one of them takes a dislike to someone, well . . ."

She fully expected Lili to explode in indignation again, or at least announce rather grandly, that in God's eyes we were all equal. She had often made such statements when she first left the convent. They were true, of course, but they did tend to bring all conversation to an abrupt halt. Encouraged by her tolerance, she went on. "There are so many things for you to learn about society, dear Lili, and rank and its privileges is only one of them."

Still her companion had no comment, and she decided now was as good a time as any to get some basic truths out in the open. Truths she had been concerned about presenting properly to the girl, for they were not going to sit well with her.

Pressing her hand again, she said, "I think you might as well know now that although your background allows you to make a respectable marriage, you must not hope for much more. It is not because you have no dowry. Alastair and I will see to that. It is because although you have some titles on your family tree, they are attached to distant relations. And your father, although I know nothing to his detriment, well, he was not even gentry. He was only a poor artist."

"I see," Lili said slowly before she called Cornelia's attention to one of the distinctive cairns by the side of the road that marked the boundaries of Wyckend. The limited future she might look forward to was not mentioned again. Lili did not intend to forget it, of course, for she had been shocked by Cornelia's words, but she set them aside to consider later when she was alone.

To her relief, there was no sign of the dowager countess when they entered the gloomy Gothic stone mansion that was Wyckend Court. The large public rooms—the dining, reception, library, and various salons were unchanged from the time the dowager had come here as a bride. Moreover she would not entertain any notion of having them redecorated. Cornelia had tried to ease her into acceptance by introducing a few small changes, but the dowager had immediately spied them out, denounced them, and ordered their removal. At last, Cornelia had given up trying. Even Alastair, with all his tact and charm, had not been successful. It was as if the dowager, forced to retreat to this, her last stronghold, had become intent on holding the Court intact with every fiber of her intense little body.

And so the vast rooms grew older and drearier with the upholstery wearing thin and the draperies fading, and the Russells retreated to their personal suite, where they were able to indulge their own tastes.

Lili was shown to the room she had occupied before. It was decorated in pastel blues and violet and so luxurious compared to the room she had called her own at the farm, there was no comparison. Still, after she excused the maid and wandered over to the windows to stare down at Wyckend's dormant gardens, she could not help missing that snug, familiar place under the eaves—her four-poster with its cozy quilts, the low rocking chair by the window where her first doll still sat, the colorful rag rug set before the fireplace which she and the maids had made last winter. And for a few moments, no doubt because she was tired, she told herself, she shed a tear for the old familiar things, and for her loving foster parents. Ben was not forgotten either. He seemed much farther away than a mere three days' drive. That was probably Wyckend's fault, Lili told herself. It was so grand.

The dowager made her appearance at dinner, in fact she was already seated at the head of the table—a position she had always refused to relinquish to her daughter-in-law—when Cornelia and Lili came in.

"And who is this—this person?" she demanded haughtily, raising her quizzing glass to peer through it. It magnified that eye so it looked huge in her little face, and Lili had to make herself smile.

"You do not remember Lili? My young relative, Mother?" Cornelia inquired as she bent to kiss her withered cheek.

The dowager looked around wildly. "Leave us!" she ordered the butler and footmen who were at the sideboard, preparing to serve the dinner. Waving her napkin at them, she cried, "Go! Go! And shut the door securely behind you!"

Nothing further was said until they obeyed, although Cornelia took her seat and motioned Lili to do the same.

"So," the dowager said in an awful voice, "it has come to this, has it? That you would dare, madam!"

"Dare what? I do not understand," Cornelia said, looking as confused as Lili felt.

"Dare to bring your ill-gotten bastard into my house," her mother-in-law hissed. "I suppose you intend to leave her Wyckend, too. Oh, the shame, the agony I suffer, knowing that although you would not give Wyckend its next earl, you dare to flaunt this—this child of sin in my face."

"You are mistaken, ma'am," Cornelia said firmly. Lili cringed back in her seat, wishing with all her heart she had never left Moorlands. "Lili is not my child," Cornelia went on. "The very idea! She is seventeen and I, as you know, am only thirty. I was not that precocious. No, she is Lili Martingale. Her mother was Thora Edson before her marriage. She was my mother's cousin. I have told you all this before."

"I do not believe you! One has only to look at the devil's mark you both have to see the truth!"

Cornelia touched her forehead. Her hair grew from a distinctive widow's peak. So did Lili's, and it was just as black and curly.

"Do you mean our family resemblance, ma'am? Think no more about it, if you please. Lili and I are distant cousins, or something like that. I have never been able to figure it out. But she has nothing to do with Wyckend, nor will she ever, so you may be easy on that head.

"Now, shall we have the servants back? I am so hungry. The inns of England are not noted for their cuisine, even the best of them, as you may remember."

"I could not eat a morsel," the dowager said as she struggled to her feet. When Cornelia would have risen to help her, she was motioned back fiercely. "No, you Jezebel, stay away from me! I have only one thing to be thankful for, and that is that my beloved Ogden never learned of your deceit."

Her back ramrod straight, the dowager marched steadily to the door and slammed it behind her. Wide-eyed with distress, Lili stared at Cornelia speechless.

Cornelia smiled at her as she stepped on the secret button on the floor near her chair, with which she was able to summon the servants. Somehow the dowager had never caught on to it, or wondered why they seemed to appear just when she wanted them.

"The dowager has decided she would prefer to dine in her rooms this evening, Bayley," she told the elderly butler as he came to pour the wine. "See that she has a tray of her favorites, if you would be so kind."

The butler bowed, and dinner progressed. Nothing of course could be said while the servants were in the room, and Lili's heart stopped pounding when Cornelia talked so lightly of their journey, the new gowns Lili was to have, and the possibility of Alastair returning from London before week's end. At last the meal concluded and the servants were dismissed.

"I can see you are still unnerved by Sarah's tirade, Lili," her cousin said. "There is no need for it. She is an old lady, and I suspect she is failing mentally. Did you notice how her left hand shook?"

"I thought it was with rage," Lili whispered.

To her surprise, Cornelia laughed. "Oh, she was furious, of course. And at eighty-six she dislikes surprises and change. Witness the decor. She has completely forgotten your visit of two summers ago. No, dear Lili, she is only old and fretful with it. Pay her no mind, my dear, no mind at all."

Lili was about to say that the accusation the dowager had leveled at her daughter-in-law could well be true. After all, one of the Moorlands' farmer's daughters had had a baby at fourteen.

But looking into Cornelia's clear blue eyes, she saw something that warned her that such a statement would be most unwise. Unwise and undoubtably rude as well, and she held her tongue.

But when she went up to her room later, she was still thinking about it. Below her in the library, seemingly intent on the post that had arrived in her absence, Cornelia Russell was thinking about it as well, until at last she closed her eyes briefly and shook her head as she drew a deep breath and let it out in a rush.

I wish Alastair were here, she thought as she picked up another letter. Oh, how I wish Alastair were here.

Chapter Four

Lili was tired but it was a long time before she fell asleep that first night at Wyckend. She found it impossible to rid her mind of the picture of the indignant dowager, or banish her ugly words of accusation. Which was too bad, for she knew she was not Cornelia's daughter. It was only *possible*—it was not probable. Cornelia was the daughter of Sir Reginald Wakefield of Berkshire, and as such would have been carefully guarded. There would have been no hot tumble in a haystack for her. Lili remembered Roy Akins then. Was that what he had had in mind for her? A quick toss-up of her skirts in the henhouse? How revolting men were, especially the young ones! She remembered Ben's embraces then and blushed.

After a while she forced herself to put the dowager's reproaches aside. She was just an old lady and as Cornelia said, she imagines things, Lili told herself. I will pray for her, but I will not heed her anymore.

But as she tried to compose herself for sleep, plumping up her pillows and pulling up her covers, she remembered what Cornelia had said in the carriage, and all thoughts of sleep deserted her.

So, she was not good enough for the likes of a titled gentleman, was she? She could only look forward to a "respectable" marriage, whatever that might be? At first she had wanted to interrupt Cornelia, argue with her, but as the horror of what she was saying unfolded, she had been on tiptoe to hear her out. It was not because she had considered marriage, for she had not. She was only seventeen. Her wedding day, or so she had thought, was far in the future. No, she had thought only of balls and parties and new friends. Yet here was not only Ben pressing her to wed him, but Cornelia laying out her future as calm as calm could be! Didn't anyone think seventeen a tender age for such a weighty business? Besides, she was not at all sure she would ever marry. She had other options, after all. She had had a wealth of education from the nuns. She could speak French of course like a native and she was also fluent in German. She had some Italian and she could read Latin and Greek. She was also versed in geography, some basic mathematics, and philosophy as well as religion—heady subjects and perhaps unnecessary for young misses to know. The captain had taught her history and military strategy, too. Perhaps she should hire out as a tutor? The very thought made her giggle.

But Nancy had instructed her in the piano and the violin. To be sure, she had no singing voice and none of her father's expertise as an artist had come down to her. Her sketches were only adequate, her watercolors, muddy. Still she thought she might make a superior governess, fit to instruct even a duke's daughters.

Lili cursed under her breath and turned over on her other side. Oh, yes, she might *teach* them even though 'Nelia had told her she could never aspire to their heights. And why? Because her father had been a poor nobody, while theirs, through no superiority of their own, but only from an accident of birth, had become exalted. It was all most unfair, and she was sure not at all what God had intended.

It was very late when she fell asleep at last, and late when she woke to find a maid making up her fire and Cornelia delivering her morning chocolate with her own hands.

"I am so sorry I overslept," she exclaimed as she sat up to take it. "But you must not wait on me, 'Nelia. It is I who should wait on you."

"Please do not," her hostess said over her shoulder as she threw open the draperies to let the weak March light steal in. It was raining and blowing, an ugly day. Lili knew she would be confined to the Court, and she stifled a sigh.

"I am not so decrepit or of such advanced age that help is necessary," Cornelia continued. "Do get up, Lili. I want you to see the latest *Godey's*. There are some charming ensembles depicted there. We will see if any appeal to us both.

"Not, of course, that we will have any say in the matter," she added as Lili finished her chocolate and climbed out of bed. "Alastair will take over, as he always does."

She sighed. "If only he did not have such exquisite taste," she complained. "I confess I still cherish a hope I might catch him in some horrid mistake, but in four years of marriage he has remained faultless. So tiresome, don't you agree?"

The ensembles depicted in the popular lady's magazine awed Lili. She could not picture herself garbed in a single one of them, and they looked as if they would be very expensive. Cornelia scolded her for concerning herself with the cost. As the relative of Mrs. Alastair Russell, she must be clothed appropriately, must she not? She wisely did not mention in any detail how many gowns and slippers and hats Lili would need, for she knew she would recoil in horror. She had decided to wait until she had Alastair beside her for that. She could still remember how he had persuaded a thirteen-year-old Lili to accept a certain cherry cloak to replace the ugly gray one the nuns had given her, and how he had overridden all her protests and purchased the scarlet trunk she still used to this day.

Lili did not look forward to meeting the dowager countess again. But when she came out of the library later that day, the lady was passing in the hall. Demurely, she dropped her a reverent curtsy. To her surprise, she was completely ignored. The dowager moved past her, giving orders to the butler as she did so. She did not acknowledge Lili in any way. Lili knew she had been seen, however, for Lady Wyckend had inspected her from head to toe before looking right through her. It felt eerie. It was almost as if she were not there at all.

However, when Lili thought of it later in the privacy of her room, she realized such treatment was vastly superior to being

called a bastard whenever they chanced to meet, which she
had quite expected and secretly dreaded.

She was ignored at dinner as well when the three ladies
gathered in the dining room that evening. The dowager spoke
only to her former daughter-in-law, and when Cornelia addressed Lili, she pretended not to hear. Cornelia was perturbed, but Lili winked at her and smiled, to let her know she
did not dislike such treatment in the slightest.

After that first stormy day, the weather changed for the better. There was even a hint of spring in the air. Lili was quick to
ask permission to ride and Cornelia said she might if she had a
groom to accompany her.

"But surely a groom is not necessary, 'Nelia," she protested,
turning around so the maid could do up her habit. "What is the
need of him if I remain on Wyckend land? I am not used to
being followed about. I know I will hate it."

"Hate it or not, it is how proper young ladies go riding," her
hostess assured her. Not blue to match her eyes. That would be
too obvious, she told herself. Would a gray habit with charcoal
trimming be too sophisticated for a seventeen-year-old?

She saw Lili was staring at her, her stubborn little chin
tilted, and she stared back, her expression growing colder and
firmer. To her surprise, Lili dissolved in giggles.

"Oh, that is perfect, 'Nelia," she exclaimed when she could
speak. "You look so strict, why, even regal. I wonder if I could
acquire such a look? I am sure it would come in handy on any
number of occasions."

"With the groom or not at all," she was told. "I will not be
diverted by these clever tricks of yours."

"Very well, if you insist," Lili replied, looking perfectly
woebegone.

"If miss would remain still, please?" the maid asked from
her knees, where she was trying to stitch up a section of the
hem that had come undone. Obediently, Lili subsided.

The groom's name was Flynn. He was a middle-aged man
with a dour expression except when he was addressing horses.
Then he crooned to them and called them pet names as he

groomed them. He told Lili she had an excellent mount and he would be obliged if she would refrain from ruining its mouth. Lili was very much on her guard all through their first ride, but soon, after they had been out together for a few days, she relaxed. Flynn might not be the best of companions, but he was not obtrusive, and she was able to ride without being forced to listen to a constant stream of instructions and warnings. It was then she knew Flynn found her horsemanship acceptable.

Cornelia read a great deal when she was not writing letters, and Lili was delighted to join her in her sitting room or the library, both of them deep in their current book. Lili had discovered a cache of old novels on a library shelf, which she found amusing. Still she had to chuckle one afternoon, and Cornelia looked up from her own book to inquire why.

"It is this novel, 'Nelia. The people in it use such overblown language. Just listen to this—'M'lord, I must beg you to moderate your speech lest I swoon at this inopportune inappropriate pleading for my hand. Surely you know it is not suitable for a lady like myself to hear until my father has given you his august approval. Desist, I say, m'lord, desist!' Now 'Nelia, can you imagine anyone saying 'desist'?"

"You must try one of Miss Austen's novels. I have found her delightful, although I wonder if I should encourage you to read novels at all. Some people consider them a terrible influence on the young. But since I myself enjoy them, I feel I can hardly censure your taste."

Lili was glad of that. Mostly she considered Cornelia a dear companion and their difference in age of no importance. It was only occasionally when she did something Cornelia could not approve, that she was brought up short and reminded of those thirteen years.

One afternoon, fresh from a bath after a morning spent in the saddle, Lili wandered downstairs to discover Cornelia was entertaining afternoon callers. When Viscount Halpern rose from his chair and subjected her to an icy inspection, Lili was glad the dowager was nowhere to be seen. The older lady with him was introduced as his mother, the Marchioness of

Braybourne. Lili regarded the lady with apprehension. She was remembering Cornelia's lecture on the nobility, and how grand and exalted dukes and marquises were. But although the lady was hardly informal, she bore her part in the conversation easily.

As she took her seat, Lili wondered why they had come. Braybourne was some little distance from Wyckend, but she did not know if calls were often exchanged between the two estates. Then it occurred to her that perhaps the viscount had come to tell them about the boy who had been injured, and she scolded herself mentally for her uncharitable thoughts about him.

During the next lull in the conversation, she turned to him and smiled so winningly he looked stunned.

"You are so good to come and let us know how the poor shepherd boy is doing, m'lord. I trust he is mending nicely?"

"I have no idea how he does," Halpern told her, frowning now. "I cannot imagine why you would suppose I would know anything about him."

Lili did not pause to think, something Cornelia had often berated her for in the past. Instead, she said quickly, "Perhaps because it was your fault he was injured in the first place? Yours and your guests? Or perhaps, since you obviously could not summon up the slightest bit of Christian concern, you might have felt some small obligation to do so?"

It was very still in the drawing room when she fell silent. The viscount had paled, and Cornelia appeared struck dumb. Only the marchioness had the presence of mind to say to her hostess, "I see the dowager still holds firm in her desire to keep Wyckend just as she first saw it as a bride. I do feel for you, Mrs. Russell. It must be so tiresome."

"Indeed it is," Cornelia agreed, and the conversation turned to elderly ladies and their crotchets. Lili wished she were dead. She was sure the viscount wished she were as well, for he ignored her for the remainder of the visit. Oh, why had she attacked him like that? Still, she had spoken nothing but the truth. The boy's injury and the loss of one of his flock must fall entirely on Halpern's broad shoulders and his rank did not excuse him. The boy was only a peasant, true, but he was a human being, and as such, he was just as good as Viscount Halpern. In the Lord's eyes, anyway. Still, she could see it had not been her place to point this out to the man, especially in Cornelia's drawing room during an afternoon call. From a marchioness, too, she remembered, and groaned. And it was not as if her scolding would do any good. The man was conceited, overbearing, and so sure of his superiority Lili wanted to shake him. She forced herself to sit quietly and limited her remarks from then on to simple statements that could not cause offense and she spoke only when spoken to. Halpern seemed to relish this penance, for she caught a light in his eyes and what she suspected to be the hint of a smile. It infuriated her but she could do nothing about it. And he knew it, which made her even angrier.

When the guests rose to leave, he spoke to her again for the first time since her outburst. "Since you are so interested, Miss Martingale, I shall make it my business to send you a complete report of the unfortunate youth's well-being. I trust you will not feel it necessary for me to go to the hovel where he no doubt lives to inquire? That it might be acceptable for me to send an agent? Thank you. You are too good."

Lili clenched her fists in the folds of her skirts. Insufferable boor, she thought as she nodded distantly before she turned to give his mother her best curtsy. As she did so, she wondered at that lady's searching gaze. But she did not have to wonder why Cornelia looked so grim and she steeled herself to endure what she was sure would be a scathing lecture on her manners and her lack of taste.

The Marchioness of Braybourne managed to contain herself until the carriage was bowling down the gravel drive to Wyckend Court's gates before she said, "Do tell me what you did to that girl to give her such a dislike of you, Graeme. It is most unlike you. Indeed, I have often disapproved your casual, easy grace with the ladies."

"That girl is no lady," came the quick reply.

Since he was seated beside her, all she could see of her son was a moody profile and the distinguished nose so like his father's. She smiled to herself. "Who is she, do you suppose?" she asked. "Mrs. Russell did say something about her being a distant relative before she joined us if you remember, but I do not recognize the name. Do you?"

"I've never heard of it," he said, his tone implying he had no interest in any Martingale, most especially this one.

"The very idea, taking me to task for my behaviour, and she but a green girl. For you must admit, Mother, if she is a minute over eighteen it would be most surprising," he added, ruining his nonchalant pose.

"Perhaps Mrs. Russell intends to present her this Season," Lady Braybourne murmured.

"One trembles for London, never mind the *ton*'s continued existence," came the swift retort. "You must be wrong, ma'am. Cornelia Russell does not lack common sense. Surely she knows how disastrous such a presentation would be."

"Miss Martingale has a charming smile. When she is not overcome with remorse, that is. And you must admit, she is truly lovely."

He did not reply for a moment, and his mother turned slightly to see why. Her brows rose when she saw he appeared deep in thought.

"She is well enough, I suppose," he said finally. "Perhaps some young man, almost as callow as she is herself, might be brought to the sticking point. Someone stupid enough to find her constant faux pas amusing rather than appalling. But do let us discuss something—anything—else."

"Not until you tell me if you were serious when you all but slayed her by saying you would find out how the injured boy did, and let her know the result. And tell me as well why I have not heard of this terrible accident."

Graeme Wilder was a man of twenty-eight, well past parental lectures, at least from his mother. Still, he colored slightly as he said, "I shall certainly send her a formal note

about the lad. He is one of Squire Meekham's shepherds and
he came to grief because Percy is such a bruiser. He was over
the wall, Gore right behind him, before I could warn them the
road there was heavily traveled. We were lucky they and their
mounts didn't come to grief as well as the boy. As it was I had
to shoot one of the sheep. The boy was unconscious. I do not
know the extent of his injuries. I have reimbursed the squire
for the sheep of course."

"I have never thought Percy Ridgeway at all sensible," the
marchioness said with a sniff. "It is to be forever regretted his
father died so young and his mother left him to tutors until he
was old enough to be sent to school."

"He means no harm, Mother. You know he means no harm."

"But he does seem to create it, does he not? Don't you remember last autumn when he came for the hunting and nearly
burned Braybourne to the ground?"

"You exaggerate, my dear. It was only a little fire involving
nothing more than his bed curtains. I know how bad he felt
about upsetting his candle."

"The fire also burned the carpet and the bed itself. And he is
far too young to be getting absentminded about candles. Unless, as I have always supposed, but am sure I will never discover from you, he was in his cups when he did it. We were
lucky, Graeme, and you know it. If that housemaid hadn't
been passing his door and smelled smoke, heaven knows what
would have happened. And I suppose I shall never discover
why she was either. Passing, I mean. At that hour. If indeed
that was her occupation.

"I wish he would marry. It might be the making of him. If
he could find anyone who would have him, that is."

The viscount was quick to change the subject, for he was on
dangerous ground here. He realized he should have known his
mother was far too astute to believe the story of the wandering
maid, but he had no intention of revealing she had been in
Percy's bed when the fire began. Instead he began to speak of
his mother's current oil painting. She was an accomplished
artist and several of her paintings had been exhibited at the

Royal Academy. He had no doubt that from Percy's deplorable single state, his mother would progress to his own. She did not tease him, or mention it often. She was far too subtle for that. But he knew she did not understand why he had never seen fit to offer for any of the pretty, suitable girls who were presented every Season by their proud, hopeful parents.

Halpern had begun to agree with her that it was time for him to be setting up his nursery. His father, although as healthy a man as you could hope for, would be sixty-seven this year and much as he disliked thinking about a future without him, he was forced to admit it was coming, whether he liked it or not. And then the careless days of being only the heir to the title would be over, and he would have to settle down in earnest to serious matters, as the seventh Marquis of Braybourne.

It was a sobering thought.

Chapter Five

Alastair Russell returned to Wyckend three days later.

Lili was delighted to see him not only because being fond of him, she had missed him, but because she knew his presence would give 'Nelia's thoughts a new direction.

The lecture she had been subjected to had not been harsh, nor had she been assigned any penance. Indeed, it was Nelia's lack of anger when it was obvious she was distressed, that made the whole experience so difficult. And the way she shook her head and said at last, "I wonder if it is a good idea to even think of bringing you out this Season, Lili. You are very young. Younger even than I thought you would be."

At first that statement made no sense. How could she be younger than her age, she wondered? 'Nelia knew she was seventeen. She had sent those beautiful gowns when she could not come to Moorlands for the occasion. The obvious answer—that her behaviour was such it was only worthy of a child, was too terrible to consider. Lili cried alone in her room, and made herself write a long essay on her shortcomings and her desire to do better, which she told herself she would read every single day.

She was out riding with the groom when Alastair's carriage pulled up before the doors that afternoon and so she did not see him untill much later when she waited for him in the drawing room where they generally assembled before dinner. She was glad when he came in alone. As usual, he was dressed impeccably in evening clothes a duke might envy. Several of them had, over the years, in fact. And he was as handsome as she remembered him—those startling clear green eyes, that cap of gleaming gold hair, his white, elegant hands and dazzling linen, his straight posture.

She ran to kiss him and hug him tight, closing her eyes to better savor the lotion he wore she knew so well. Lili had loved him from first meeting in a rocking coach on a French road at dawn. Thirteen then, she had wished she were older, so she might have some chance of marrying him someday. But that was not to be. He loved 'Nelia. She was thirty now, and Alastair—my goodness, he was almost forty. It hardly seemed possible.

"I hear you have been making mice feet of your reputation, Lili," he said as he released her. "Is this true?"

"I don't think it is quite as bad as that, but yes, I did speak before I thought. My wretched tongue! I never meant to scold Halpern like that, especially in front of the marchioness, but he is such a—such a conceited, pompous, overbearing . . ."

"Very like I am," Alastair murmured as he poured himself a glass of sherry. "Do sit down, Lili. Hovering and wringing your hands will not undo the damage. We must think how that can be accomplished."

"He is nothing like you at all, the very idea," Lili protested as she sat down and arranged her skirts with one graceful motion. Russell watched her critically over the rim of his glass. He thought she was even more lovely than he remembered, and now she was older, she had an enticing figure as well. That tiny waist, the hint of shapely hips under the empire gown she wore, her elegant high bosom. And she was but seventeen. Cornelia had warned him, but still she was a picture. Now, if they could only persuade her to keep a civil tongue in her head, they might yet see her married creditably. And although he had been surprised to find her here at Wyckend, for he had not thought she should be presented until she had had her eighteenth birthday, he quite agreed with his wife there had been no other way to handle what had surely become an explosive situation. And Lili Martingale would never be a farmer's wife, not if he had anything to say about it. It was too bad he liked Ben Moorland so much, he thought as he silently begged his pardon for rearranging his life. Still, he felt better when he realized Lili would have made the man a dreadful wife. And marriage was more than those first few ecstatic weeks. Much more.

Cornelia arrived just then in a whirl of skirts. Her face had a lovely color, almost as if she were blushing, and Lili envied her the smile Alastair gave her as he seated her.

"Lili and I have just been discussing Halpern," he said. "I saw him in London a few months ago. He seemed a reasonable man to me, but I bow to your superior understanding. What did you call him, Lili? Conceited, overbearing, and er, pompous? Very like I am myself, wouldn't you say, 'Nelia, my love?"

"I would," she agreed a little too quickly. He looked at her askance and she smiled at him as she added, "But you have such an air about you, my dear, you make it seem the most normal thing in the world. Halpern has not acquired your finesse. I am afraid, not content with crushing Lili with a withering gaze, he was so foolish as to give her a severe setdown as well."

"Good for him," Russell said before he sipped his sherry. "I am sure she deserved it. The world would be a better place if more young women had them on a regular basis."

"My dear countess! How delightful to see you again. You look well."

As he spoke he went to greet the elderly lady being helped into the room by her almost equally elderly maid. Her tiny wrinkled face was wreathed in smiles and she laid her hand on Alastair Russell's sleeve and allowed him to take her to her favorite chair by the fire. He even knelt to adjust the footstool kept ready there, for without it, the dowager's feet would have dangled several inches above the floor.

"Should you care for a drop of Madeira, ma'am?" he asked.

"I should not—that will be all, Jenks—you know I should not, but in honor of your homecoming I shall indulge."

"Lili, if you would be so kind?" he said over his shoulder.

She hastened to do his bidding, pouring the wine into the fragile crystal glass the dowager preferred.

Until Bayley summoned them to the dining room, the dowager and Alastair Russell conversed, with Cornelia occasionally contributing a word or so. Russell did not notice that the elderly woman never acknowledged Lili's existence; she certainly did not speak to her. But once they were all seated at the dining table, it became obvious.

Russell had been describing some of the new fashions he had seen in London, in particular a gown he was sure would become Lili, and he asked the dowager's opinion.

"I should think Cornelia would look very well in it. She appears to advantage in almost every shade of blue."

"But it was Lili I had in mind," Russell reminded her. "Thank you, Bayley, I believe I will have some chicken."

Busy serving himself, he did not notice at first that the dowager did not answer. Still, when he looked up at last, he saw Cornelia's eyes were full of warnings, Lili was staring at her plate as if fascinated with her dinner, and the dowager sat plainly indignant. "Now what is this all about?" he asked. "Never tell me you have been upsetting our dear Sarah as well as the neighborhood nobility, Lili?"

"I will explain everything later," Cornelia murmured across the table, waving the footman away when he would have poured her more wine.

"I am sure there is no need for all this secrecy," the dowager proclaimed, loath to cease being the center of attraction. "This—this girl Cornelia has brought to reside here—at Wyckend, mind!—is none other than her own child, born out of wedlock before her marriage to my dear deluded son, Ogden. I do not acknowledge her. I shall never do so. I am only sorry it has been necessary for you to learn of her existence, my dear Alastair."

Russell dismissed the servants with a wave of his hand. He did not speak until the door closed behind them, but when he did his voice was icy. "I do not know where you had your intelligence, madam, but let me assure you, Lili is the legitimate daughter of one of 'Neila's distant relatives. She is not a bastard. I helped 'Nelia fetch her from that French convent four years ago."

"You must be mistaken, sir," the dowager insisted. "I would not have thought you could be taken in so easily. Why, just look at her—that peak in her hair, so unusual, is it not? And her eyes, her nose, exactly like her mother's."

There was a silence so complete, Lili fancied she could hear the clock ticking three rooms away. She wanted to slide under the table and curl up in a small ball of misery, she was so humiliated. When she dared peek at Alastair, she almost gasped. He was furious, so furious the dowager cringed in her seat, her hands clasped to her heart.

"I will try to forget the insult you have just given my beloved wife, madam," he said. "I say again, you are mistaken. There are often resemblances in families. And I beg you to ask yourself why we would bring Lili here if what you believe is true. It would be stupid of us to invite gossip, and we are not in the least stupid.

"Finally, I must remind you that as the present owner of Wyckend, I would be well within my rights to insist you remove from here permanently."

"Ah, no, Alastair," Cornelia said, reaching out a hand to him in supplication.

"Ah, yes, my love. I will not have you insulted in your own home, at your own table. Not even by Sarah. You will apologize at once, madam."

For a moment, the dowager remained defiant, but she could tell from Russell's rigid posture, the way he looked at her, that he had meant every word he said. She did not dare take the chance he might make good his threat, but even beyond that, she could not bear to alienate him. She loved him, and she often compared him to her son, the late earl, although anyone who had known them both would have protested, for they were not at all alike.

"I—I beg your pardon, 'Nelia," she said finally, so softly it was hard to hear her. "If Alastair says this person is not your daughter, I suppose I am forced to accept it."

"We will excuse you, madam," Russell said, relentless in spite of the pitiful glance she sent him. "This has been upsetting for all of us. 'Nelia, summon the servants. The dowager will go to her own rooms now."

Lili felt starved for breath, and as the dowager tottered from the room on a footman's arm, she inhaled rapidly. She wondered what the servants would make of this, wondered whether they believed, as their former mistress did, that she had been born out of wedlock to 'Nelia.

"How ridiculous she is," Russell said when they were alone at last and he and Cornelia were enjoying a glass of port. "She probably has little skill in mathematics, but surely even such as she can count back and see you would have had to be indiscreet at the age of twelve in order to produce Lili. And that would be impossible, unless you have been lying to me about your age, love?

"I am sorry, Lili, that you have been subjected to such rot. If she continues to misbehave to you, I shall have her removed to the dower house. By rights, she should have spent the last ten years there."

"It is all right. Truly," Lili managed to say, but she was quick to excuse herself after dinner to flee to her room. She did not call a maid but undressed herself. Then she sat down in the low slipper chair at the fireside and wept. Wept because her coming here was making everyone so unhappy. Cornelia first, then Alastair, even the dowager. She was an old lady and excuses should be made for her.

And on top of all that, she had behaved idiotically in front of the Marchioness of Braybourne, and given her son a disgust of her. It was more than too bad, it was awful. She was nothing but a disaster from beginning to end.

She rose then and went to fetch the note that had arrived from Halpern today. She read it again slowly, every cold, formal word.

"Miss Martingale may be reassured that the shepherd boy

she has managed to make her concern, suffered a broken left leg in the accident. It is believed he will make a full recovery."

The note had no salutation, nor any closing except for his title.

A tear dropped on the paper and caused the capital "H" of that title to run. Lili told herself she should go home, and she would have if she had felt safe in doing so. But she knew full well there was no home for her at Moorlands anymore, unless she was prepared to marry Ben.

And even now, beset with troubles and homesick for the familiar faces and scenes of Moorlands, she did not think herself ready for such a final ending. Why, it would be like putting a book away, just when the story began to get exciting.

The dowager kept her word, speaking to Lili at every chance meeting. She was hardly effusive unless Alastair happened to be somewhere near. Then she smiled and nodded, and pretended to be delighted. But her eyes were cold, so cold Lili knew she was hated more than ever. She often fled the house to escape her. She would have liked to discuss this with Cornelia, but now that her husband had returned, Cornelia had little time for her. Lili found herself dreading the numerous rainy days, and she spent most of the clement ones on horseback or on long walks.

One morning early, she decided to walk around the lake that could be seen from Wyckend's north terrace. She did not think to take a maid with her. There was no need for that on Wyckend land, she told herself stoutly as she laced up her sturdy boots. Besides, she had suddenly become very conscious of the servants, wondering what they were thinking and why they looked at her a certain way. She was almost positive they were smirking at her behind her back; calling her a bastard. She knew some of them believed the dowager's accusation, believed Alastair had just been covering up an unpleasant truth. One upstairs maid in particular had let her know by her scornful expression that she was one of their number. Lili dreaded it when she answered the bell.

It was the first week of April now, and the air was softer. Lili felt better with every step that took her farther from the Court. She breathed deeply as she strode along, sorry it was too early for flowers. As she went on her way, she thought of Moorlands. Nancy wrote to her often, adding the captain's thoughts to her own. She never failed to tell Lili how she was loved and sorely missed. But she also never failed to say what a lucky girl she was to have this chance with the Russells.

As Lili entered a small wood, she frowned, remembering. It almost felt sometimes as if Nancy were warning her not to try and come back. Was it possible she knew of Ben's proposal and disapproved of it?

She had covered several miles when she began to tire. But it was too cold to sit down and rest, for the sun had disappeared behind dark clouds and a nasty wind had come up. Pulling her cloak close, Lili smiled down at its homely brown color. 'Nelia had declared their first purchase in London would be a more fashionable one. Lili agreed her cloak was not pretty, but it kept her comfortable.

Looking across the lake, she saw she had come almost three-quarters of the way, and she decided it would be quicker to go on than retrace her steps. Still, surveying the gray water spattered now with whitecaps made by the wind, Wyckend seemed far away. Still, she was a countrywoman. She had trudged many a mile during her stay at the farm.

Half an hour later, she came upon a brook blocking her path. There was no footbridge across it and she paused in confusion. To go back now would be foolish, she knew. Perhaps there were stepping stones somewhere? She had been following a well-marked path that echoed the contours of the lake itself. Strange, no one had thought to make a safe passage here. She walked along the brook for some time, but although it narrowed in places, there was no help for walkers. Retreating to the original path, Lili decided she had no choice but to chance a crossing. The brook was wide and it looked deep, but she was sure she could jump it. Picking up her skirts and holding them above her knees she backed up to give herself a running start. She was just ready to launch herself over the water when she heard a horse neigh somewhere nearby. It startled her, for she had thought herself quite alone, and she checked her jump. For a moment, she teetered on the bank, but the ground under her feet, softened by the spring rains, broke away under her weight. Unable to help herself, she slid forward into the rushing water. The stones she landed on shifted under her feet, and before she knew it, she was on her hands and knees in the icy water.

Struggling to escape, she managed to crawl to the opposite bank. It was higher than its fellow, and she could not get out. Her sodden skirts held her captive, and her cloak felt like a lead weight on her shoulders. She cursed long and loud in her frustration.

Chapter Six

"Well, that's a charming expression for a young lady to know, never mind voice," a deep, amused voice remarked. Lili looked way up to see Viscount Halpern regarding her. He was astride a bay gelding and as she stared at him, he dismounted and came to hold out his hand to her.

"Here, take hold," he ordered.

Lili obeyed. She never even thought of telling him she could manage without his assistance, thank you very much. That would have been foolish beyond words, and she was not foolish. Not when she was cold and wet and thoroughly miserable at any rate.

"T-t-t-thank you," she managed to say when she was on dry land again. The wind battered her wet skirts against her legs and she shivered. Her hands and feet felt like ice, too.

"You are a long way from home, Miss Martingale," the viscount said. "Did your mount throw you?"

"I w-w-was w-w-walking," Lili told him, shivering even harder, no matter how she tried to hide it. Even grateful as she was for his help, she couldn't stop herself from wondering why it had to be he, of all people, who had found her here in this lonely spot. Was she cursed, somehow?

The viscount hid his surprise that she could walk so far as he said, "We must get you out of those wet clothes as soon as possible. I think it best to take you to Braybourne. It is closer than Wyckend Court. In fact you are on Braybourne land here. Were you aware of that?"

As he spoke, he put his arm around her and half carried her

toward the gelding that stood patiently, head down as it sniffed the dead grass before it.

"I h-h-had better g-g-go h-h-home," she protested.

He ignored her. Putting his hands on her waist, he lifted her easily onto the gelding's back, speaking to the horse to calm it as he did so.

"You will go to Braybourne, Miss Martingale," he said as he mounted behind her and pulled her into the crook of his arm.

Lili wanted to protest this sweeping, omnipotent statement, but her teeth were chattering so, she knew she would not be able to get the words out.

"However did you come to fall in the brook?" he asked as he wheeled the horse and set out the way he had come.

Lili was struggling to sit independently, but there wasn't any room for such modesty. Like it or not, she was crammed against Halpern's broad chest. Resigning herself to this intimacy, she said, "I w-w-would not h-h-have d-d-done so if y-y-your h-horse hadn't s-s-startled m-m-me."

He chuckled, a warm chuckle she could almost feel had started deep in his belly. It was an infectious chuckle, too, and somehow she found this unsettling.

"So, this is my fault too?" he asked lightly. "Dear me, I seem to be involved in one bad turn after another, don't I?" Then he added quickly, "Don't try to talk. I will have you safe in a little while, and warm as well."

Lili shuddered in response, and he urged the horse to a trot. It seemed an endless time before they entered an open gate and rode cross country until they reached a formal drive. It wound through a large beech wood, where they encountered some men gathering kindling. As they bowed to the viscount, Lili knew Braybourne could not be far now.

When it came into view below them as they left the wood at the crest of a rise, she gasped. Set among acres of lawn and formal gardens, and fronted by ornamental water, Braybourne Hall stood proud and tall. It was made of the same gray stone as Wyckend, but the end result was one of almost fragile elegance that was unusual for a building so massive. And it seemed to grow even more massive the closer they came to it. At last the gelding clattered over the cobblestones as they went under an arched entrance and came to a halt before a set of graceful curving marble steps. Large urns stood on those steps. They were empty now, but Lili was sure they would be filled with flowers by May.

The viscount dismounted and threw the reins over the gelding's head. He reached up for Lili, who sat in a miserable huddle.

"Put your hands on my shoulders," Halpern ordered. She did as she was told. She not only had no choice, she had no desire to remain where she was a minute longer than she had to. She could feel the wind now even through her sodden clothes. She had lost all feeling in her legs as well. She wondered how she was to manage the steps without falling, but the viscount did not let her try. Instead, he swung her up into his arms and mounted the steps two at a time. Lili's heart began to race and she stared at him, aghast. Their faces were only inches apart. She saw he had a pair of handsome hazel eyes flecked with gold, and his mouth was finely formed. She also saw where his valet had nicked him this morning, shaving him. The cut made him more human somehow.

Since he had his hands full, Halpern kicked the massive door with its carved panels and shining brass. It was swung open immediately.

"There you are, Pickett. This young lady had the misfortune to fall into a stream. I am taking her to my room. There's a fire there. Have the maids bring hot water, towels, brandy—you know the drill. Oh," he called over his shoulder as he strode across the massive hall to the stairs, "ask my mother's maid to come to me. At once."

Lili was aware of a broad set of stairs, a long hall lined with what appeared to be family portraits, and a maid flattening herself against the wall to allow them passage, her mouth a perfect O of astonishment. Then they were in a room that was obviously a man's private domain. The furniture was dark and

imposing, and the draperies and bed hangings were a deep
scarlet with gold trim. A handsome Oriental rug covered the
floor. The fire in the grate burned brightly, and Lili was delighted to be set down before it, although she found herself
clutching the viscount's arm for support.

"Put your arms out wide so I can take this cloak off," he
said. Lili obeyed, but deep inside she had stiffened at the orders he threw at her, one after the other. "Good, now sit down
and let me get your shoes. Oh wait, first this ridiculous bonnet." He tilted her chin up so he could undo the ribbon. He
seemed to be having trouble with it—perhaps it had knot-
ted?—and she reached up to help him. She found her hands
being pushed away, and once again felt some resentment.

"There!" he said at last, tossing it to the floor before he
pushed her gently into a big wing chair. "Can you manage
your gloves?" he asked as he knelt and pushed her sodden
skirts up to begin unlacing her boots.

"My lord!" A shocked female voice cried from the doorway.
"Whatever do you think you are doing?"

As she spoke, a middle-aged maid marched into the room,
her arms full of towels. Behind her, two maids held copper
cans of hot water.

"I am divesting this poor child of some very cold, very wet
garments," he explained.

"I see," the maid said, raking Lili from head to foot. Her
gown clung to her body. It was obvious she was no child, and
the maid sniffed.

Halpern rose. "Best you take over now, Keating. I'll just
fetch something for her to wear before I leave . . ."

He dashed into the adjoining dressing room to return in a
moment with a handsome dressing gown. It was made of dark
green wool with black velvet cuffs and lapels. "Put this on
her," he instructed. "You there, put the water can down and go
across the hall and make up the fire there. And the bed," he
added as he followed one of the maids to the door. "I will just
see what's keeping Pickett and that brandy . . ."

Still talking, he disappeared and Lili was left with the middle-

aged maid, who looked as if she did not approve these goings-
on, no, not the least little bit.

"If you will just stand up, miss," she said coldly. "We'll see
about getting that gown off you. Shut the door, Bessie," she
added, sniffing again.

Lili could not help it. She was cold and tired and depressed,
and the hot tears began to flow in a steady stream down her
cold cheeks. "I-I-I'm sorry to b-b-be such a b-b-bother," she
managed to get out.

The maid looked up sharply, and when she saw that woe-
beogone little face, her indignation vanished. Folding Lili in
her arms against her massive bosom, she crooned, "There,
there, miss. Don't cry now. We've quite enough water to deal
with without you adding to it, now don't we?"

For some reason, this pleasantry cheered Lili considerably,
and she stood docilely as she was undressed, rubbed briskly
with warm towels, and at last enfolded in the viscount's dressing gown. Her hands disappeared in the long sleeves and the
hem puddled around her on the floor, but it felt lovely and
warm. It smelled lovely as well, of some spicy scent that had a
hint of summer in it.

"There now, here's some hot tea, miss," Keating said as another maid came in with a tray. "Just let me fold back these
cuffs for you, and sit down here and drink it while I see how
Agnes is coming along. We'll soon have your room ready, and
you can climb into bed for a good rest."

Lili took the cup she was handed and cradled it in both
hands. She almost hated to drink it, it made such an excellent
hand warmer. The maids gathered up her wet clothes and curtsied themselves away.

Left alone, Lili stared into the fire and tried to think what
she must do. Of course she should not go to bed here, but what
else could she do without any clothes to wear? She would
have to wait until hers dried. But perhaps someone might ride
to Wyckend to tell 'Nelia of her misfortunes. She was sure
Alastair would come for her with dry clothes and she need not
impose on the viscount much longer. She looked around the

large room as she sipped her tea. There were papers on the desk, and books stacked beside it. A coat lay over the end of the bed, and several white neckcloths were draped over a doorknob. Near a walnut armoire, there was a large dog's bed. That surprised her. She had not thought the haughty Viscount Halpern the type of man who liked dogs.

"There you are. All right and tight now?" Halpern asked as he entered the room. Lili was sure he should not be here with her alone. She was undressed, and never mind she was covered from head to toe in his dressing gown. She saw his face change as he looked at her, soften almost, and she wondered at it. Something seemed to have come into the room with him and brought an atmosphere that unnerved her even as it heightened all her senses. She was alarmed, although she didn't know why.

Of course, she had no idea how adorable she looked, huddled there in the big chair, lost in a dressing gown made for a man many sizes larger, with her black curls tumbling on her head and her blue eyes still bright from crying.

After a silence that seemed to stretch endlessly, the viscount recalled himself. "How are you feeling?" he asked gruffly. "Better, I hope. Warmer."

"I am fine now, m'lord," she said. "I must thank you for everything you have done for me," she added as she put the teacup she held down on the table beside her.

"You will need that," he said, showing her the bottle of old brandy he carried. "This will help warm you."

"But I don't need it, thank you, and I—I don't drink brandy. Or anything else, yet," she added, as if determined to be honest.

He was busy pouring a tot of the amber liqueur and she doubted he had even heard her. When he held out the cup and smiled, she took it without a word. And she had to admit, even the fumes that reached her nose were warming.

She only sipped a little of the brandy, but still, when she swallowed it, she was thrown into a fit of coughing. The liqueur burned her throat all the way down to her stomach. But after Halpern had pounded her back, and she was only gasping, she could tell the warmth it provided was far superior to tea.

"Perhaps I should have diluted it," he said, checking the teapot to see if it was empty.

"No, no, please. This is quite enough, I assure you."

"M'lord, what are you doing here?" Keating demanded as she bustled back into the room. "Just you go along now. I'm going to put miss to bed across the hall, and I would appreciate it if you made yourself scarce.

"What's that you're holding? You've never been plying the poor little thing with brandy, have you, at her age? I never!"

"In this case, it was only for medicinal purposes, Keating," he said, sounding amused. "I wish you a good rest, Miss Martingale. I have sent a groom to Wyckend with a note to inform the Russells of your whereabouts, and your misadventure."

"Thank you," Lili said, wondering why she still felt so strange, so uneasy.

After he was gone, Keating helped her across the hall. They found one maid adding coal to the glowing grate while another passed a warming pan slowly between the sheets of a large bed.

Keating waved them away as she held out a night rail fragile with lace before the fire to warm it. "This is one of m'lady's gowns," she said. "No, no, she would be delighted to lend it to you. So, you are a Miss Martingale. Strange, that. I knew a family of that name once, in my home village. Of course I left there years ago when I went into service as a girl," she said as she whisked off the viscount's robe and lowered the night rail over Lili's head. It fit her much better, and it was certainly lovely, but still she missed the robe that had been discarded.

Telling herself she was being very silly, she allowed Keating to tuck her into bed, and worn out from her walk and all the subsequent excitement, she fell asleep before the maid even closed the door.

An hour later, Keating was back with a tray. "A Mr. Russell of Wyckend has arrived, miss," she told Lili as she opened the draperies to let the light in. Lili stretched and yawned before she sat up. She would have been happy to sleep longer. But of course, she told herself as she eyed the portmanteau another maid was setting down, she had to get dressed and go home. As she began to devour a scone she had slathered with strawberry jam, she wondered if she would see the viscount again. It was strange how he had changed. Why, he had been all kindness, all gentle concern for her. Of course, she thought as she cut a piece of ham, he had also ordered her about shamelessly. Somehow that had not bothered her too much, probably because she was so miserable it felt good to be told what to do. Not that I would care for it on a regular basis, she told herself, her eyes growing stormy.

Keating accompanied her down the massive staircase to show her the drawing room where Alastair waited with the marquis. Lili had not cared to learn he was there. It would have been so much easier if she had just been able to slip away, without having to meet someone she was sure would scorn her even more than his son did. But when Keating left her at the door with a nod and a smile, she had no choice but to knock and enter.

The drawing room was huge. As she came in, two gentlemen rose from chairs set near a bow window. The light was behind them and she could not see their faces. Still, she recognized Alastair from his bearing. The other man was just as tall but he was heavier, and as she drew closer she saw he had a head of white hair and a florid complexion. He raised his quizzing glass to inspect her as she curtsied.

"May I present our ward, Lillian Martingale, m'lord?" Alastair said. "Lili, the Marquis of Braybourne."

She curtsied again, glad to be able to look down. She fancied the marquis's intent eyes were able to see inside her head and read her thoughts, and she didn't like it.

"So this is Miss Martingale," he said in a weary voice. He sounded as if she were just what he had expected, whatever that was. "You intend to present her in a year or so, do you? Well, she's pretty enough."

"Cornelia is thinking of this year, sir," Alastair told him. "However, Lili's escapades must give us pause.

"How are you, my dear?" he asked then, coming to hold her hand. She wondered why he looked at her so searchingly. "You don't look as if you fell in a cold stream only a while ago."

"Everyone has been so kind," she said, smiling to include the marquis. His brows rose and he nodded.

"Of course," he said curtly. "I see it all now."

"We will not trespass here longer, sir," Alastair said as he held out the shawl Cornelia had sent to replace Lili's cloak. As she put it on, he added, "My thanks, and my wife's as well, for everything you have done for this tiresome girl. Be sure to convey my compliments to your son. Lili was fortunate he was about when she fell into the stream."

"It would not have happened if he had not been there," she said impulsively. "It was the neighing of his horse that startled me just as I was about to jump the brook."

"Indeed?" the marquis drawled. Lili wondered why he sounded so skeptical. She decided she did not like this old man at all.

"Yes, m'lord, indeed," she said, tilting her stubborn little chin at him.

"She's right, you know," Halpern remarked as he came down the room toward them. Lili turned. She had not heard him come in.

"I apologize that any action of mine—or my horse—caused you to suffer a ducking, Miss Martingale."

Lili felt her cheeks reddening and she began to study the handsome Axminster carpet beneath her feet.

"We were just about to leave, Halpern," Alastair told him. "However, I am glad of the opportunity to thank you for Lili's sake. No matter whose fault it was, she surely would have suffered from exposure if you hadn't been there."

"No need to go on about it, man," the marquis interrupted. "She is obviously bloomin' now, isn't she?"

His tone was so sarcastic, Lili was glad when Alastair led

her away. Halpern escorted them to the carriage, chatting of London to Alastair as he did so. He helped Lili to her seat himself, waving the groom away. Lili stammered as she said good-bye. Halpern grinned at her, amused again. She felt distinctly miffed as they set off for home.

"Well, that was a fine thing," Alastair remarked mildly. "You must tell me, my dear, what you were doing on Braybourne land, jumping a Braybourne brook this morning."

"I went out for a walk around the lake. I didn't know I was on Braybourne land. There was no cairn to mark the boundary as there usually is."

"Strange, wasn't it, that the viscount just happened to be there? You weren't by any chance looking for him, were you, minx?"

"Looking for Halpern?" she echoed, turning to stare at him. As usual he was impeccable. The Marquis of Braybourne might be a noble gentleman but he could not hold a candle to Alastair Russell. Today, however, Lili did not notice.

"Of course I wasn't looking for him," she said indignantly. "I barely know the man and what I do know about him, I dislike."

"I only ask because it is obvious his father thinks you were stalking him. He's quite a catch, Viscount Halpern."

Lili grasped his arm. "Is that why he did not like me? But it is not true! You know it is not true, Alastair!"

"No, I didn't, but I will take your word for it. You do not lie, Lili. I know that. But I beg you not to form any sort *tendre* for the eligible viscount. He is not a suitable prospect for a husband, my dear. Not at all. He has a noble and revered name. They are proud, the Wilders. I expect Halpern to marry high, perhaps to a duke's daughter. He is not for the likes of you, Lili."

Lili stared at him, speechless with dismay. Here was Alastair, much as 'Nelia had done, telling her about her low estate, too. Warning her it would be impossible for her to hope for a marriage to any titled gentleman. It stunned her, as did his assumption she could be so devious as to deliberately seek

Halpern out, hoping to either intrigue him or entrap him. For the remainder of the short distance to the Court, she stared out the window, lost in some very unpleasant thoughts.

Back in the drawing room at Braybourne, the marquis was echoing Russell's words. "You're too old for that chit, Graeme, and I'll thank you to remember it, sir," he growled as he accepted the glass of Canary his son handed him.

"Do you think so?" Halpern asked, lifting his own glass in a mock salute. "Let me see now. I am twenty-eight. Since Miss Martingale is at least eighteen, I suppose I . . ."

His father snorted. "Eighteen, you say? Where are your eyes? I would wager she's not a day over seventeen if she is even that. A schoolroom miss, for all she's so clever. She'll have you, Graeme, if she can catch you, so be on your guard."

The viscount was sure his father must be wrong about Miss Martingale. Seventeen? Surely not! But he said nothing that would have provoked the old man to an argument. It wasn't worth it.

"You need not concern yourself, sir. I am not easily taken in," he said mildly. "Tell me, does Mother join us this afternoon or is she still locked away in her studio with her paints?"

Chapter Seven

Lili did not see the viscount again, for the only one who came to Wyckend from Braybourne was a groom bearing a neatly tied bundle of the clothing she had worn the morning of her mishap. They had been freshly washed and ironed, the brown cloak brushed as carefully as if it were the queen's.

She put the clothes away herself, wearing a serious expression as she did so. She could not seem able to put Alastair's words from her mind, nor those of the sarcastic old gentleman who was the Marquis of Braybourne. That he should think her interested in his son was ludicrous, she told herself. Halpern was an older man. Much too old for her. Yet somehow, if she were to be honest with herself, she had to agree he did not seem paternal. Indeed, she often found herself thinking of him, remembering things about him—how his hair fell back from his forehead in a broad wave, the gold flecks in his deep-set eyes, the faint dimple next to his expressive mouth. The clean, chiseled line of his jaw. And most importantly, the way she had felt held in his arms before him in the saddle.

And something had really surprised her later. 'Nelia, instead of being upset with her for what had happened, had only laughed and said she wished she might have been there to see such a comical thing for herself.

"And I wish you had been there, too," she had told her fervently. "Your presence would have stilled all the horrid suspicions the marquis harbored. Why, he seemed to consider me some kind of—of adventurer!"

"I cannot imagine *why* he would think such a thing," the dowager contributed. Lili started. They were in the drawing room after dinner at the time, and she had forgotten the old lady was with them. Generally, she went to her own rooms as soon as the meal was ended. But then, she had smiled at her young guest. Lili could almost feel the poison in that smile from across the room. She hid a shiver.

"I expect the dancing master I engaged in London, as well as the mantua maker, to arrive in the next day or so, Lili," Alastair said, changing the subject neatly.

"You may be sure Alastair has chosen all the nicest colors and patterns for your clothes, my dear," Cornelia said. "Not that he will tell me a single thing about them. Men can be so provoking!

"But, Alastair, what do you think of a light gray habit trimmed with darker gray or black? It might be attractive with Lili's dark hair. Understated, too. Unless you consider it too drab for a young girl?"

"No. But perhaps too sophisticated?"

"I suggest a brilliant scarlet," the dowager said. "It will call attention to the gel, draw all the young bloods' eyes. And surely that is what we want, ain't it? To marry her off quickly?"

Alastair turned to look at her, his handsome face intent. For a moment, the two stared at each other, then the dowager looked down. She was flustered as she gathered up the belongings she always carried. Her reticule, a fan, a large handkerchief, a silver-capped bottle of salts.

Alastair was there when she struggled to her feet, to escort her to the door, where he assigned a footman to see her safely to her rooms.

"She is becoming more and more unpleasant," 'Nelia remarked when the three were alone. "I hope you are ignoring her jibes, Lili. Her age, you know . . ."

Lili bit her lower lip to keep from bursting into speech. She did not think it at all fair that old age allowed people to say any nasty thing they chose, and excused them from the censure a younger person would have had to suffer. Alastair must have agreed with her, because he said, "That is no reason for her to attack Lili. Well, never mind, my pet. We will be leaving for London soon and you will not have to see Sarah for a long time."

"When?" Lili demanded, inching forward in her chair, the dowager forgotten.

"In a week or so," he promised. "After your gowns are fitted and you have mastered all the dance steps and figures you will require. And I have set all in train here for the spring planting, et cetera. 'Nelia, my love, you did not tell me a gentleman farmer's life would be so circumscribed. I am mired in duties and scarcely have a moment to myself."

"But you have no rooster to contend with," Cornelia told him, smiling. "You must admit, sir, there is no rooster."

They both chuckled, and as she often did now, Lili felt forgotten and very much in the way. The rooster was a private joke between them. She had never been told what that joke was. And there were other moments like this one when the two of them seemed to forget she was even in the room, so lost were they in a world of their own. She could feel tears forming in her eyes, and she jumped up to excuse herself, lest they disgrace her. She could not imagine why she suddenly wanted to cry. Surely the dowager had not upset her to that extent. Could it be she was missing Moorlands again? And Nancy and the captain? Ben? Especially Ben?

"Don't leave just yet, Lili," Alastair ordered, and obediently she sat down again. "I have been meaning to ask you why you so often look lost and sad. You are not homesick, I trust?"

Her tears forgotten, Lili considered her answer carefully. "Sometimes," she admitted. "It is so different here."

"I should hope so," he replied, looking affronted. Cornelia smiled. Lili could not.

"But is there some other reason as well? Confess now."

Lili twisted her hands in her lap. She knew she must say something. "Well, yes, I have been unhappy ever since the dowager said I was born out of wedlock," she admitted. "I knew it was not true. You told me so, 'Nelia, and I believe you. But you see, the servants believe the dowager. At least some of them do. You may be sure word traveled swiftly after that scene at the table that night."

"It always does. It is impossible to keep anything from servants," Alastair said, frowning now. "Have they been rude to you? Disobeyed an order of yours?"

"Not all of them. In fact, not very many. But there is one upstairs maid in particular who sneers at me and hesitates when I ask her to do something. It is unpleasant."

Alastair held up a hand when Cornelia would have spoken. "I see we have forgotten an important part of your education, Lili. When a servant is insolent, you have merely to stare at them—hard. When they begin to look uncomfortable, and I assure you they will, you raise your brows. Like this."

He glared at her for a moment, then looked so haughty and surprised, she almost giggled.

"And if that does not resolve the matter, you threaten them with dismissal."

"In this case, I think dismissal is what is needed," Cornelia said crisply. "Who is this maid, Lili?"

Lili hesitated. Even now she did not want to bring trouble to another. But at last she sighed, and said, "It is Dorcas, ma'am."

"She shall leave our employ tomorrow. After dismissing her, I shall inform both Bayley and my maid the reason I did so. I am sure you will find a drastic change in the staff's attitude by tomorrow evening, my dear."

"And don't you start feeling sorry for the maid, as I know you are longing to do," Alastair instructed. "She does not deserve your pity, my girl, so do not waste it on her."

The dancing master arrived. His wife came with him, to play the piano while he taught Lili all the latest steps. She was forced to spend over an hour a day with him. When the fashionable dressmaker and her assistant arrived as well, she found she had little free time. All the fabrics and colors were beautiful, as Cornelia had said they would be, but when she saw how many outfits were planned, she rebelled.

"You do not realize how unfortunate it would be to have to appear in the same ballgown on every occasion," Alastair told her when she went to him and protested. "That is only done by people down on their luck. Or squeeze pennies, of course. And if you are thinking of telling me of all the destitute girls who have only one ragged gown, spare me! Instead of dwelling on such as they, I would suggest you consider how many you are keeping happily employed plying their needles for Madame Duprés while making your gowns."

Lili scorned his reasoning, but when she had had her first fitting of a pale yellow silk gown trimmed with rosettes of the same color, she was won over.

She went to church that Sunday alone. Alastair never attended, something that disturbed her, for she was concerned for his soul. Cornelia often went with her, but this particular Sunday she had not appeared for breakfast. When Lili inquired for her, her maid said she was still sleeping.

Dressed in a smart new carriage gown with a hat Cornelia had lent her until they could shop for hats and bonnets of her own in London, Lili rode in solitary state. She had refused to take a maid, and Alastair had not insisted when she told him that surely she was perfectly safe with not only the coachman to protect her, but the two footmen in livery up behind as well.

To be truthful, she preferred to attend church alone. She was not that religious, one of the reasons she had been eager to escape the convent, but still, attending daily Mass had been a habit not easily broken. Of course, there was no chance of attending Mass here in the country. Catholics were still hated here; there were no churches or abbeys that she knew of. But even though she found the Church of England liturgy plain and undistinguished compared to the Latin spoken in the Catholic Church, she was able to replace that liturgy in her mind with the familiar words she knew by heart. And sometimes, if she concentrated really hard, she could see in her mind the nuns of her childhood as well, kneeling with their rosaries and praying, and she was comforted.

This morning she found she was not the only one from a great house to attend services. Shortly after she was seated, there arose in the congregation a whispering and stirring that told her the nobles of Braybourne must have come, too. She kept her eyes closed, but she was listening so intently she could hear a shiver of silk that could only be the marchioness's gown as she passed, and she fancied she caught a whiff of that intriguing lotion the viscount wore.

She heard little of the service that morning, and if anyone had asked her what the sermon had been about, she would have been hard put to answer. Instead, she sat and fretted about how she was to escape after the service without having to speak to the party from Braybourne. At least the marquis had not come, she told herself, peeking at the back of the viscount's head and the handsome hat his mother wore.

As soon as the final benediction had been pronounced, Lili fled, praying her rush to the door was not too obvious. The vicar smiled at her and held her hand in his as he inquired for the Russells. He was a kindly old man and she could not escape him without being rude. Only when he was forced to reach up and smooth back his white hair when a sudden April breeze disarranged it, was she free to leave. But by then it was too late.

"Miss Martingale, well met," the viscount drawled. "Give you good day, sir," he added as he passed the vicar, leaving his mother to deal with the man.

"I trust you suffered no ill effects from your earlier, er, dip?" he asked as he took Lili's arm and strolled with her to the carriages.

"I am well, m'lord," she answered, carefully not looking at him. "Thank you."

He paused and she was forced to do so as well. "You have no maid with you?"

"Surely there is no need. The coachman and two footmen

are protection enough. I see they are waiting for me. You must excuse me, sir."

He did not reply. Instead he stepped in front of her and grasped both her arms. Lili was aware everyone who had attended morning service was lingering in the churchyard, and all of them were intent on the fascinating scene being played out before them.

"What are you doing?" she demanded, unable to break free under the circumstances. "Let me go at once!"

"Perhaps I will, now I have forced you to look at me," he told her. "I find I dislike conversing with a profile. Not that is not a lovely profile, but still . . . You should have a maid, you know, if for nothing more than to lend you consequence."

"At church, in the country, such niceties are ridiculous," she retorted, delighted to be able to correct him. "Besides, what I do is none of your affair, sir. Now let me go."

Before he could reply to this crisp order, his mother arrived and he was forced to release her. As she curtsied, Lili could still feel the pressure of his hands on her arms, and she prayed her face did not betray her confusion.

"Good morning, Miss Martingale," the marchioness said with her faint smile. "Charming to see you again. Did you find our humble little church acceptable?"

"Why yes, of course, but if Wyckend had had a church, I would have gone there, believe me, ma'am," Lili stammered, sure she was being criticized for treading on Braybourne property again. Then she blushed even more, aware she had sounded very rude, and very, very young. The marchioness must have agreed with her, for as she took the viscount's arm, she nodded her dismissal.

Lili was only too glad to curtsy in farewell before she hurried to the Wyckend carriage. Only when it was leaving the churchyard did she exhale audibly in relief.

Behind her, Halpern lingered to watch her departure before he joined the marchioness in their carriage. "You came too soon, my dear," he scolded lightly. "I especially wanted to find out the prickly Miss Martingale's age, and I did not have time.

Father tells me she can be no more than seventeen, if she is even that, but I find that hard to believe. Surely she must have had her eighteenth birthday. After all, the Russells are considering her come-out."

"Your father has always been very astute when it comes to my sex. Very astute," the marchioness said tartly. "She may well be only seventeen. She is certainly gauche enough, wouldn't you say? And she is awkward to a fault."

"Perhaps it is only awe of you and your high estate that makes her so, ma'am," he suggested.

"Then why does she not appear in any awe of you, my son?" she inquired sweetly.

He did not answer and for the time it took them to return to the Hall, he was deep in his own thoughts. The marchioness left him to them, although she was perturbed. Then she told herself Graeme was not some impressionable young man, easily caught by a pretty face and graceful figure. Heaven knows he must have grown immune to such charms after so many years' exposure to them. And the girls of noble families who had been brought to his attention had been well-mannered girls, accustomed to society, trained to become a countess or a duchess or a marchioness. This Miss Martingale was not at all like them. But could it be possible, she wondered, grasping the side strap as the carriage rumbled over a rough patch of road, that the girl's artless candor had intrigued him? It would not be the first time a man had fallen in love with an unsuitable female. Why, every Season it seemed there was some ghastly *mésalliance* that caused a storm of gossip. And while a few of those marriages succeeded, most of them turned out to be as disastrous as everyone had gleefully predicted. But her son would not be one of those lovestruck fools. Not Graeme!

When she recalled the trouble she had had carrying him and giving birth, after four disappointing miscarriages, she was more determined than ever that he would do his duty. He was a Wilder, the next Marquis of Braybourne. He would honor his name and his title as he had been trained from childhood to do.

As the carriage turned in between the gates that marked the entrance to Braybourne, she let go of the strap. She told herself it was silly to worry, become upset for no reason whatsoever. Graeme was as haughty a man as his father, and just as proud. She could trust him to see Miss Martingale for what she was; a very young, very gauche little nobody with nothing to commend her.

Thinking rationally, Halpern would have been the first to agree with her. But there was no denying Miss Martingale intrigued him. She was so maladroit he found himself waiting gleefully for what she would do—or say—next. Of course it could be his interest in her was due to nothing more than boredom. He had had to cancel a visit to friends right after Christmas because his father had fallen ill. He had made a complete recovery, thank heavens, but it had meant he himself was kept tied to Braybourne. Then the weather had been unpleasant with late frosts and heavy snowfalls. When he returned to town, as he was even now making arrangements to do, he was sure he would forget the girl entirely.

But wait. Perhaps it would be amusing to treat her to an idle flirtation. And of course that would delight the gossips, who would then have something rich to chew on over their tea trays. And when he wandered away, as of course he would eventually, Miss Martingale would have gained prominence as his latest flirt. Any number of men might rush to take her up to see what had attracted him. Really, when you considered it, it was positively magnanimous of him to give the girl such distinction.

That evening at dinner, while Cornelia and Alastair were discussing some details of the removal to London, Lady Wyckend interrupted them.

"I received a most interesting letter yesterday from my dear friend, Fanny Parmeter. You do remember her, don't you, Cornelia? I believe she was in Vienna while you were there.

"Fanny begs me to come to London this spring. She says it has been an age since I have done so, and she is right. Why, I quite long to see the gracious house on Upper Brook Street where I came as a bride. Did you know Ogden was born there, Cornelia? The earl insisted on it, for he wanted me to have the finest care."

Lili looked down at her plate in despair, all her appetite gone. She had been counting the hours until she could escape the dowager, and now it appeared she was to have no escape.

"Are you sure this would be a wise move, ma'am?" Alastair asked, raising her spirits. Perhaps they could persuade her not to come. Wouldn't that be grand! "You have not traveled for some time and you are not strong. There is no doubt you would find it taxing, moving households. And do forgive me for even mentioning it, but you are not a young woman anymore."

Since it was Alastair who spoke, the dowager only smiled. "How like you, dear Alastair, to be concerned for me," she said.

"London has changed, Mother," Cornelia said, adding her mite. "It will not be at all as you remember it. Why, you have not seen it for over twenty years. Many things you remember will be gone, old friends as well. And there is a constant racket there. Such noise and traffic, and the smells!"

"If it is so unpleasant, what draws you and Alastair there so often, daughter?" the old lady said tartly. "You need not worry. I do not intend a long visit. I shall probably only remain for a month, or six weeks. I assume there is still a room for me in the house my dear husband built for me as a bride? Some small cubby out of everybody's way?"

"Of course there is a room for you," Cornelia said. "I was not trying to dissuade you from the adventure, ma'am, only pointing out its perils. I am sure if you travel slowly and allow Alastair to choose your grooms, perhaps even an outrider to serve as courier, you will make the journey in splendid form."

She smiled warmly, and Alastair lifted his glass in a toast. Lili knew a stranger would have assumed the thought of entertaining the Dowager Countess of Wyckend was something they were looking forward to with delight.

Her convent training told her she should condemn such devious behaviour, but a part of her had to applaud their tact and aplomb. And she wondered if she would ever, ever be so accomplished. Or so cunning.

Chapter Eight

Although the mantua maker and her assistant had returned to London, they had not finished Lili's new gowns. She was to have many more fittings as soon as she reached town. The dancing master and his wife had left as well, after she had spent a strenuous morning dancing with Alastair to prove she had mastered the steps.

"You must dance perfectly and with grace," he told her. "You are Beau Russell's ward. Always remember that."

Lili nodded, trying to hide her discomfort from him. As usual, Alastair was perfection. Not even a tiny fold of his cravat had wilted, nor was a single hair on his head out of place. She was hot and wrinkled and out of breath and love him though she did, she could not help but resent him.

It seemed an endless time to her before they set off for London near the end of April. Lili told herself she was going to enjoy every moment away from the dowager countess. Lady Wyckend did not intend to leave the country til mid-May.

London was a revelation to Lili. She almost pressed her nose to the carriage window in her eagerness to see it all. First there was the pall of black smoke that hung over it. It was visible for many miles before they reached London proper. And when at last they were rattling through the streets, Lili was stunned. She had thought the walled city of Vienna impressive, but it was nothing compared to London with its grand squares, handsome churches, and state buildings, its busy commercial streets. And the people! There were throngs of noisy humanity all rushing about their business, more carriages and carts than she had ever seen—why, even the smells of London were exotic! Only the parks set down like quiet green jewels in the madness surrounding them were a reminder of the countryside they had just quit. Lili never even heard Alastair remark that if she went about here with her mouth hanging open as it was now, she would be thought simple.

At last the carriages turned into a large square and Cornelia leaned forward herself and said, "I fear the coachman has made a mistake, Alastair. This is not Upper Brook, it is Grosvenor Square. And we are stopping. What can be the matter?"

As was customary, Lili sat facing back, and she saw that Alastair looked positively smug.

"Come and see the surprise I have for you, love," he said, jumping down before the grooms could position the steps.

Cornelia seemed about to speak, but then she shrugged and obeyed. Soon the three of them were standing before a large house built of Portland stone. It was fronted with Corinthian columns and faced east. Cornelia stared at it for a moment before she said in a wondering voice, "Now what have you done, my love?"

"I will tell you all in a moment," he promised, shepherding them both up the marble steps. They were followed by his valet and her maid, who had traveled behind them in another carriage.

They were admitted to the house by a strange butler who snapped his fingers at a footman to take their wraps.

"We will have sherry in the drawing room, Marks," Alastair ordered. Lili noticed the servants who had come with them had already gone upstairs with the dressing cases and portmanteaus.

"I am sure you would enjoy a glass, my dear. Traveling is so tedious, isn't it? And there is nothing so pleasant as journey's end."

As he spoke, Alastair led them down a broad hall and opened a set of double doors. Lili gasped. It was a beautiful room, large and well lit with a bank of tall windows on one side that overlooked a garden. French doors led to a narrow terrace. The room itself was done in golds and cream and a deep royal blue and it had a number of handsome oils gracing its walls. It was beautiful and rich, and at the same time, welcoming. Perhaps that was due to the number of flower arrangements, and a small coal fire that brought warmth and cheer.

Cornelia managed to contain herself until the sherry had been served. Even Lili had a small glass, for Alastair said the occasion warranted it. At last, when they were alone, Cornelia said, "You did this, did you not? Decorated this room? I detect your expert hand, my dear."

Alastair smiled. "Of course I did, the rest of the house as well. This is to be our home in London from now on. I had it from the Earl of Hayford."

"I have always thought the house in Upper Brook Street more than adequate," his wife remarked as she picked up a porcelain cherub and examined it.

"Have you? But you must admit it is a bit cramped and not at all suitable for entertaining. And if you remember, we were forced to stable our horses elsewhere. So inconvenient. Here we have a private garden as well as stables, and wonder of wonders, a ballroom that is not at all despicable."

"And what of the dowager?" Cornelia asked, putting down the figurine to reposition a drooping rose in one of the vases. "She was so looking forward to returning to the house she came to as a bride."

"And so she shall," he said promptly. Lili turned abruptly. She had gone to study a painting on the far wall, to give them some privacy, but now she almost skipped in her hurry to rejoin them.

"She is not coming here? Truly, Alastair?"

"Do try not to sound quite so delighted, child," he scolded. "No, she will reside in Upper Brook. We may have to endure the woman in the country, 'Nelia. I see no need to do so in town."

"She will be furious," his wife said, but Lili noticed she did not sound perturbed at the prospect.

"No, she won't. Have you forgotten my powers of persuasion? How she adores me? I have given her Bayley and the cook to soothe any ruffled feathers she might have. I shall also point out how much more comfortable she will be, mistress of her own establishment, and free of all the confusion, late hours, and alarums Lili's first Season is sure to produce. And I will tell her she could even invite that bosom bow of hers to stay—what is that woman's name?"

"Parmeter."

"Yes. Dreadful woman. Besides, we are very near and in an emergency can reach Sarah in minutes. It will all work out, you will see."

"I think it is a grand plan," Lili said. Then, waving her hand at the drawing room, she added, "Did you accomplish all this just since the dowager announced she was coming to town?"

Alastair laughed at her, she sounded so awed, and after a moment, so did Cornelia. "No, I am not that marvelous, Lili. I purchased the house last September. The rebuilding and decorating have been going on for months. But come and see for yourselves."

The next hour was spent exploring the house from attic to cellars. Lili thought it the handsomest, most impressive mansion she had ever seen. Her own room, which overloooked the garden, was so lovely she hugged Alastair tight to thank him. And the library, the parlors, and the ballroom he had mentioned were each one grander and lovelier than the last.

The next few days were busy getting settled in and acquiring more servants. Cornelia alerted her friends to their arrival and her new address, and Alastair began to plan a number of dinner parties, a reception, and even a ball. Lili drifted through the days in a haze of happiness. She was often reminded of their days in Vienna, just the three of them.

Lili had never been able to break the habit of early rising she had been used to in the convent and now she began to go for a ride even before she had her breakfast. It was easier then, trotting Josephine through the almost empty streets to Hyde Park. She was always accompanied by the faithful Flynn, but although Alastair came with her occasionally, Cornelia never did.

"And you will not do so much longer either," she said one day when Lili came in for breakfast, her cheeks flushed from the fresh air and exercise. "Not when the parties begin in earnest. Why, sometime we do not get to bed till four in the morning."

"I cannot imagine it," Lili said from the buffet where she was selecting her breakfast.

"It has already begun," Alastair told them, holding up a sheaf of thick cards of invitation. "This morning we have been asked to three receptions, a musical salon, an afternoon of silver loo—oh, I beg your pardon, my love. That one was addressed to you—a Venetian breakfast, and a grand soiree."

"Are we going to all of them?" Lili asked in awe as she took her seat.

Mr. Russell eyed her heaping plate. "Really, Lili," he murmured. "Two eggs? Ham *and* sausage? A scone and a muffin?

"But to answer your question, no, we only accept the most select invitations. Some hostesses ask everyone but the butcher's boy, in the hope their parties will gain society's ultimate accolade, being called a perfect crush."

Lili ate her breakfast and listened carefully. She knew she had a lot to learn about society and she was determined not to make any more mistakes. When Alastair retired behind his newspaper, and Cornelia was deep in her correspondence, Lili went over her engagements for the day. The mantua maker was coming for fittings this morning, 'Nelia had mentioned shopping for sandals and hats this afternoon, and at five o'clock they were to go for a walk with Alastair in the park. She knew that would not be a walk but a leisurely stroll. They would stop often to greet any friends they chanced to encounter. Lili didn't care. She was anxious to make friends of her own, friends her age. Especially some girls she could talk to, gossip with, and ask their advice. And she must meet some young men, too, she supposed, so she would have partners when they started going to balls. As she ate the last bite of muffin and one of the new footmen poured her another cup of coffee, she sighed in delight. London was wonderful. She was so glad to be here.

She did meet a number of the *haute ton*'s finest that afternoon. Unfortunately, only a few were young, and none so young as she was herself. For the most part she had to make do with the warm smiles and the compliments of gentlemen Alastair's age, and women like Cornelia, whose interests were mainly domestic. But there was a Miss Gwendolyn Austin and her brother, Reed. Miss Austin was also making her come-out this Season, although she seemed much older and more sophisticated to Lili. And Lili doubted they would ever be real friends. Miss Austin spent most of their time together peeking at Alastair. Her brother's behaviour was much more acceptable, for he made it obvious he had taken an instant liking to her. He was dressed finely, although Lili was sure Alastair must deplore his elaborate cravat. She found herself fascinated by the narrow mustache he sported. Mr. Austin touched it often, as if to make sure it was still there. Lili told herself not to laugh at him and she promised him a dance if they should meet at some future party.

"Know I shall hold you to that promise, Miss Martingale," he said as he and his sister prepared to take their leave.

"We Austins are so fond of dancing," his sister contributed, sending Alastair a melting glance as she did so. Alas, he missed it entirely.

"Do girls often make such a cake of themselves over Alastair?" Lili asked Cornelia as they strolled on together. Alastair had paused to greet another friend, so they were private for a moment.

"All the time," Cornelia told her cheerfully. "And women who should know better, as well. Oh, there is Alva Potter! Do you remember her, Lili?"

She waved as she spoke, and an elderly little woman seated all alone in a magnificent open landau ordered her coachman to halt. Lili smiled. They had stayed with Mrs. Potter in Vienna. She was a rich widow who had tried to buy her way into society.

"My dear Cornelia, how delightful to see you," Alva Potter said as loudly as she could, so everyone within hearing would know she was on intimate terms with the elegant Mr. Russell's wife. "And if I am not mistaken, this is that young chit you had with you in Vienna. Howdedo, Miss Martingale? You've turned out fine, you have, if I do say so. Still dress too plain, both of you, but there! I shall never understand why the *ton* shy away from a little finery."

Since Mrs. Potter was attired this afternoon in a scarlet driving dress with rows of large gold buttons and three flounces, and a hat that was adorned with royal blue and gold plumes, Lili could see she took her own advice and she struggled to hide a giggle. As the two older ladies arranged a future meeting, she looked around and saw Viscount Halpern riding toward her with a group of friends. When he saw her, he pulled up and bowed over the saddle to her. Lili was startled, his smile was so warm. She even looked over her shoulder, to see if there might not be some other lady he was honoring. Seeing no one, and observing how his smile broadened at her confusion, she bowed slightly and turned away.

"Who is that?" Mrs. Potter demanded. Lili wished she would lower her voice.

"Viscount Halpern, ye say? Speak up, Cornelia! You've taken to mumbling, and it is not at all the thing. I know of Halpern. He's to be Marquis of Braybourne as soon as his father goes, ain't that so? Well, well! Mind you behave yourself, missy, and you might have a chance of catching him. But not if you give him stupid little bows and colder smiles, ye won't."

While Cornelia extricated them, Lili tried to look unconcerned. She did not think Halpern had heard the old lady, and she was feeling rather proud of the way she had handled their encounter, and never mind Alva Potter's advice. Of course, she thought as she and Cornelia went on their way, it was easy to do when he was on horseback and she, on foot. But she was sure she would be able to act creditably when next they met. She was to attend the theater with the Russells this evening. Perhaps he might be there, in a box across the way? She would smile at him, she decided. After all, even though he was old, he might be of some use to her. He might even have younger male relatives. Yes, it certainly would be to her benefit to cultivate the arrogant viscount.

Halpern was not at the theater, but by then, Lili had forgotten him completely. She was fascinated by the performance, the first she had ever seen, and although she was sure the nuns would think it scandalous, she enjoyed every moment, especially the farce at the end. And the well-dressed society people in their boxes, inspecting the audience through their glasses, the orange sellers hawking their wares, and the common folk crowded in the pit, shouting advice or booing the performers—it was all so new and so exciting.

Cornelia had insisted she keep to her normal routine while she was in town, and so Lili spent part of her days practicing her violin and the piano, reading a worthy book, often in a foreign language so she would not lose her skill, and helping Cornelia oversee the staff. She also ran errands for Cornelia, as soon as she became more accustomed to town. She was always attended not only by a maid but by a footman as well on these expeditions.

"I do feel so silly, like someone pretending to be the queen," she complained one evening at dinner when the three of them were alone. "Surely a maid *or* a footman would do? It is not as if I have large, heavy parcels to be carried."

"Both. Always," Alastair said. "And there will be no more discussion. Surely you must admit 'Nelia and I are better judges of what is proper in town; the dangers that might befall a green girl."

Lili opened her mouth to protest, caught a glimpse of Alastair's face, and just as quickly closed it.

The Dowager Countess of Wyckend arrived as scheduled, and if there had been any kind of dustup about the new

arrangements, Lili was not there to see it. Alastair told her that
things had been settled nicely and Sarah was looking forward
to their visit the following afternoon. "Just Cornelia and me,"
he added and shook his head when she grinned at him in relief.

As it happened, Cornelia had asked her to fetch the second
volume of a novel they were both reading, and when the Russells set off for Upper Brook Street, she went in another direction, attended by her usual retinue.

When she was leaving the booksellers, she chanced to meet
Viscount Halpern again. He was alone this time and they came
face-to-face at the door. After greeting her and inquiring how
she did, the viscount began to walk beside her. This flustered
Lili, who felt she had behaved admirably up to that moment.
How she was to go on if he continued by her side, she did not
know.

"Oh, you must not, sir," she tried to protest. "You were
going into the booksellers, were you not? I would not keep
you."

He laughed down at her and Lili found herself admiring his
handsome hazel eyes again. "No dusty book could equal the
pleasure of your company, Miss Martingale," he said easily as
he took her arm in his and patted her hand. "Fall behind, you
two," he told her servants, quite as if they were his to direct,
Lili thought indignantly. She was even more indignant when
they obeyed.

"You have another errand?" he asked. "I would be glad to
escort you there."

Lili had intended to visit the fascinating stalls at the Soho
Bazaar, but now she said, "No indeed. I am merely going
home."

"To Grosvenor Square then. I understand Mr. Russell has
bought the Earl of Hayford's mansion. I presume he caught
him when he was under the hatches and desperate."

Lili sensed some condemnation in his voice, and she hurried
to Alastair's defense. "I am sure Mr. Russell may purchase any
house he pleases. And if this earl did lose his fortune I think it
serves him right. He must have gambled it away. Besides, it

has been done up so fine, even the Prince Regent might envy the decor."

"I shall look forward to seeing it," Halpern said.

Lili was not fooled. She could almost hear the laughter behind that meek statement. "And so you shall, if, that is, you are invited to attend one of our evenings," she said grandly. "I am not entirely sure who is on the guest list."

Her maid coughed behind her, and she realized she had just made a gaffe. But as she was searching for something to say that would redeem her, the viscount said, "May I hope you might put in a good word for me, Miss Martingale? I am sure if you were to do so, I could look forward to receiving one of those prized invitations.

"I am not being sarcastic," he added, just before she could put him in his place, all her good resolutions forgotten. "Beau Russell is unique. He always has been. And his parties are exclusive, much as the Duke of Severn's are. Neither of them bow to the current mode of hot rooms, so overcrowded not only ladies, but some elderly gentlemen as well have to be carried outside to be revived. I commend him, and I would be honored to be included.

"Do you perhaps go to the Banners' soiree in two days' time?" he asked next. Lili had been looking forward to that party. It was to be her first ball and she was going to wear her prettiest gown, a drift of white silk with tiny peach roses embroidered in bands at the empire waist and the hem. She even had embroidered satin sandals to match.

"Yes, we have been invited," she managed to say. They were walking up Duke Street now. Grosvenor Square was just ahead, and perversely, she wished it were farther. She had suddenly realized it was very nice to be escorted by a gentleman who took such good care of her. He had paid a boy a penny to sweep the crossing for them, and when a sausage seller had accosted them, had sent the man on his way without any fuss. Besides, she liked his fashionable attire and jaunty top hat. Still, she was not completely lulled into complacency and a part of her wondered why on earth he was bothering with her, even going out of his way to see her home. It was most unlike the man she had first met on the road to Wyckend. What was he up to? For surely he had to have a reason for behaving this way.

"May I hope you will save me a dance, Miss Martingale?" he inquired, and she was so startled, she stumbled. He was quick to support her.

"Why, certainly, m'lord, if you would care for it," she heard herself saying. Just like some witless ninny, she scolded herself as they reached the marble steps that led to what was now Russell House. Why had she not thought to make some excuse? Still, she had to admit that even as old as he was, the viscount did have presence. She was sure any attentions he might bestow on her could be nothing but advantageous, so she made herself smile warmly as she bid him good day and thanked him for his escort. And as she ran up the steps, followed more sedately by the maid and footman, she made a note to ask Cornelia the correct way to deal with older gentlemen who sought one out and treated one to gallantry.

Chapter Nine

L ili accomplished very little the day of the Banner soiree. She tried to practice the piano but soon lost interest, and she did not even tune her violin. The book she settled down to read in the most uncomfortable chair in the library, which she had chosen to help her concentrate, went unappreciated. Between the lines she found herself picturing her silk gown, the satin slippers, and how her hair might look. One of London's best hairdressers was to visit this afternoon. She could hardly wait. Finally, after reading the same sentence twice and not understanding a word of it either time, she closed her book and went to the window to inspect the Square.

It was not a pleasant day. A light rain was falling, which she hoped would stop before evening. Across the square she saw a glum footman walking two equally unhappy pugs, and she smiled. Then she saw a carriage pull up at Number 24, two doors away. A lot of baggage was lashed to the roof and she leaned forward. An elderly couple lived at Number 24. She wondered who their visitors might be.

A man left the carriage first to seek shelter under the large umbrella the groom handed him. As he looked around, Lili saw he was young. She thought he might even be called handsome if he were to stop frowning. Two girls joined him on the pavement, and when he would not share his umbrella with them, scurried inside. At last, a thin, older lady came down the carriage steps to lean heavily on the groom's arm. The man with the umbrella took her other arm, and between them, the two men half carried her up the steps and into the house. Lili

wondered who they all were and how long they intended to
stay. She had noticed the elderly owners seldom had visitors
and rarely left the house themselves. Perhaps she might make
friends with the girls? She did so long for friends!

She meant to mention the new arrivals later, but in the excitement of preparing for her first evening party, she forgot all
about them. She was pleased with how she looked. The hairdresser had exclaimed over her widow's peak and dark curls,
and after washing her hair and cutting it, had combed it back
from her face to fasten it high on the back of her head. From
there, it fell in a cascade of curls. When Cornelia saw the
arrangement, she pulled a few peach rosebuds from the posy
Alastair had provided, and put them in Lili's hair. And as if
that were not enough, the Russells gave her a pearl necklace,
to mark the occasion. Before she could start to cry, however,
Alastair told her he would be obliged if she would remember
whose ward she was, and conduct herself accordingly.

The Banners' large mansion on Park Lane was ablaze with
light. It took almost half an hour for the Russell carriage to
reach the front steps, and it was an agonizing time for Lili,
who dared not move lest she crease her gown. At last she mentioned how much quicker it would have been if they had
walked the short distance from Grosvenor Square. Alastair
agreed but he told her such a thing was never done.

Admitted at last and relieved of their wraps, the three went
up a flight of stairs to where Lord and Lady Banner were receiving. Lili smiled gratefully at them when she was introduced, before she trailed Cornelia and Alastair around the
large drawing room as they greeted their friends and made her
known to them. She was glad when two gentlemen asked her
to dance. Mr. Austin came up to ask as well, reminding her of
her promise. Of Viscount Halpern there was no sign, and she
was surprised at how disappointed she was. These boys she
was pledged to were all very well, but she had been looking
forward to seeing Halpern and noting his expression when he
saw her in all her finery.

Several sets later, while she was sitting beside Cornelia and wishing she had a fan to wield in the increasingly hot room, the viscount suddenly appeared.

"Give you good evening, Mrs. Russell," he said as he bowed. "Miss Martingale.

"May I?" he asked, indicating the chair Alastair had just vacated. Cornelia nodded her permission. Halpern spoke almost exclusively with her, which annoyed Lili until she realized it was all he could do, for Cornelia was seated between them. At last, as the orchestra returned to their seats in the gallery, he said, "Perhaps you would be so kind as to give me permission to dance with Miss Martingale, ma'am? I promise to take the greatest care of her."

"Why, certainly, m'lord," Cornelia said, smiling at the incongruity of playing chaperon at the age of thirty. "If Lili would care for it, that is."

The viscount was already bowing to her, and he checked, as if he had not expected this response. "And would you care for it, Miss Martingale?" he asked softly, extending his hand to her.

"Yes. I would," she managed to say, and gave him her hand. They walked together to the floor and waited for the music to begin.

"You are looking very fine this evening," he said. "I like the flowers in your hair."

"I had a French hairdresser today," she confided. "And see, the Russells gave me this pearl necklace. Isn't it grand?" Then she looked down, her lips compressed. How could she have blurted out such things? The viscount must think her a witless child!

"No, don't feel badly," he said, keeping his voice low as other couples assembled nearby. "Is this your first ball? I am sure that must be exciting. Ah, the quadrille. I was hoping for a waltz."

"I am not approved to waltz," Lili said as she took her place opposite him and he raised both their hands.

"When you are, I hope you will dance the first one with me," he said. She did not smile, for she was minding her steps.

Somehow this dance was a lot more difficult in a group with the sophisticated viscount partnering her. She managed to acquit herself without stumbling, and when the set was over, discovered Halpern had no intention of returning her to Cornelia. In fact, Cornelia was nowhere to be seen. She did spot the Dowager Countess of Wyckend however, seated beside another elderly lady, as fat as she was thin. Both of them appeared to be studying her through their quizzing glasses, and Lili was glad when Halpern took her to the supper room. They were joined at their table by Lord Gore and his sister, and Mr. Percy Ridgeway and a stunning blonde who proceeded to ignore him in her effort to attract Halpern's attention. Most of the conversation was over Lili's head, for she did not know the people or the places discussed. Still, she smiled and pretended to laugh when the others did. Then there came a moment when Halpern stopped smiling. The blonde had just told a story about a Harriet Wilson that appeared to upset him, for he frowned at her and shook his head.

"Oh, to be sure, not before the infantry," she said carelessly, tossing her head and pouting. "Are you and Miss—Miss . . ."

"Miss Lili Martingale."

"Yes. Are you related, m'lord? Is she some young cousin of yours come up to London to see the sights? How good of you to squire her around, although she is young to attend a soiree."

Lili was annoyed to find herself talked about as if she were not even there. "We are not related," she said before Halpern could speak. "We are acquaintances."

"Are you indeed?" the blonde asked, her eyes bright with mockery. Gore and his sister chuckled. Lili did not see there was anything amusing about being ridiculed. She wished she could leave.

"My word, never say you are the girl we met in the road," Percy Ridgeway said. "How different you look! I did not recognize you until just now."

"In the road? Now there's a story and I would hear it, if you please, Percy," her tormentor said with a sideways glance at Halpern. "It certainly seems a singular place to meet."

The viscount rose and held out his hand again. Lili was quick to take it and even quicker to rise. "If you will excuse us?" he murmured before he led her away. Lili could feel the eyes of the people they had just left on her back and she wondered what they would find to say now they were alone. No doubt the story of her defense of the injured shepherd would be embellished beyond recognition. It was just as well she never learned what was said, for there was a great deal of conjecture about her and her background, and the viscount's interest in her, this young miss with neither family nor wealth to commend her so far as they could tell.

"I would like to return to Cornelia now," Lili said as they entered the drawing room again. All her delight in the evening was gone and there was a large lump in her throat.

"In a while," he said, standing close beside her and pretending to watch the dancers. "I hope you are not upset because of the things Miss Wharton said. You should not be. She is only jealous of you."

"Because you were escorting me instead of her?" Lili asked.

His brows rose slightly. "I would not say that. But she is embarking on her third Season not only unwed but unpromised as well. It seems to have turned her sour."

"Who is Harriet Wilson?" Lili asked next. "She sounds a lively girl. Is she here tonight?"

She wondered why Halpern seemed startled for a moment, why he turned so quickly to look at her. "No, you really don't know, do you?" he said as if to himself. "Perhaps it would be wiser for me not to tell you, preserve your innocence as it were. But this is London, Miss Martingale, and things are very different here, as you shall learn. And I do think it better for you to know as much about life here as you can, so you can navigate your way through dangerous waters. Miss Wilson, along with at least two of her sisters, is a *demimondaine*. Do you understand the word?"

Lili had been listening to him in some confusion, but now her face cleared. "Oh, you mean she is a man's mistress," she said, not bothering to lower her voice. A couple nearby turned to stare at her. The viscount took her arm and led her farther away.

"Whose mistress?" she asked.

"I have no idea whose gold-filled purse she is interested in at the moment," he said. "She is, er, easy with her favors. But what do you know of such things?"

"Only what I have read in books," Lili confessed, feeling more cheerful. "I thought she must be someone in society. I am glad to know I should not mention her name in polite circles."

"Heavens, no," he said, laughing down at her. "That would never do."

"Perhaps you might tell me other things I should not mention," Lili prompted. "I admit I am very ignorant."

He stared down at her, his face turning serious. Lili wondered at it as he said, "I think you should ask Mrs. Russell for guidance. It is hardly my place to instruct you. Some might even say such a thing would be indecent."

Lili cocked her head to one side to ponder this statement. "Yes, I can understand why," she agreed. "But I do feel you might be more open and honest than Cornelia. She would probably tell me these things were nothing a young girl should know. Why, she could not bring herself to explain how babies are made and I was ignorant of that for a long time until I went to live at the farm."

"You have lived on a farm?" Halpern asked, grasping at the safest part of that sentence. He wondered what the girl would say next.

"Yes, after we came here from France. I was born in France you see, but when my mother died giving birth to me, my father gave me to the nuns at the abbey at Blamont to raise. I was there until I was thirteen. 'Nelia and Alastair rescued me. My mother was 'Nelia's mother's cousin. I think. But we are related somehow."

Halpern took two glasses of champagne from a footman's tray and gave her one. Lili looked at it suspiciously before she took a sip. It was very dry and she wrinkled her nose.

Halpern studied her over the rim of his glass. She was flushed from the heat of the room, and the color became her. Her dark blue eyes sparkled now and she was smiling and at ease. He saw one of the rosebuds in the topknot she wore was coming loose and he reached out to fix it. She looked taken aback, but she kept still until he was satisfied.

"Miss Martingale, may I ask you a personal question?"

"Of course. Well, I suppose so."

"Then tell me, if you would be so good, just how old are you?"

"I do not think I should answer that," she said, peeking up at him from under her lashes. Halpern admired the effect without being at all carried away by it.

"Somewhere I have read a lady's age is her secret to keep," she added. "How old are you?"

He bowed. "I am twenty-eight."

"As old as *that*? My word! I was sure you were younger," she exclaimed, frowning as she began to count silently on her fingers.

"Careful now," he said, although he found her shock uncomplimentary. "You will be revealing your age in spite of your wish to keep it to yourself. But enough of ages. What did you learn in that French convent besides French?"

"Many things. Alastair says I have a superfluous amount of knowledge, but I do not think anyone can be too educated, do you? To answer your question, I speak German as well as French. I have some Italian and I can read Latin and Greek. I have studied the great philosophers, and geography and history, as well as mathematics. I must admit I have little fondness for that last subject."

"And what did you learn at the farm? What else, I mean?"

"How to behave mostly, you know, in society. How to dance. How to play the piano and the violin. And manage a household. But I hate sewing." She gazed up at him for a moment before she confessed in a softer tone, "And although I loved the Moorland family, I could not learn to love farming. I found it boring and confining."

"You are not the only one to come to that conclusion," he said. "Drink your champagne, Miss Martingale. It is over time for me to return you to Mrs. Russell. I fear I have monopolized you for much too long."

"And people would look askance at that? But there is no need," she told him before she obediently sipped her champagne. When she saw he looked puzzled, she added, "You are so much older than I. I am sure if they think anything of it, it will only be to commend you for your kindness to someone Alastair calls 'a green girl.' They would be right."

"Tell me, are you trying to be insulting or is it just all naiveté?" he demanded.

"Insulting? Dear me, not at all! Oh, I do apologize if I have said anything to insult you, sir! I am aware I am not very good company as yet, for I am so ignorant. But I intend to improve as you might discover if you seek me out again," she added. The words had no sooner left her mouth before she began to wonder if two sips of champagne were responsible for such abandon. She decided that could not be the cause. No doubt she was just intoxicated with the evening, the handsome albeit older man standing beside her, and her first London party.

"You should not say such things, Miss Martingale," he scolded. He sounded just as Alastair Russell might. "Many men would misinterpret your remarks. Think you were doing more than innocently flirting with them."

"And what could I be doing besides flirting?" she asked as she disposed of the almost-full champagne flute on a passing footman's tray.

He did not answer. Instead he tucked her hand in his arm and hustled her back to where Cornelia was sitting. He did not linger over his farewells, either, and Lili settled back in an ornate gilt chair, feeling chastened. She could see Cornelia wanted to question her, but before she could begin, the Dowager Countess of Wyckend arrived, her large friend in avid attendance. Both Cornelia and Lili rose quickly to their feet.

"I see you have seen fit to bring this person to the Banner soiree, daughter-in-law," the dowager began, her voice stiff. "I must admit I am shocked. Emmeline Banner is top-of-the-trees. I doubt she will think a nobody a proper guest."

"Good evening, Mother," Cornelia said. Her voice was even, but Lili sensed her anger. She was angry herself and she hoped none of the nearby guests were listening.

"Mrs. Parmeter, allow me to present my cousin to you. She is Lillian Martingale, hardly a nobody."

"Who was her father?" Mrs. Parmeter inquired, raising her quizzing glass. The magnified eye was hideous. It reminded Lili of a fish's, but she did not feel like giggling. Here were two more people acting as if she were invisible. It was very rude of them, not that she expected anything else from the dowager.

When Cornelia did not answer, Mrs. Parmeter turned to her.

"I cannot imagine why such a thing is important to *you*, ma'am. You are a stranger," Cornelia said. As the color rose in the old woman's face, she added, "It is not a secret, however. Thomas Martingale married my mother's cousin. She was Thora Edson. They lived in France until Thora died in child-birth. I have no idea where Mr. Martingale is now. Alastair and I have assumed the role of guardian."

"But where has the gel been all these years?" Mrs. Parmeter insisted.

"In a French convent. It was near—"

"In France? That decadent country that was of late our enemy?" Mrs. Parmeter asked in horror. "And raised by nuns, too! I wonder you dare to present her to good English society, indeed I do. I know you dote on the man, Sarah, but I must say it was probably all Russell's idea. I have never thought him anything but a fop and a wastrel."

"You will excuse us," Cornelia said before the dowager could protest. She was rigid with anger. "I will not listen to you insult my beloved husband. Come, Lili."

Lili was only too glad to walk away. When she looked back from the safety of the other side of the room, she saw the two had their heads together and they were both talking at the same time.

"Why does she hate me so much?" she asked, swallowing her tears.

"She doesn't hate you. How could she? She doesn't even know you."

"I meant the dowager. She had to have told Mrs. Parmeter all about me."

Cornelia sighed. "I expect she still believes you are my daughter and I am afraid you have become a fixation with her. She has concentrated all her disappointments and sorrows on your shoulders; she probably even blames you for them. You must forget her, Lili. Or at least ignore her. She cannot hurt you. Alastair will not let her do that. Nor can Mrs. Parmeter. No one will pay them any heed, for any girl presented to society by Beau Russell must be accepted.

"Now tell me, how did you enjoy your dance with Halpern? It was quite an honor for him to take you in to supper as well."

Lili was not able to answer, for a young man was bowing and asking her for the next set. She saw another man behind him turn away, looking disappointed, and she wondered if Halpern's attentions had indeed brought her into favor. If they had, she had something else to thank him for, she thought as she smiled at her new partner.

The soiree lasted till the early morning hours and Lili enjoyed every minute of them, dancing and meeting other young people. She fell asleep as soon as she had been undressed, the dowager and Mrs. Parmeter forgotten completely. And when she woke at the decadent hour of ten, dressed and went down to breakfast, she found three posies at her place. None of them, however, was from Graeme Wilder, Viscount Halpern, and she wondered why that was so disappointing.

Chapter Ten

The man in question was being shaved at that moment and finding it hard to keep from frowning while his valet was engaged in the ticklish operation.

Damn it, he was not old, he told himself as he stared fixedly at his reflection in the shaving mirror. Twenty-eight was not old. It is if you are eighteen or nineteen, his common sense reminded him. In fact, ten years or more is an eternity at that age. Now why did he find that such a depressing thought?

Attired at last in town clothes, he went down to his solitary breakfast. He did not expect his father and mother to arrive in town for another week or so. Until they did so, he was the sole inhabitant of Braybourne House on Park Lane, if you did not count the army of servants who were employed to take care of his every whim. This morning he was glad he was alone.

He still did not know how old she was. But why did her actual age matter, he asked himself as he buttered his toast. She was young, very young. He recalled her figure then, charmingly displayed in the yellow silk gown. No, she was not a little girl. Perhaps the only childlike things about her were her occasional gaffes and her flawless skin. It was as soft as his nephew's, and Harry was only two.

He stared unseeing out the window of the breakfast parlor. It overlooked the mansion next door, something his mother deplored. When she was here, the undercurtains were kept tightly closed, for the owner of that mansion was a notorious cit's widow, a Mrs. Alva Potter. He himself preferred to let the light stream in, and if he chanced to see her staring at him through her quizzing glass and smiling, he ignored her. Once she had even waved. Affronted, he had ordered the butler to close the draperies. She never waved again.

He was a Wilder of Braybourne, and as such was aware certain lines must be drawn between him and the rest of humanity, although he had never thought consciously of it that way. If you had asked him, he would have said he was easy with the other classes, for he could not think his attitude might be condescending. This innate sense of worth, his haughtiness, had been bred into Wilder men, bone and sinew, for generations.

Halpern did not see the first post next to his place, the newspapers his butler had ironed smooth for his perusal. Instead, he stared unseeing into space and considered his age. It was not until it occurred to him that in twelve years he would be forty—forty!—that he put his head back and laughed at himself. To think he had become blue-deviled over such a thing was ludicrous, he told himself as he reached for the letter on top of the pile of mail. Still, he supposed it might be a good idea to look about this spring with an eye to marriage and setting up his nursery. Time was passing. It had a way of doing that. Unfortunately.

Lili did not have to wait very long before she met the visitors to Number 24, for after she had had her breakfast, she went out with her maid for a stroll. It was a glorious day, warm and sunny with a little breeze, and she had missed her early morning ride. As soon as she stepped from the house, she spotted the two girls about to enter the little park in the center of the square. They had no maid with them. Perhaps they were considered adequate chaperons for each other? If only she had a sister, she thought, hurrying to catch up with them before the gate closed.

"Good morning," she said brightly with her warm smile. "Thank you for opening the gate."

"Are you a resident?" tho older girl asked stiffly. "I do not recall seeing you in years past. If you are not, go away. The park is private."

She sounded so stiff and disapproving, Lili paused before she said, "Why yes, I live at Number 20, two doors from you. I saw you arrive yesterday. My name is Lili Martingale. I am the ward of Alastair and Cornelia Russell."

"Beau Russell?" the younger girl whispered, her eyes huge in her pale face. "Are you really?"

Lili nodded. "What are your names?" she asked when they did not identify themselves.

"I am Miss Elizabeth Rowley and this is my sister, Bettina," the elder said almost grudgingly. "Our brother is Arthur Rowley. *The* Arthur Rowley. No doubt you have heard of him?"

Lili was sorry she had to deny any knowledge of Mr. Rowley. "Are you here for a long visit?" she inquired instead as the three began to stroll the perimeter of the park. "I myself have come to spend the Season."

"We, too," Miss Rowley admitted. "We stay with our grandparents, General and Mrs. Westford."

"A general!" Lili exclaimed. "Did he fight with Wellington?"

"Hardly. He is very old. He fought in the war with our American colonies many years ago. He was badly wounded there. Wars are stupid."

"Yes, they certainly are," Lili said, glad to have something in common with the prickly Miss Rowley. She suspected the girl was in her twenties. Even her sister seemed a few years older than she was herself.

"Where are you from?" Miss Rowley demanded.

"I was brought up in France and lived there during the war. In a convent," she added almost defiantly, thinking to get over that hurdle quickly. "My parents were English, of course. This is my first Season and my first visit to London."

"*We* have been here numerous times," Miss Rowley said with a thin smile. Lili was sure they would never be fast friends.

"I do not like it here," the younger sister admitted. When her eyes met Lili's, she blushed scarlet and lowered her eyes to stare at the path beneath their feet.

"Why not?" Lili asked, to draw her out. "Is it the noise? The crowds? The odors?"

"It is everything," the girl whispered.

"Bettina is of a retiring nature," her sister said. "She prefers Hampshire where our home is located. *Parlez-vous Français?*"

"Mais oui, mademoiselle," Lili replied, but when she continued in that language, she discovered Miss Rowely had only the most rudimentary knowledge of it and was indignant to be caught out.

"Yes, yes, I am sure," she muttered in reply to a question about Hampshire. She seemed relieved they had reached the gate again. "We must leave you now, Miss Martingale. We merely came out for our daily exercise."

Lili was astounded anyone could think a gentle stroll around the little park constituted exercise, but she only smiled and said, "I shall hope to see you again sometime, then."

Miss Rowley did not reply, nor did her sister, and they waited until Lili stepped out on the pavement so they could lock the gate behind them.

That evening at dinner, Lili told the Russells of the meeting. Alastair thought for a moment, then nodded. "Yes, I do remember a Mrs. Rowley from several years ago. She was a woman much afflicted by ailments no doctor seemed able to cure. But when her husband died suddenly, she made a miraculous recovery and became quite active in society. Alas, she was struck down with a rheumatic disease and finds it hard to even walk now. You may take that as a lesson, Cornelia, my love."

Lili could tell 'Nelia was having the greatest difficulty trying to contain her laughter, and she wondered at it. She did not see the jest, but she sensed it was something it would be better not to ask about.

"Perhaps you have heard of an Arthur Rowley?" she asked Alastair as she took some mushroom fritters from the plate a footman was offering. "Miss Rowley seemed to think I must have heard of him, for she called him *the* Arthur Rowley."

"Never heard a peep of him," Alastair said cheerfully.

"Well, I am glad these Rowleys have arrived in the Square, Lili. It will be good for you to have young friends to go about with."

She frowned a little. "Yes," she said slowly. "Except I do not think Miss Rowley especially is at all friendly. She seemed so stiff and proud. And her sister is so shy, she barely speaks at all."

"We will find you someone, dear," Cornelia consoled her. "There are many young girls here in London at this time."

"Indeed," Alastair said as he indicated his empty wineglass. Marks hastened to fill it and he went on. "It seems to me the metropolis is fair swamped with them. Everywhere you look there is another gaggle of 'em giggling and sharing secrets and flirting with the young men."

"I thought it was only a group of geese that was called a gaggle," his wife said.

"You have obviously not been paying attention, my love," she was told. "Gaggle, I said, and gaggle I meant.

"Lili, has your new evening gown been delivered? Lord Garrett's reception is tomorrow evening."

Later, getting ready for bed, Lili wondered if Cornelia had told her husband of their encounter with the dowager and Mrs. Parmeter at the soiree. He had given no indication that he had heard of it. Was it possible Cornelia had kept it from him? Lili had never seen Alastair in a temper. When he was angry or annoyed, he only became colder and more sarcastic than usual. But she knew he would not take any insults to his wife lightly. Lady Wyckend had better be careful, she thought as she dismissed the maid.

She had ordered her horse brought around early so she could ride before the park became crowded. Later, she had another fitting. They seemed endless to her, and all her protests about the excessive number of ensembles she was acquiring was ignored. Cornelia was dressed even finer. Lili thought she must protest, too, but when she mentioned it, Cornelia shook her head.

"I would not do so for the world, Lili, and I beg you to stop fretting. It is a point of pride to Alastair to have his ladies looking better than anyone else. Accepting his standards is the least we can do, don't you think?"

Lili had gone away chastened and determined she would never say another word about her clothes except "thank you."

That afternoon Cornelia intended to make some calls; Lili was to go along. She smiled to herself. Perhaps she might meet some girls who would be friendlier than the Misses Rowley? And of course tomorrow evening was Lord Garrett's reception. The gown she had chosen to wear was luscious. There was no other word for it, she thought, yawning as she climbed into bed. It was made of fine lilac muslin and deceptively simple, the bodice consisting of hundreds of tiny pleats that released under the bosom to a soft float of color. The only decoration was a tiny bouquet of dark silk violets, placed at the center of the *décolletage*. She had long white gloves to wear, of course, and a dainty reticule and fan. She doubted any girl at the reception would be dressed so fine. There was only one Beau Russell.

The next morning was windy, and it promised rain later. Her mare was skittish, sidestepping and ducking its head as it stamped the cobblestones.

"Feelin' peckish, today, she is, miss," Flynn warned her as they set out. "Best be ready."

"Perhaps Josephine wishes she were back at Wyckend, out at pasture," Lili remarked, leaning forward to pat the mare's neck.

Flynn mumbled something Lili thought sounded like "—not the only one" but before she could remark it, she had her hands full. The mare seemed determined to run away with her.

The park reached safely, she let the mare have her head, with Flynn thundering after. After several minutes, Josephine settled to a canter. Lili smiled. She was still smiling when a man on a handsome black gelding came abreast and nodded.

The mare took offense at the gelding and would have run off again if Lili had not had control. But she sensed

Josephine's nervousness as Halpern continued to ride beside her.

"Shall we trot, Miss Martingale?" he suggested. "I would talk to you.

"You keep early hours, Miss Martingale," Halpern remarked as she slowed the mare obediently and prayed it would behave itself. "Perhaps too early for your mount?" he added, as the mare tossed its head and snorted. "Or is it only as tempermental as any female?"

"Good morning, my lord," Lili said, determined not to be baited into an indiscretion. "You are out early as well."

"I prefer to exercise when there are no crowds showing off their clothes, their mounts, and their horsemanship.

"Tell me, are you enjoying London, Miss Martingale? Is it everything you expected?"

"Indeed I am. There are so many things to do and see. I fear I will not have time for everything, for we are beset with invitations to parties. Are you attending Lord Garrett's reception this evening, sir?"

"I suppose I must put in an appearance at least. Garrett and I are distantly related. But then, it seems everyone in the *ton* is kin one way or the other."

"Except for me. I am only related to Cornelia and her family. As far as I know."

"What of your father?" he asked idly, raising his crop to salute a couple strolling along beside Rotten Row.

"I don't know anything about my father's family," she admitted. "He was an artist. That is why he and my mother were living in France, so he could paint there. I wish I knew where he had gone, where he was now. I—I miss him even though I never knew him."

"It is greatly to your credit that you say so, Miss Martingale. But do consider. It might not be advantageous to you to meet him. You might not like him. He might be overbearing, loud, and rude, intent on whisking you abroad again, and you so happily situated with the Russells now."

"I never thought of that, sir," Lili replied, a picture of such a man coming easily to mind.

Josephine took exception to a noisy cart clattering by outside the park and Lili had her hands full for a moment.

"You ride very well," Halpern remarked.

"I had an excellent teacher," Lili said. As she did so, she remembered Ben and how patient he had been with her, how insistent that she be prepared for anything her mount might conceive, and she felt a wave of sadness wash over her. She missed Ben, missed all the Moorlands so, yet she could feel them slipping away from her. Day by day their faces grew dimmer, their voices fainter. Letters came and were answered, but it was not the same.

She saw they had reached the gate at Hyde Park Corner, and she reined in. "This is where I must leave you, sir," she said, blinking away some tears. "I have a number of things to do today, and best I get to them."

As she stopped speaking, her stomach growled with hunger and she was thrown into confusion. She was angry as well. Here she had been going on so well, making no embarrassing gaffes, and her stomach had betrayed her. And she suspected Halpern would not do the gentlemanly thing and ignore it. She was not mistaken.

"May I suggest a hearty breakfast head your list of activities, Miss Martingale?" he suggested politely, a devil dancing in his eyes. "I shall look for you this evening at Garrett's affair. Good morning."

He had a wonderful seat, Lili thought as he trotted off. Such a fine, straight back and broad shoulders. He was a handsome man, too, for all he was so old. Somehow he made her forget that when they were together.

That afternoon she and Cornelia visited several ladies, sitting with some, leaving cards with others. Not all of them were of society, either, for Cornelia had many intellectual women friends. Lili enjoyed both kinds of visits, especially those where other young people were present.

Finally, they were driven to an address on Park Lane. Lili

was astounded when they were shown to a small drawing room and found Alva Potter sitting there alone. Her wrinkled old face broke into a warm smile as Cornelia bent to kiss her. Lili hastened to curtsy.

"Well, so you did come and call again," the old lady exclaimed. "Benson, some tea and pastries and look snappy, man," she added to her butler. "Come and sit down, do," she went on, clearing the table beside her of the fringe she had been knotting.

"This is such a lovely house," Cornelia remarked. "It is so handy to everything. But surely it is very large for you alone, ma'am."

"As you say. But then, anything smaller would look mean. And I have hopes of entertaining some of the nobility I met at the Congress of Vienna. Remember how popular I was?"

Cornelia nodded. It was true Alva Potter had been taken up by several of the English elite there, all eager to be the first to hear what Cornelia knew was called "a Potterism." But as so often happened, the *ton* lost interest when everyone returned to England. The lady's funny remarks, elaborate costumes, and the wealth her husband had made through trade, ceased to amuse. Now Mrs. Potter languished alone, all her invitations either ignored or brusquely refused. Cornelia wished she would forget society, see there were others of her own class who would make her happy and content. The *ton* had a long memory. Mr. Potter's rise to fame as a rag and bottle man had not been forgotten.

While the two older ladies continued to discuss Vienna, Lili wandered over to the window. There was another mansion next door. She could see inside one of the rooms on the ground floor. A footman was busy there, arranging some silver on a sideboard. As he was leaving, he caught sight of her and he blew her a kiss and leered.

Lili drew back, shocked. "My word," she exclaimed. "What on earth does that man think he is doing?"

When she explained what had happened, Alva Potter bristled. "High and mighty they are, them Wilders," she muttered. Lili stared at her, astonished.

"They think they are so fine," the old lady went on, tossing her head so violently her fancy cap of lace and ribbons fell over one eye. "Not a bit friendly, they ain't. When I first moved here, I went over to leave my card. The butler gave me such a look! Well! And he told me the Marquis and Marchioness of Braybourne were not at home to the likes of *me*. And here we have an ordinary servant taking his cue from his masters. It is too bad!"

"It is indeed," Cornelia murmured as the butler and footman brought in an elaborate tea tray and arranged it on the table. As they did so, she said, "That is a lovely color you are wearing today, ma'am. It is forester's green, is it not?"

Her attempt to stave off any more of Mrs. Potter's complaints about her neighbors before the servants was not heeded.

"I waved one morning when I chanced to look out and spot the viscount at his breakfast. Halpern, y'know. He at least keeps the draperies open, unlike his mother. But do you know what he did, and me just trying to be friendly? He had the servant close the curtains and he kept them that way for several days. Wouldn't you think he could at least smile? Proud he is, and far too high in the instep, if you ask me. Because when he takes his breeches off at night, he's a man like any other, now ain't that right?"

Lili stifled a giggle and nearly choked on the delicious piece of cake she was devouring. Fortunately the servants were leaving the room and Cornelia could relax.

"I am sorry to hear it, ma'am," she said as she refused the plate of cookies her hostess was pressing on her. Lili took three.

It was well past the allotted visiting time when they were released at last. As they went down the steps to the carriage, Lili said, "Isn't she the funny one? She does make me laugh."

"Rather her situation is sad, poor old dear," Cornelia told her. "She is all alone. She has no family, none she will acknowledge now she has all that wealth. In a way she is just like the Braybournes, but she cannot see it and would be astounded if it it were pointed out to her. I worry about her, all alone in that huge mansion. And Alastair and I are the only ones in London who continue to see her."

"It is very good of you," Lili remarked.

"Nonsense," Cornelia said briskly. "I enjoy her. As you said, dear Lili, she is amusing. One never knows what she will say next, except to be sure it will not be at all suitable. Besides, she was very good to us in Vienna.

"Ah, we are home," she remarked. "A rest will be lovely, won't it, before we must dress for the evening?"

Chapter Eleven

Looking back on it a long time later, Lili realized that the evening of Lord Garrett's reception was the first time she should have noticed something was wrong. There was nothing she could point to and say, "There! That is when the trouble began," for it was too slight and subtle a change for that. Still, when she had awakened the next morning, she had felt remnants of a vague unease. She pondered it for a long time before she rang for her morning chocolate.

It was not that she was not familiar with what she called "The Look" now, that hesitant, considering gaze from which all expression was carefully erased. That gaze that seemed to ask who she was, where she had come from, and why she was there, and more importantly, why she was being presented. Once in a while she would even be treated to a smirk, or a quizzing glass raised in inspection then dropped with a sigh, or even the slight shrug of a shoulder that told her more than any words could do that she was not at all important. She had even had to endure an abruptly turned back, surely the most devastating snub of all. Still, there were those who smiled and seemed glad to make her acquaintance, those who extended a cordial hand or bowed. It had not all been superiority. Nor was it the night of Lord Garrett's reception. Halpern had been there and he had been attentive, introducing her to friends of his, especially a young cousin who was making her come-out, too. And when an elderly gentleman had pushed her back against the wall in the crush, Halpern had been quick to call such cavalier behaviour to the gentleman's attention. Later, he had even demonstrated how a well-placed elbow or quick pressure of the foot on another's toes could gain some much-needed space. Lord Garrett believed in crushes. His reception was most memorable for being one.

Cornelia had been with her for part of the time of course, and several of the people she had met earlier had had a friendly word for her. She had even been invited to join a riding party on an expedition to Greenwich, and a shopping spree with two sisters who begged her advice on bonnets. All very heady and comforting. And yet . . . and yet . . . ?

As she lay in her comfortable bed, the noise of London muffled by the trees outside her window, which were now in full leaf, she went over the evening again. Her nemesis, the Dowager Countess of Wyckend had not been present at the affair, nor had her friend, Mrs. Parmeter, unless she had missed seeing them in the crowd. But Lady Watson had been standoffish, Miss Hatheway distinctly unfriendly. And then there had been the time she had been standing beside Cornelia and had seen two ladies studying them both, then turning away to whisper some secrets. What had they been? she wondered. Surely the dowager had not spread any gossip about her being Cornelia's bastard daughter abroad, had she? Lili wondered in horror. Then she told herself she was being ridiculous. If she had felt uneasy on the drive home, and was still so this morning, it must have been something she ate. The footmen had passed trays of sweetmeats and she had had several of them, as well as two glasses of wine, it had been so warm and close in the drawing room and even on the stairs. Several people had fainted, and one lady had had to be carried out to the street to be revived. But even so, now that she thought it over, she could honestly say that for the first time since her arrival in London, she had not had a good time. It bothered her, and it was bothering her still when she went down to breakfast. There was a bouquet at her place—a tight collection of violets surrounded by their heart-shaped leaves all wrapped in a lace paper frill. She smiled when she saw it and picked it up to inhale its faint, woodsy scent.

"I did tell you the violet gown would be a huge success, didn't I?" Cornelia teased from her place at the head of the table. "Who has honored you, my dear?"

The stiff white card bore the title *Viscount Halpern*. There was no message or pretty quotation; he had not personalized it in any way. For some reason this irked Lili as she held out the card for Cornelia to see.

"Halpern?" she said slowly. "Now why should he be sending you a nosegay? I did think him very attentive last evening; why, he spent considerable time with you. I admit I do not understand it. Perhaps you do, Lili? Has he said anything that would explain this unusual flirting he is engaged in?"

Just the word "flirting" made Lili feel better. Of course that was what it was, just casual dalliance. "I am sure I do not understand it either, ma'am," she said. "He has been kind to me, introducing me to various people, and if you remember, he did dance with me at the soiree. Last night he remarked my gown and said it was becoming. I can think of nothing else."

As she finished, Lili felt a stab of guilt. Halpern had not merely complimented her; no, he had told her the color of her gown turned her blue eyes to smokey violet. He had also called them bewitching. She could not forget that. In fact, she had tucked it away to remember always. Still, she had heard enough flowery compliments by now to take Halpern's attentions with a grain of salt. For even though she would not be eighteen until next January, she was hardly a ninny to be taken in by some gentleman's smile and easy words. Both Cornelia and Nancy Moorland had told her how to value compliments and the fervent promises that were given by moonlight only to be forgotten at dawn.

She wished Halpern had written a message on his card though. Why bother to send the violets otherwise? Unless he had not dared do so, lest it be misinterpreted? And not only by her, but by Cornelia, too. After all, 'Nelia was in effect her guardian, and as such might well insist on reading her correspondence.

Lili shook her head as if to clear it. She was becoming fanciful, silly, even. Halpern had tossed a message to his butler on his way to bed, ordering the flowers be delivered, and then he had no doubt forgotten all about it. She wondered why she found that such a depressing thought.

Lili did not leave the house that day. For some reason she had no desire to shop or go to the booksellers or the park. Instead she wrote a long letter to the Moorlands, read, and practiced her music. She even spent an hour on her needlework. By late afternoon she was not only bored, she was fretful and irritable. Not even a glimpse of her violets, placed on her dressing table, could cheer her.

She was seated in the drawing room alone when the butler announced a caller. Cornelia and Alastair had gone to visit a friend. Lili had been invited, but in her present mood had declined the treat. Now she stared at the butler in wonder.

"Who is it?" she asked, noting his disapproving face, no doubt the result of Cornelia's absence.

"I'm sure I cannot say, miss," he told her. "He did not tell me. And he had no card for me to present. I suspect he does not have one."

This last promouncement was accompanied by a distinct sniff. Lili did not notice, for she was so excited, sure she knew who was standing even now in the mansion's splendid foyer, covertly being watched by the tall footmen on duty there.

"Tell me, Marks, is the gentleman dressed in town clothes?" she asked, edging forward in her chair, her needlework slipping, forgotten to her feet.

"I would have to say he is not, miss," he replied even more haughtily, if that were possible. "There is a distinct look of the country about him, if I may be so bold as to say so."

"Then you may show him in at once. He is an old friend of mine from my former home."

"But Mrs. Russell is not here, miss," Marks protested. "It is not proper . . ."

"Show him in, Marks," Lili ordered as she rose. "He is a Mr. Moorland and he is like a brother to me. No doubt he has

news of the family, and I would hear it. Besides, you will be in
the hall, will you not? Go! Go at once!"

For a moment the butler hesitated before he went to do her
bidding. Lili clasped her hands tightly before her to hide their
trembling. It had suddenly occurred to her that perhaps there
was trouble at home, and that was why Ben had come himself
at the busiest time of the year for a farmer. She knew Captain
Moorland had been failing when she left. She even knew he
did not have long to live. Perhaps he was gone?

When Ben entered the room watched by a careful butler, she
ran to him to grasp him by the arms. "Tell me, Ben, tell me at
once!" she demanded. "Is it the captain? Has he . . . has
he . . ."

She could not say the word, but Ben, staring down at her
face and the tears filling her eyes, made haste to say, "No, no,
everyone is fine, Lili. If it isn't just like you to think the worst
and take on so."

These brotherly words must have reassured the butler, for
he not only left the room, he closed the door behind him.

Lili was uncomfortable now as she saw the look on Ben
Moorland's face. She knew why he had come; she wondered
she could ever have mistaken his intent. "Do sit down," she
said, letting him go and indicating a chair across from her
own. "I am surprised to see you, sir, in May. Surely the farm
claims your attention."

"It does," Ben said tersely as he stared at the handsome
fruitwood armchair with its elaborate gold brocade covering.
Lili saw he was dressed in his best clothes, although anyone in
the *ton* would have known in an instant his navy coat and
fawn breeches were the work of a provincial tailor. Even his
white cambric shirt and cravat, fashioned carefully by Nancy's
expert needle, showed their origin. She wondered what the
servants here had made of them and was instantly ashamed of
herself. She had certainly changed for the worse, she thought
bleakly. This was *Ben,* her beloved friend and mentor and she
loved him. His clothes did not matter.

"Could we go outside?" he was asking now, indicating the

French doors that led to the terrace and the narrow garden beyond. "I feel as if I were suffocating in here, lass, it's all so grand and rich."

"Of course," she said, jumping up to lead the way. "It is a nice afternoon. I won't need a wrap."

As they went down the steps to the garden path, she added, "Oh, please tell me everything, Ben. Letters are all very well, but they do not tell nearly enough."

His smile was fleeting, for his face was still taut and strained somehow. "Nancy sends her love, my brother as well. Of course, his is all wrapped up in warnings about London and the dangers here. What else? We had a wet spring and so we were late sowing. The pig has had a litter, nine piglets she had, all good-sized. I sold two at the last market day. The fruit trees set late because of the rain. We must hope for a good harvest. But the wheat is growing well—"

"Ben, I am not interested in pigs and wheat!" Lili interrupted. "Tell me about *people*."

"Do you mean Roy Akins?" he asked stiffly. "He's run off to the army, he has. Always was no good, was Roy."

Lili had to think for a moment before she remembered the boy and his stolen kiss in the henhouse. She laughed. "Of course I don't mean him. How can you think such a thing? Tell me instead of Nancy and the neighbors. And has Ellie convinced Hod Jackson to wed her? I know she has been trying to, this age."

She was to be sorry she had said that, for it reminded Ben of his own errand. He stopped walking and turned her to face him. They were out of sight of the drawing room now, behind the tall elm in the center of the garden.

"You know why I've come, don't you?" he asked roughly. "You know why I couldn't stay away, don't you, lass? Because every day, every night, I've wanted you. I've come to take you home with me, Lili, as my wife. Yes, my wife, for I'll wait no longer. There's a place here in town where you can get a special license so you don't have to have banns called. I've the money for it with me and as soon as you give the word, I'll be

off to get that license. I love you so, lass. It's been eating me
inside that love, all because you haven't been with me."

He kissed her then and a wave of despair swept over Lili,
for his lips claimed hers as fervently as she remembered. She
had as good as told him before she left the farm she did not
love him, and she knew now nothing had changed. Indeed,
days went by and she did not even think of him. His kiss grew
more passionate and demanding, and his hands caressed her
back, molding her body to his. She tried to pull away, but he
was having none of that. He had been starved for her too long.
He was not about to let her go now that he had her close.

Graeme Wilder stood some little distance away and watched
them. He had called at Russell House this afternoon on a
whim, or so he had told himself. Finding the Russells absent,
and Miss Martingale entertaining a strange gentleman in the
drawing room, he had, by the simple act of raising an eye-
brow, reduced the butler almost to incoherence. Waving a dis-
missive hand to that butler, he had gone unchecked to the
drawing room. There was no sign of Lili or her guest there, but
the terrace door stood open and it did not take him long to discover the two sheltering behind the elm tree and engaging in
what he saw was a passionate, consuming embrace. It was a
few seconds before he noticed Lili was trying to break away.
He would have gone to her aid except the stranger lifted his
head. He did not release her, however. Moving closer to step
behind a flowering bush, Halpern began to eavesdrop without
a qualm.

"What is it, Lili?" he heard the man ask in a hoarse whisper.
"Why do you try to get away? You kissed me back the night
before you left. In your bedroom, remember? Has London
changed you so much that you think you do not love me anymore?"

"Ben, let me go," Lili pleaded. "I cannot breathe if you hold
me so tightly."

Halpern saw the man obey although he did not seem at all
happy to do so. "Answer me," he growled.

"I do not remember kissing you back," she began, and when

he stepped forward, she moved back, her hands raised as if that would hold him off. "I love you, Ben, you know that. No, no, wait and hear me out. I love you as I would love my brother, if I had one. You are very dear to me; why, you are part of my family. But you are not the man I love. I cannot feel that way about you. I know I never will. And nothing you can say, nothing you can do, can change that."

There was a long, silent moment. Then the man named Ben said, "You do not know your own mind, Lili. You are too young and the love of a man and a woman is new to you. But after we are married, you will see how that love will grow. I promise you it will be so. For, Lili, you are my life. I have waited for you for four long years, waited for you to grow old enough for marriage, ever since you came to the farm that first night so long ago, all big eyes and with that mop of black curls of yours, and your sweet voice so shy and hesitant. You were so frightened of the new place, the strange people. But that worked out, did it not?

"Our marriage will work out as well. And when you have a baby in your arms, when you are mistress of Moorlands, why, then, you will be content. And I will love you every moment for the rest of our lives together."

"But I won't be content," Lili said baldly. "Listen to me, Ben! You don't listen because you don't want to hear what I am saying."

"It is this damned town that has changed you, spoiled you," he said as he reached for her again.

Retreating a safe distance, she said, "No, London has nothing to do with it. I tried to tell you at Moorlands. I cannot love you the way you want. I never will. I don't want to be mistress of Moorlands. I don't love the place as you do. I find it small and confining, even boring. But it is your life, Ben, we both know that. You deserve a wife who will care for it with you, not the indifferent rebel I would be. Please, please, go back to Moorlands and forget me."

Halpern found he was holding his breath, watching the two people before him. He could hear a carriage rumbling by in

the Square beyond the wall, and in the boughs of the elm over-
head, some birds twittering, but all his attention was focused
on Lili Martingale and the man who loved her.

"You mean it, don't you. And, my love—all the time I've
waited for you—it was all for nothing," he said in a bitter
voice.

"I'm sorry," Lili whispered. Halpern saw she was making a
valiant effort not to cry.

The man named Ben did not try to persuade her further, nor
did he bid her good-bye. Instead, he turned on his heel and almost ran back to the house. As he passed by, Halpern saw he
was weeping, his open, handsome face distorted with pain. He
felt a pang of sympathy.

When he looked at Lili again, she was weeping, too, her
hands covering her face and her shoulders shaking. As he
watched, she reached into her pocket for a handkerchief, and
she cried harder when she did not find one. He went to her
then and took her in his arms as naturally as if he did it every
day. "Here, Lili," he said. "Take mine."

She took the handkerchief he gave her gratefully and buried
her face in it as her tears continued to fall. Halpern held her
softly and rocked her to and fro, murmuring words that made
little sense but at least conveyed comfort. "There, there," he
said. "It will be better soon," he told her. "Yes, it is too bad,"
he added.

It seemed a long time before her tears and sobs died away to
a few sighs and hiccups. Still Lili remained in his arms, her
head resting on his chest and his handkerchief, now thoroughly damp, clutched in her hand. He was sorry when she
suddenly remembered who he was, where they were, and the
impropriety of their positions, and broke free.

"What are you doing here?" she whispered. "Why did you
come? Oh, did you see? Hear?"

"Yes, everything," he told her, wondering why a shiny
runny nose should be so endearing. "Don't fret about it. Wipe
your eyes and blow your nose, Lili. No doubt he was a worthy
man, but since you cannot love him, what you did was for the

best. You do not love him, do you? You were not just teasing him?"

Her eyes flashed with sudden anger. "Of course I wasn't! How can you think anything so base? I love Ben Moorland. He is family to me and I have little enough of family to my name. I wept because I had to hurt him, and I would not have done so for the world. Oh, dear, why does life have to be so *hard*?"

Halpern did not smile at her dramatic words. No doubt what she had just done had been hard for her. She was so young, younger still in the way she thought and spoke and behaved. "Come and sit down," he suggested, indicating the bench set under the tree. "You will feel more the thing presently."

She frowned as she obeyed. He saw she was twisting and pulling his handkerchief and he removed it from her frenetic grasp. He was sure if she ripped it in two it would only turn her into a watering pot again and he had no desire for that.

"I hurt him so," she said, quite forgetting he was even there. "I didn't explain it right, tell him in a way that would not be so painful. No, I just blurted it out coldly. Why, I even told him the farm *bored* me. How could I have said such a thing to Ben? He loves that farm; why, he would defend it with his life!"

"You did it the best you could," Halpern reassured her. "Those kinds of scenes are never easy. And later, everyone wishes they could do them over. Better."

She looked at him. "Have you . . . ?" she began. Then she shook her head. "No, of course you have not had to repulse another. That is something only women must do. How silly of me. But perhaps some girl long ago told you the same things I told Ben? Someone you loved? Oh, sir, is that why you are still unmarried at your age? I am so sorry, indeed I am, that I should cause you to remember it after all these long years."

Halpern rose so quickly, she gasped. "It is no such thing," he said, sounding as if his cravat were choking him. "I beg you to compose yourself, Miss Martingale. I will leave you now so you may do so. Try not to brood or blame yourself further. Give you good day."

As he disappeared into the house, Lili stared after him, wondering about his sudden anger. For he had been angry and she had no idea why. Nor did she know why he had come this afternoon or how he had happened to end up in the garden. Perhaps Marks had thought he might serve as a substitute chaperon since 'Nelia was not at home?

Yes, of course, that must be it. Halpern was an older gentleman and although he was not family, he could be considered a respectable replacement. Remembering how upset Marks had been when she had insisted on seeing Ben alone, she applauded his quick thinking. Really, it was very clever of him to make use of the viscount.

Chapter Twelve

Halpern left Grosvenor Square quickly. His top hat was placed on his head at its usual smart angle and his face revealed nothing untoward. Still, he was glad when he reached Braybourne House without encountering any of his acquaintances. Gaining the privacy of the library, he poured himself a glass of sherry and paced up and down, too agitated to sit still.

The nerve of the girl to assume just like that that he had been so disappointed in love it had put him off women from then on, he told himself as he took a healthy sip. Too bad Miss Martingale had no idea the number of lovers he had had—beautiful women, charming and intelligent. Too bad she did not know that rather than ever being dismissed, he had always been ardently pursued, and any endings there had been had been initiated by him, and him alone.

He suddenly remembered she had also dared to imply he was so old any love affairs he might have indulged in must have occurred long ago. This annoyed him so he marched to the window and stood brooding there before he tossed off the rest of his sherry. She was impossible. Naive, unsophisticated, rustic, too prone to say whatever came into her head—impossible!

Then why was he in such a state, he wondered. Why did this bother him so much? Why couldn't he laugh at it and forget it? It certainly would have caused any of his friends to laugh long and loud, if they had happened to overhear it. And thank heavens they had not, he thought, bringing out his handkerchief to mop his brow.

He stared down at the still-damp ball he held in his hand. Damp with Miss Martingale's tears, he reminded himself. No, not Miss Martingale, Lili. He had called her that when he had her in his arms. And how grand she had felt there. She was so soft in all the right places, such a delicious, seductive, innocent armful. And that mop of black curls the man Ben had mentioned—how they had tickled his chin when she clutched his coat and wept into his chest. He remembered wanting to kiss her himself. Well, of course he had, he told himself stoutly. Surely that was a normal reaction, wasn't it? To kiss her and make it better, as he would have kissed a child who fell and hurt herself?

Somehow he did not think this was the correct interpretation of his feelings at that moment, but it would have to do. He knew it would be most unwise to try and define his thoughts further. Suffice it to say, he had felt a tenderness for her, a tenderness made up of regret for her weeping and her hurt.

And even that was unusual, he realized, retreating to a chair by the fireplace and sitting down to stretch his legs out before him. He had had his flirts over the Seasons, as well as his lovers. None of them had ever inspired him to anything remotely resembling tenderness. Certainly he had never felt the urge to ask for anyone's hand in marriage; the very idea of spending the rest of his life with one woman had never appealed to him. And he felt that way still, even though he had as good as set himself to searching for a wife this Season. He was reminded he had yet to begin looking, for of course one could not count Lili Martingale. As his mother had so correctly pointed out, she was nothing but a green girl. He knew she was unsuited for the post of Marchioness of Braybourne.

What he needed was a not-too unattractive titled girl of a good family that was not too closely related to his own. One who had been brought up to wealth and privilege and knew the life she could expect as his wife. One who was prepared for that life, accepted it, and would do his name honor. At least until he had his heir and perhaps one other son, he thought with a grimace. He wondered why such a suitable course was so unappealing. And why did Lili Martingale's woebegone face keep appearing in his mind's eye? Why could he still hear her sobs and the hearty way she had blown her nose when he ordered her to do so? Why did he wish even now he had her back in his arms so he could hold her close and comfort her?

He rose and left the library, calling for his horse to be brought around as he took the stairs two at a time. A good, hard ride would clear his head of these ridiculous fancies, he told himself. It had better.

Halpern did not see Lili for several days, and he told himself that was just as well. He realized now it had been foolish to send her that nosegay, and foolish to call at Russell House the same afternoon. Indeed, it had been foolhardy to make her his latest flirt and it would be prudent to extricate himself before things went any further.

Since that was the case, he had to wonder why he found himself riding beside her on the expedition to Greenwich to which he had also been invited.

Lili gave him a warm smile as they trotted out of town in the large troop of riders their hostess had assembled. Lady Coburn had twin daughters to bring out this Season. She had planned a number of festive occasions, for there was no denying both Edna and Florence were bran-faced and no lotion had proved strong enough to remove their freckles. Still, they were good-natured girls with pretty chestnut hair and big brown eyes, and they were excellent riders. To their credit as well, and certainly more importantly, were their excellent dowries and the fact their father was the Earl of Coburn. Their mother had great hopes for them, although she would have admitted Viscount Halpern was a long shot. Certainly he had never shown any interest in very young girls, which made it all the more puzzling he was so attentive to Beau Russell's ward. Perhaps he was not such a long shot after all? For as the future Marquis of Braybourne, he would not choose some nobody to wed. To flirt with, yes. To marry, no. She vowed to alert the girls to this possibility as soon as they reached their destination.

It was a warm day for May, warm and sunny, and Lili was enjoying the ride. Her mare seemed at ease, too, as soon as London's streets were left behind.

"That's a handsome mount you have, Miss Martingale," Halpern remarked. "I thought her high-strung that day we rode in the park, but I see she is no such thing."

"Oh no, Josephine is a lady. It was only she was not used to London," Lili told him.

"Josephine?" he asked. "There must be a story there. It's an unusual name for a horse."

Of course Lili explained her mare's connection to the former Empress of France, and Halpern laughed as she had known he would. Today, however, it did not bother her, she was so relieved he was not still angry with her.

She had felt remorse over Ben for an entire day, even after she had had a long soul-searching talk with Cornelia. Eventually she had gone to Alastair. He had assured her she had done the right thing, and because the advice came from him, she accepted it and set herself to forgetting. For some reason she had not mentioned Halpern to either of them after she discovered the butler had somehow forgotten to tell them of his visit.

A short time later Halpern and Lili found themselves leading the party after a spirited canter. Without discussion they halted their mounts by the side of the road and waited for the others to catch them up.

"I am glad we have this moment, my lord," Lili began formally, determined to get any unpleasantness over quickly. "You were very kind to me the other day when you found me weeping. I was most remiss not to thank you."

"To say nothing of thanking me for the use of my handkerchief which you certainly needed," Halpern replied, equally determined to keep the discussion on a light note.

"Yes, of course, that, too, as well as your comforting shoulder. It was good of you and I appreciate your concern, sir."

"Well, now you have thanked me shall we say no more

about it?" he asked, staring down the road as if willing the rest of the group to appear.

Not quite through, Lili refused to be diverted. "When you left me so suddenly, I feared you were angry," she went on. "I must have said something that offended you, and I would not have done so for the world. I have no idea what that might have been. Won't you tell me so I may watch my tongue another time?"

"You are mistaken. I merely remembered a prior engagement and realized I was going to be unforgiveably late for it if I did not make haste. Do not always be relating things to yourself, Miss Martingale. The world does not revolve around you to the exclusion of all else."

Now it was Lili's turn to look down the road for their party. Halpern, however, was too skilled to allow the situation to disintegrate into an awkward silence, and he began to discuss a masquerade that was planned for the following week, and like subjects until the others appeared.

He soon found himself alone, for Lili had dropped back to ride beside his shy cousin. He reined in beside Lady Florence. When he saw her mother the countess smiling at him, he realized he had been neatly scooped into the lady's net. Not that it mattered, he told himself. Lady Florence was exactly the kind of girl he had envisioned as his marchioness. By the time they reached Greenwich, however, he had crossed her from his list of possible candidates. The lady had an irritating high-pitched laugh that Halpern knew would drive him to do murder if he was forced to listen to it at the breakfast table. He was quick to make his escape. Somehow her twin attached herself to him a short time later. Lady Edna—"my family and friends call me Teddy, m'lord, just imagine!"—had a more musical laugh, but she had an equally annoying habit of sniffing after every sentence.

After a picnic luncheon most of the party went off to explore the Greenwich Observatory with its outstanding view of London. Others took the King William Walk that led to Greenwich Pier and the Thames. Halpern, seeking to avoid the ladies of Coburn ducked into the church of St. Alphage, where he found Lili Martingale. They were the only people there. Dust motes danced in the sunlight that slanted through the tall narrow windows. It was very quiet.

"Henry the Eighth was baptized here," Halpern told her as he joined her at the baptismal font.

"Indeed?" Lili asked distantly and he smiled to himself.

"A lesser mortal is associated with this church as well," he continued. "Her name was Lavinia Fenton. She became the Duchess of Bolton after an illustrious career in the theater. In fact she was the first actress to play Polly Peachum in Gay's *Beggar's Opera.* Her burial is recorded in the register."

"I am not familiar with the play," Lili admitted.

"Perhaps you might see a revival someday." he said.

As they left the church, they both blinked in the sunlight and Halpern had to shade his eyes as he looked for the rest of the party. Seeing no one familiar, he said, "Should you care to walk down to the Thames, Miss Martingale?"

Lili nodded and took his arm. Halpern thought her very subdued. He wondered if he had destroyed her spirits by criticizing her for thinking everything in the world began and ended with her. It was a typical failing of the young. If his mother were to be believed, he had had a terrible case of it himself once upon a time and he suspected he still suffered occasionally from it.

When they reached the Thames they paused to watch a small coaster beat its way up the river. Lili was reminded of the crossing she had made here from Belgium three years before, how she and Alastair had stood at the bow of the ship, watching the waves, how 'Nelia had had to go below, the motion bothered her so.

"What are you thinking?" Halpern asked. "A wealth of emotions just crossed your face; amusement, delight, even distaste."

Lili told him. "We left Vienna suddenly," she confessed. "I do not know why. But I do remember how upset I was about it. I had made friends with an elderly gentleman and I did not like to abandon him. Strange, that. I cannot even remember his name now, and he was so nice."

They had reached a stone wall. Some cows were pastured behind that wall and with one accord Halpern and Lili turned to retrace their steps. Lili fancied she could smell the brine of the channel although she knew they were miles away from it still.

Nothing had been said for quite a time when suddenly her escort said, "What did that man Ben mean when he claimed you had kissed him back in your bedroom?" he asked.

Lili was so startled, she stopped walking. "Why, what a singular thing to ask me, sir," she managed to say.

"I notice you do not answer," he replied, never taking his eyes from hers. "And why is that?"

When she only stared at him helplessly, he went on. "What was he doing in your room? I know things are different in the country, but I did not think they were as loose as that. Men do not visit a girl's bedchamber, not even men in the immediate family. Well, Miss Martingale?"

It was only later Lili realized she could have refused to answer, and she would have been well within her rights to do so, for the information was none of Halpern's concern. But with his hazel eyes searching her face so intently she felt strangely unable to resist. "It happened the night before I left for Wyckend," she confessed. "I had gone to bed. Everyone had gone to bed for we were to make an early start. I suppose Ben did not want a public leave-taking. He had asked me to marry him earlier that day; I had not said I would."

"So he kissed you," Halpern said, taking up the tale. "And I believe he said you kissed him back?"

"I have no recollection of doing such a thing," Lili said, thoroughly flustered now. "I may have. I do love Ben, you know."

"So you said," he persisted. "Tell me, Lili, did you like that kiss?"

Lili did not notice the use of her first name for she was confused. Confused and warm with embarrassment and unable to turn him away with a light jest because she had been brought up by the nuns to be truthful and confess her failings.

"Yes, I did," she said softly. "It was like nothing I had ever known before. It made me feel all—oh, I do not know how to describe it!—all warm and boneless and it reminded me that all I—oh!"

She stopped, horrified at what she had almost revealed. She wondered why he continued to stare at her, his gaze so forceful it made it impossible for her to look away, and she was stunned when he took her in his arms and bent his head to kiss her. She closed her eyes. Her heart had begun to pound. Why was he doing this, she wondered. He was Viscount Halpern and he was almost as old as Alastair. Still, the feeling she had had when Ben kissed her came flooding back. Halpern's lips were insistent and not a bit gentle, but she did not feel threatened. She could feel his hands on her back right through her habit and shirt and shift. She prayed he would not let her go for she was sure she would collapse in a heap on the ground if he did not support her.

It seemed an age before he lifted his head an inch or so and said in a hoarse voice, "Did you like it better than my kiss, Lili?"

Her eyes flew open. What did he mean? This was not some game they were playing. Was it?

"I beg your pardon," he said then. He did not let her go, for which she was very grateful. "I should not have asked you that."

"No, you shouldn't," she said. Her voice was little more than a croak and she did not wonder when he smiled at it.

"I suspect we had better be getting back," he remarked, looking around as if for the rest of their party. And thank heavens he did not see them, or anyone else for that matter, he thought. Only the cows could have noticed the embrace and they were more intent on the fresh spring grass than any antics human beings might be up to.

As he took Lili's arm, he said, "I suppose I must also apologize for that kiss I stole. I do not want to. I enjoyed it too much. It would be lying for me to say I regret it. But perhaps you will at least forgive me for the liberty I took, Miss Martingale?"

You called me Lili a moment ago, she thought. "Certainly, my lord," she replied aloud.

"You are too good. If you had not, I should have had to seek Mr. Russell's permission to ask you to marry me."

"Marry?" she echoed, stopping to stare at him. "Oh no, I do not want to be married, not for years. And I couldn't marry you in any case. You are to be a marquis. Besides that, you are much too old for me."

Halpern had been wondering why he had even mentioned marriage. She had forgiven him his kiss, there was no need to be conventional. But now, instead of feeling grateful she was denying him, he was indignant that she could think him old.

"I am only twenty-eight. As I believe I told you earlier."

"And I am seventeen," she replied. As a look of horror passed over his face, she added, "Well, I will be eighteen in January, but still . . ."

"Only seventeen? I had no idea you were so young," he muttered, for all his usual finesse had deserted him. "My father did say . . . but I refused to believe him. I must beg your pardon again. What I did was twice as heinous in your case, you, who are little better than a child."

Lili knew she was no such thing but she kept her lips tightly pressed together. As she did so, she wondered why she wished she had her crop handy, then she realized that more than anything else in the world, she wanted to strike him with it—hard. She sensed he was sneaking glances at her, but she did not give him the satisfaction of returning them.

"Well, we will say no more about it, pretend it never happened. I see the coaster has made some progress. Do you suppose the tide has changed?"

Lili did not care a bit for the coaster, but she could tell the viscount did not intend to discuss what had just happened anymore. She did not know if all London gentlemen behaved this way when they found themselves alone with a girl. Perhaps it was all her fault for going off on a walk with him? Perhaps he had thought she was expecting him to kiss her since she was such a bold piece, and once trapped had felt he must mention marriage? The fact that he had not gone first to Alastair showed it had been a sudden decision, one he now regretted. For if he loved me, she thought as she marched along beside him, the skirt of her habit thrown over her arm, he would have ignored my protests, pleaded for my agreement, and kissed me until I was breathless.

I wish he had done that, she thought, and her face paled.

Surely she was not becoming wanton, was she? What had just happened was not at all the thing. She knew that. She also knew that most young ladies in the *ton* did not have to deal with situations remotely like it. And she could not understand why it had fallen to her lot. It seemed very unfair.

She was reminded then of Halpern's comment this morning that she must not take everything so personally. It had wounded her at the time; recalling it was just as painful.

He is a terrible man, she told herself as she stumbled over a pebble and quickly regained her balance before he could help her. Truly terrible.

But you did like his kiss more than you liked Ben's, her honest conscience reminded her, and it was all she could do not to stamp her foot in frustration.

Chapter Thirteen

Lili was back in Grosvenor Square by four that afternoon. She found Cornelia and Alastair had gone driving, leaving her a note reminding her of the reception they were all to attend that evening.

She went slowly up the steps to her room. For the first time she realized she had no desire to attend a party, and instead, wished she might have supper in bed and spend the evening alone. To brood? Perhaps. Or perhaps to reread that essay she had written about her faults? She had not studied it for a long time.

As she rang for a maid, she knew she could not excuse herself by saying she was tired from the day's riding. For one thing she was never tired. For another, she suspected they would know something was wrong and tax her with it. She could not discuss today with 'Nelia, and most certainly not with Alastair. She suspected he would take a very dim view of a stolen kiss and he might well insist the viscount be held accountable.

For a moment, she stood still in the center of the room, daydreaming. Alastair, of course, would insist on a wedding for royalty. St. Paul's or Westminster Abbey, a throng of little bridesmaids and a train at least twenty feet long. And trumpeters naturally, as well as a full choir of boys' angelic voices. And she would carry white roses and . . .

She gritted her teeth and threw her crop and gloves at the bed. Fool! she told herself. Idiot!

For the next hour she kept herself very busy. First she had

a bath and had her hair washed, then she sat down at her desk, wrapped in a warm robe to write to Nancy Moorland and try to explain why she had refused to marry Ben. It was something she had dreaded doing and managed to postpone. Now it was merely a chore to keep her from thinking too much about this afternoon at Greenwich. At the end of the letter, she added her dear love to the captain, and to Ben as well. She knew Nancy would understand that last message, although Ben would scorn it. After she sealed the letter, she bent her head and prayed that God would help Ben find someone worthy of him; a girl who loved him with all her heart.

At the reception later she found herself looking around nervously, but of Graeme Wilder, Viscount Halpern, there was no sign. She was both relieved and disappointed. She did see the Rowley sisters and she smiled warmly to them. To her surprise, Miss Rowley turned her back. Perhaps she needed glasses, Lili thought. Her sister Bettina sent her a shy little smile, so quickly gone Lili was not sure she had not imagined it. She saw they were with their brother, the noted Arthur. He was a man in his twenties, so slim he was almost gaunt, and quite ordinary-looking with nothing to commend him but a superior expression. He only conversed with a select few, Lili noted. She saw his sisters were not well dressed. Even she knew that, after being under Alastair Russell's wing. Their gowns were plain, almost dowdy, and she was sure they had been made at home. Could it be Mr. Rowley was a nip cheese? How unfortunate for his sisters if it were so. And why had they chosen to ignore her? Perhaps because they had not been properly introduced? Yes, that must be it. She must not read too much into what was probably an innocuous situation.

She saw the Dowager Countess of Wyckend was present this evening. She was seated with that Mrs. Parmeter and two other elderly ladies, all of them with their heads together as they exchanged gossip.

"Lili? Have your wits gone begging?" she heard Alastair inquire, and she turned to find he was waiting to present a handsome young man to her. Mr. Warfield had only recently arrived in town. He professed his delight in meeting Miss Martingale, and begged her to indulge him in a stroll about the room. Lili thought him overly optimistic. The reception was very crowded. But she misjudged Cary Warfield. He found a room at the back of the house where only a few people were talking and admiring the oil paintings that lined the walls. Lili found her eyes drawn to one painting of a group of young men about to set out on a hunt. One of them looked very much like Halpern.

"Do you know who painted that large oil, sir?" she asked.

"I've not a clue. Shall we investigate?" he said as he led her up to it. A large sideboard separated them from it, but Lili had no trouble seeing the signature was that of the Marchioness of Braybourne, and that yes, indeed, the proud-looking man bestride the large gelding was none other than her son. An enormous dog of some breed she could not identify stared up at him adoringly. Perhaps the very same dog who used the bed in his room at Braybourne?

"I say, there's Percy Ridgeway and Lord Gore," Warfield declared, raising an elaborate quizzing glass to look more closely. "And Halpern, of course. I see his mater did the painting. She's a dab hand at painting, you know. Have you had the chance to meet the viscount, Miss Martingale?"

Lili allowed she had had that honor.

"He is really top of the trees, is he not?" Warfield asked eagerly. Lili decided if he was a day over twenty-one, she would be surprised.

"Always so elegant, so fashionably turned out, and never at a loss for a jest or a bon mot," her escort continued. "They say he has been asked to join a race to Basingstoke next week, he and three other bloods driving their perch phaetons. There is to be a time limit, and whoever beats it by the largest margin will win a hundred guineas. I can tell you, my money is on Halpern. If he enters, that is. He is such a driver, and his cattle so superior!"

"He is quite a hero of yours, I see," Lili said sweetly.

"But not of yours, Miss Martingale?" he asked, peering at her closely.

She managed a chuckle. "How you do take one up, sir," she protested. "I only know the gentleman slightly. He is, er, quite old, is he not?"

"Old? No, no, he is not old. M'father's old, but Halpern is in prime twig. Never a doubt of it, 'pon my word."

He continued to talk of his idol so reverently Lili was almost tempted to reveal the man had feet of clay. She told herself she was delighted when Mr. Warfield returned her to Cornelia and Alastair. They remained only a short time longer, for they were pledged to another reception that evening. Later, Mr. and Mrs. Hugh Carlyle were giving a supper for a few friends in their mansion on the Bath Road. Viscount Halpern was not at any of these parties and when Lili tumbled into bed shortly before dawn, she did not know whether to be relieved or disappointed. She fell asleep wondering which parties he had honored instead.

As it turned out, the viscount had not gone out at all. Instead, he had sent his regrets to both receptions and the late supper, and spent the evening at home in the library. He had a book on his lap, which he did not read, a glass of brandy and water beside him, which he almost forgot to drink, and a cozy fire to stare into while he brooded.

Seventeen! She was only seventeen. Strange, that. She had seemed older to him. She had a degree of sophistication unusual for a girl that age. Perhaps it was her poise. She had lived abroad for so long, been educated far beyond the simple subjects that were all most girls were thought to require.

And just this afternoon, as they had been strolling toward the Thames, she had overheard two Frenchmen talking. She had asked them if she might not be of service, and that was the last he had understood of the fast-paced conversation that followed. As they left them bowing and smiling, Lili had confided they had been deserted by the waterman who had brought them down from London that morning, and had no

idea how to get back. She had told him they were recent émi-
grés and their English was very bad. He remembered how useless he had felt on the one hand, and how indignant on the
other that Lili would speak to strangers, and foreigners at that.
How very *English* of him, he thought now, mocking himself.
He was sure she would have done the same if the men had
been German. He recalled she had said she was proficient in
that language as well.

He remembered a reception then when he had seen her conversing with Sir Angus McAdam. He had edged closer to
eavesdrop, they were so intent. Sir Angus was a noted author-
ity on India, its people and geography and native plants. Most
girls would have been bored as well as out of their depth, but
Lili listened carefully, posed some excellent questions, and
thoroughly captivated the crusty old gentleman without trying
to do so in the least. He had heard Sir Angus tell a friend of his
later that same evening that Miss Martingale was a most intelligent lass as well as being as bonny as a bluebell. High praise
indeed from the crusty old Scot.

She *was* bonny, there was no denying that, he thought as
he got up to add more coal to the fire. Lovely and intelligent
and charming—everything he could want in a wife except for
two glaring faults. First, she was a nobody. Outside of her
distant relationship with Cornelia Russell, he had no idea of
her family. And secondly, she was much too young for him.
Seventeen, he thought again, despairingly. Only a few years
from childhood. This weighed more heavily with him than
her family background did. Other men had married beneath
them in the past. If he chose, he could do so as well, although it would not sit well with his parents. He shrugged.
He had been of age for years and he could do as he pleased.
It was then another large disadvantage came to mind, and he
frowned. If he married her, he would look ridiculous. Everyone would mock him, tell jokes about it, murmur of April
and August. Why, even the print shops would have a day of
it, putting out caricatures of the two of them that would be

snapped up and laughed over. Could he bear that, he who had always been so proud?

It was late when he decided he must forget her. It was the only thing to do. But as he came to this excellent conclusion, Halpern remembered the kiss they had shared, how she had felt in his arms, so warm and sweet, her soft lips that had trembled under his until he coaxed them to respond, and he groaned. How could he forget her?

When Lili saw Viscount Halpern again she was disappointed, he seemed so intent on ignoring her. Disappointed but not surprised, she told herself as she smiled at Cary Warfield and agreed to the first set. Halpern had kissed her, but he had regretted that kiss. And she must remember how both Alastair and 'Nelia had stressed that with her background, she could not expect a great marriage. Not that she wanted to marry him, of course.

She was attending a ball with the Russells that evening, given by the Duke and Duchess of Severn. The gown she was wearing was a warm rose silk, and it had caused a heated discussion between Alastair and Cornelia. She had claimed it was not at all the thing for a young girl in her first Season; the color, the cut of the neckline, the narrowness of the skirt. Alastair had laughed and said anything that looked so ravishing on Lili had to be correct.

"She will carry it off, my dear, you'll see," he reassured his worried wife. "Besides, she is Beau Russell's ward. Who will dare to question it?"

Lili had clapped her hands in delight, but now she was not so sure. She had seen several people, gentlemen as well as ladies, inspecting her this evening, then turning aside to comment to friends. And it seemed to her she was receiving a greater number of questioning looks than she ever had before. None of them were obvious of course, still she did not think she was being too sensitive, or thinking the world revolved around her, as Halpern had claimed she did. But Mr. Austin had not asked for his usual dance, and his sister had moved away when Lili would have stopped to speak to her. And then there was the unwanted attentions of a young sprig of fashion whose conversation seemed very warm to her. It was almost as if Mr. Fairmont had discovered he did not have to treat her as a lady, and he told her stories she was sure he would not repeat to his sisters or his mother. She escaped his company as soon as she could.

It was quite late in the evening, after she had had supper with Cary Warfield and some of his friends, that she was approached again by Freddy Fairmont. Since she had left him earlier, he had had too much champagne and was none too steady in his step or his demeanor, something Lili was to discover to her distress before much more time passed.

The Severn ballroom had grown progressively warmer as the late May evening wore on. When Fairmont suggested they seek a breath of air on the balcony, Lili agreed. A quick look had shown her that several people were out there; indeed, the doors that led to the balcony were wide open. She was sure she would not be engaged in anything that could be remarked.

"Y'er very beau-ful, Miss Martingale," Freddy said as soon as they reached the balcony. Lili leaned against the balustrade, taking deep breaths of the cool night air.

"Thank you," she said distantly, moving away as he edged closer. Behind them, the orchestra began another set, and to her dismay all but one of the couples left to join it. She recognized the two remaining. They were newly promised and she was sure would be of no help to her.

"I would like to return to the ballroom now," she said with as much dignity as she could muster. "Everyone else has gone in. I cannot be out here alone with you, sir."

"There'sh someone else," he told her, fondling her arm. Lili was glad she was wearing long white kid gloves. She was about to leave by herself if she had to, when Freddy grabbed her and pulled her toward him. She began to fight him, kicking and squirming to escape, and moving her head from side to side to avoid the kiss he was so determined to plant on her lips. She wanted to cry out, but she knew if she did, it would only cause a scandal.

"Shtop that! Shtand still," he muttered. "Why're you bein' so diff-cult? You're nobody shpecial."

Lili realized he was so tipsy desperate measures were called for, and she bit his ear as hard as she could. He bellowed in pain and let her go, and she almost stumbled in her eagerness to put as much space between them as possible. As she did so, she looked around. The other couple had disappeared, but fortunately they had shut the balcony doors behind them when they went in. No one inside seemed aware of the fracas taking place a few feet away, and for that she was very grateful.

"Who t'hell do ye think y're ter be bitin' me?" Fairmont demanded, rubbing his ear, his face very red. Then he was silent, his mouth falling open as he stared over her shoulder in dismay.

"She is Miss Lillian Martingale. Did her name escape you, sir?" a familiar voice asked. Lili did not have to turn to know it belonged to a very angry Halpern.

"Beg y'pardon, m'lord. Dint see y'there," Fairmont mumbled.

"Much better to beg Miss Martingale's pardon, don't you think?" Halpern asked. His voice was deceptively mild, still Lili shivered at the pent-up menace she could hear in it.

"Ter be shure," Fairmont was quick to agree. "Beggin' yer pardon, Mish, er, Mish . . . My mishtake. Beg yer to 'cuse me. Not feeling quite the thing . . ."

As he spoke he edged closer and closer to the doors that led to the ballroom. As soon as he reached them, he turned and fled. Lili watched him disappear around the dancers, heading for the hall and a safer distance from Halpern's wrath. She saw he was clutching his ear still and it was bleeding, and she wondered how he would explain that to his friends.

"You bit him," the viscount said, coming close. He sounded almost amused now. "My, what sharp teeth you have, Lili."

"It was all I could think of to do," Lili confessed. She was still breathing hard and when she saw him admiring the rise and fall of her breasts in the pretty rose gown, she crossed her arms over them. "I could not scream for help; consider the scandal," she continued, at a loss for something better to say. "And I couldn't kick him hard enough to hurt him in these dancing slippers. There was nothing left to do but, er, bite him."

"I see," he said, taking her chin in his hand and raising her face to his. Lili only dared look at him for a brief moment before she lowered her eyes to his cravat. She noted he was wearing a sapphire in it this evening. It was a handsome stone.

"It is no good, Lili," Halpern said. "No good at all."

He sounded so shaken, she looked up again. She was surprised to see how anguished he appeared, and more confused than ever when that anguish changed to determination.

"I have tried to stay away this evening; indeed, I was sure I was succeeding, but somehow I knew where you were and with whom from the moment you arrived. And when I saw you coming out here with Fairmont, I came to the window to watch. And then when he tried to kiss you, even just dared to touch you, I wanted to kill him. It is a very good thing for that idiot that I did not have my pistols with me. Have I lost my mind?"

"Perhaps you are just overwrought, sir," Lili volunteered. The statement sounded inadequate but she was at a loss to think of anything else. What could he mean? Had he really been watching her? And did he care enough for her to consider murder? Surely not!

"Yes, I think I have gone mad," he went on as if she had not spoken. "I had thought this all out so carefully, made a reasonable, considered decision, one that was as good for you as I told myself it was good for me. And all it took was watching that lout trying to maul you, to wipe away my logical thinking.

"I am talking too much, and saying too little. Lili, I cannot forget you, put you aside. There is no way I can do that, for I am only a man. And I love you."

"You do?" Lili asked in a wondering voice.

His answer was a kiss that far surpassed any she had received so far in her young life. When it ended she was surprised to find her arms around his neck, both hands tangled in his dark hair.

"Just don't bite me," he growled before he bent his head to kiss her throat and all her skin down to the neck of her gown.

"I would never do that," she assured him but he wasn't listening.

When he straightened up, he led her away from the light streaming through the balcony doors. He did not care who saw them, not really, but he intended to observe all the proprieties now that he had decided on his course.

"I must beg your pardon as well as Fairmont, my dear," he told her. "I should apologize for falling in love in you. You are too young for the likes of me. I know that. I know you deserve two Seasons at least before you give your hand to some young man closer to your own age. But I find I want you for my wife so badly I intend to do whatever it takes to make you forget that deserving young man you should have."

"But I can't. I can't marry you," Lili said. "It wouldn't be right."

She was speaking of the title he would hold someday, and how inappropriate it would be for someone like her to become his marchioness. The young man he had mentioned was unimportant—unknown, and unregretted. But Halpern thought she meant the gulf that stretched between their ages, and for a moment he despaired. Then he pulled himself together, and before he lost what little control he had and began to kiss her again, he said, "I will speak to Russell tomorrow. Get his permission to court you. Please do not say no right now," he added hastily. "Think it over. Think of the life we could have together. Please, Lili, my dearest, say you will at least consider it . . ."

Lili looked up at him in wonder, her eyes troubled. He

sounded so eager and so earnest. She had never seen him this way before. Strangely, she did not feel any exultation at humbling him, as she might have a few short weeks before. Now she was the one to feel humble that he said he cared for her so much, she, who was not worthy of him. She saw he was waiting for her answer, and she made herself say carefully, "I promise I will try."

His smile when it came was blinding.

Chapter Fourteen

Lili did not say a word to the Russells about the miraculous thing that had happened to her. Even after they reached Grosvenor Square, she only kissed them good night and fled to her room. She was sure she was in for a sleepless night, she was in such a state. Surely this cannot be happening, she told herself as she stood patiently for the maid to remove her gown. Surely I am only imagining Halpern saying he loved me, and begging me to marry him. Halpern! A viscount who would someday be a marquis. A marquis! The rank that was only one step below dukes, and two removed from royalty.

She could not become a marchioness. Even now she could hear 'Nelia and then Alastair warn her she was not to aspire to a title—any title—that it would be neither possible nor appropriate. Well, it might be possible now, but deep down inside she agreed with them that such a union would not be appropriate.

Dismissing the maid with an absent word of thanks, she got into bed to pull the covers to her chin as she sat and stared at the dark corners of her room. Marriage. To Halpern. "Graeme," she said aloud, experimenting. Graeme and Lili. The Marquis and Marchioness of Braybourne request the honor of your company at a soiree to be given . . . My lady. Dear Lady Braybourne . . . Lili Wilder.

Perhaps Lillian Wilder would be more dignified?

Never mind the title, she told herself fiercely, collapsing on her pillows to stare now at the canopy over her head. This is not only about a title. This is about marriage. Marriage lasts all your life.

She found herself remembering his kiss then, how his hands had felt. How gentle they had been. They had stayed on the balcony until the quadrille was over and they were once again joined by others. Later, when they went inside he had whispered "Tomorrow" to her just before he left her with 'Nelia.

What would Alastair say to him when he came tomorrow; no, later today. If he does come, she thought, reverting to gloom again. It was more likely he would have second thoughts about marriage to a girl as unsuitable as she was, once he was alone and at home. She told herself she would not blame him if he did, even as she realized she would die if he did not come. Because she did love him. She suspected she had been tumbling into love with him for quite a period of time, only refusing to admit it because she had not thought there was any chance her love would ever be returned.

She fell asleep eventually, but when she woke at dawn she was still tired. She dared not call for a maid. If she did, everyone in the house would know there was something in the wind, and suppose Graeme did not come? she asked herself as she washed in the cold water left in the pitcher. She put on a warm robe and sat down near the window to watch the sun rise. Down below the garden was peaceful, the only sound that of the birds greeting the new day. Still, she could hear the traffic building a few streets away. London was never really quiet, not even here in Mayfair. For a moment she thought of all those carts bringing the day's supplies from the country; the animals being herded to their death in Smithfield, the crates of squawking hens and ducks, the barrels of beer and wine, the milk, fish, vegetables, and fruit—but such things were not enough to keep her mind from Halpern.

She wondered if he was awake, too, then laughed at herself. Her eyes widened as she pictured him asleep in bed in that handsome mansion on Park Lane. Did he sleep on his back or his side, she wondered, or was he sprawled on his stomach? Did he wear a nightshirt to bed? A cap? Somehow she could not picture him in a cap, and she was sure he never pulled the bed curtains. Perhaps he slept nude? She rose quickly to pace the room, disturbed by her thoughts and the mental picture they conjured up.

He won't call before ten, she told herself, perhaps not even until eleven. Morning calls were tricky. But how shall I bear to wait if he does not come till afternoon? She suddenly recalled they were pledged to attend a Venetian breakfast late this afternoon. Surely he would come before then! She did not think she could survive another night of suspense without disintegrating into a million jagged little pieces.

Viscount Halpern arrived at ten-thirty. He was dressed to a nicety that even the gentleman he was calling on must approve. The butler bore his card to the breakfast room, where Mr. Russell was lingering over his coffee. He was alone, for his wife had gone to consult the housekeeper about the day's menus, and Lili had fled to her room, sure if she remained she would give the game away. Russell's brows rose as he read the card, but he instructed the butler to bring the viscount to him here.

"A good morning to you, sir," Russell said as his guest came in. He looked perplexed, as well he might Halpern thought as he bowed and took the seat at the table indicated.

"That will be all, Marks. And how may I be of service, sir?" he went on. There was an undertone of amusement as well as curiosity in his voice, for he and the viscount had had few dealings over the years.

"I have come to ask your permission to pay my respects to your ward, Lillian Martingale," Halpern began. He had thought it over carefully before he sensed there was no best way to broach the subject, and decided just to be direct.

Not a muscle moved in Russell's face, although if asked he would have had to admit he had seldom been more surprised. "Indeed?" he managed to say.

"Indeed," the viscount said rather grimly.

"I must ask you to elaborate on your theme. You said you want to court Lili? Are you aware she is only seventeen? Little more than a child? And you yourself, sir, are somewhat older, I believe?"

"Nice of you to put it that way," Halpern replied. "As a matter of fact, I am a great deal older. I will be twenty-nine this coming October."

"I do strive to avoid stating the obvious, but in this case I have no choice. That birthday will make you twelve years older than my ward. It is a rather daunting sum of years, wouldn't you say? Twelve?"

"I would indeed. If our positions were reversed, sir, I would be showing you the door. But I beg you to hear me out. I know there is no need to tell you of the advantages Lili would have as my viscountess, and someday, my marchioness. The wealth, the privilege . . ."

"And perhaps the many years of widowhood?" Russell concluded, his voice gentle.

He watched Halpern's face darken. The man did not look well this morning in spite of his elegant appearance, he thought. But probably he had not gotten much sleep, if any, fretting over this interview. Still, he saw no reason to make it easy for him. He had serious doubts about such a union. It was too unusual. It was not only the age difference but Lili's rather ordinary, perhaps even suspect family background as well. Russell felt a weight of years he had never acknowledged and did not care to now, to be serving as guardian to a young lady whose hand was being sought in wedlock. It reminded him he was almost forty. And next he would probably be forced to be a surrogate grandfather. Horrors.

"Have you spoken to your father about this?" he asked.

Halpern looked grimmer than ever. "I have not," he said shortly. "I am not some naive sprig, after all. I make all the decisions about my life, I, alone."

Russell nodded. He knew Braybourne was entailed and Halpern an only son. The current marquis could not deny him the title or the estate. But he did not like to think of Lili marrying into a hostile family. She could be so easily wounded in spite of her poise and education. From things she had said in the past, he knew she missed having a family of her own. He and Cornelia had tried to fill that void, as had John and Nancy

Moorland, but it was not the same. Those thirteen years as an orphan with the nuns had taken their toll. But to marry into a family that hated her? Could she survive that?

He saw Halpern was regarding him steadily, his fine hazel eyes intent. "And how does Lili feel about your suit, sir?" he asked. "We have not discussed that. And none of the advantages of your birth or your wealth will mean a thing to me if she does not desire the match. If memory serves me right, she once described you to me as pompous, conceited, and er, was it overbearing?"

He saw a glimmer of amusement in his guest's face. So, he can laugh at himself, he thought. A point for Halpern.

"I can hear her saying it. We began on an unpleasant note. In fact, the first thing she called me to my face was a Levite."

"I beg your pardon?"

"She was implying I was far from a Good Samaritan and would surely have passed by on the other side of the road after my guests nearly killed a shepherd boy while jumping a wall, if she had not come upon us and forced me to see to his care. In turn, I thought her gauche and strident, but even then I admired her beauty."

"Marriage has nothing to do with beauty," Russell pointed out. "And you still have not told me how she feels about you now."

"I think she begins to love me. I know she likes me at least, although I suspect marriage frightens her. The permanence of it, perhaps. But that is understandable at seventeen."

"And you would try and win her even so?"

"Yes. I cannot wait for her to reach eighteen. I want her too much. But I assure you it is more than mere lust that moves me to take this step at long last. I love Lili. Now that I know her, I do not see how any man could not, and that is what I am afraid of. I fear someone else will come along and win her and I am not ashamed to tell you, I could not bear that."

"I am happy to hear you say so.

"Shall we adjourn to the drawing room, sir? I am sure a glass of wine would be welcome," Russell added as he led the way to the door. He spoke only of casual matters until they were seated in the handsome room and the wine had been served. Then he raised his glass in a silent toast and said, "I feel strange about this situation, uncertain even. I think I should consult my wife. She is Lili's relative, not I."

"Is Mrs. Russell at home? Could you possibly ask her now?"

He saw his host's brows rise and hurried on. "And would it be possible for me to see Lili while you do? I told her I would call this morning and ask your permission to approach her."

"You move quickly, sir," Russell complained. "And what if Mrs. Russell denies your suit? What then?"

"Then I will at least have had half an hour or so more of Lili's company," came the quick retort.

Alastair Russell set his glass down and rose. "Very well, I shall send her to you. If she knew you were coming I am sure she is probably so addled now, she could make an ascension without the aid of a hot air balloon."

His little pleasantry went unremarked and he sighed to himself as he left the man. Probably to pace the floor, he thought as he sought 'Nelia out in her morning room for a most unusual interview. Love did have a way of stifling a man's wit and humor, more's the pity.

Lili barely waited a minute or two before she ran down the stairs in the wake of the footman who had brought her Alastair's message. As she went into the drawing room she wondered if she was supposed to leave the door open. Since no one had told her not to, she closed it and stood with her back to it, staring down the room to where Halpern was waiting for her. Her heart was thudding in her chest, still she made herself walk toward him. He met her more than halfway, and before she could speak, he had his arms around her and was kissing her just the way she remembered.

"Alastair gave his permission?" she asked when he allowed her to speak. "I am surprised."

"Not yet. He has gone to speak to his wife about it,"

Halpern admitted. "You know her better than I, Lili. Will she agree?"

He sounded anxious and Lili smiled to herself. She was surprised at how much power she had over this proud man; she even found herself humbled by it. "I've no idea," she said. "I imagine she will want to discuss it with me . . ."

"And what will you say?" he demanded. "Will you tell her you agree, or will you ask her to send me about my business?"

Lili stared up at him as she leaned back in the circle of his arms. "And what would you do in such a case?" she teased.

"I would kidnap you. I've no intention of losing you, you see."

There was a hint of menace in his voice and his jaw was set hard. Lili knew he meant every word and she shivered deliciously.

"It does sound exciting," she said. "I think I would like to be kidnapped."

"Shall I put you to the test? I can have you out of here in a moment, you know. Just ring for your maid and have her bring you your hat and a wrap."

She laughed. "How tame! Do you remember Wordsworth's Lochinvar? He did not allow the bride to collect her things before he had her up before him to gallop off with her into the night."

"And therein lies the advantage of being a fictional lover," he said with a smile. "But I trust we will have no need for such dramatics. I intend to woo you conventionally, see you are treated to every courtesy and honor a bride of Braybourne deserves."

"Oh, how I hate that," she said sadly.

"What?"

"I hate it when you get all adult and pompous, as if I were nothing but an ignorant child. I am not a child, sir, and I am not lacking in understanding."

Halpern bit back the retort he longed to make. She was more a child than she liked to think, and as such, was as taken as any young girl would be with the idea of being carried off by an impetuous suitor. He would remember that; humor her. "We must hope Mrs. Russell agrees to allow me to pursue you, for if she does, there will be no need for scandal," was all he said however.

"Would you still want me if I found I could not love you?" she asked, suddenly curious.

"Yes. I would even marry you, in spite of it," he said swiftly. "But I will do my best to convince you. To love me, that is."

The Russells came in then after making what Lili considered an unusual amount of noise before they opened the door. On the other hand, she had to admit it did give her and Halpern a chance to seek chairs somewhat apart. She saw 'Nelia looked doubtful but resigned, and she smiled at her in relief.

"After careful consideration, my wife and I will allow you to continue, my lord," Russell said, his handsome face somewhat grim. "There are some conditions, however."

"And they are?"

"No one must suspect what you are about. In order to ensure that, you will have to woo Lili secretly and you must allow other men to see her, dance with her, converse. Do you agree?"

"Reluctantly, but I do," Halpern said. Then he turned to Cornelia and said, "You may be sure I love Lili very much, ma'am. I promise I will do my best to make her happy."

Cornelia bit her lip. She had been tempted to remind the viscount he had only begun his suit; that it was not at all a sure thing, but she could just imagine the reaction such a statement would have received.

"And if you are successful, my lord," Russell continued, "there will be no wedding until Lili's eighteenth birthday. I believe that is on January twentieth."

Eight months, Halpern thought grimly. I must wait for her for eight months. Perhaps Lili was right. Perhaps it would be wise for me to consider playing Lord Lochinvar.

He took his leave shortly thereafter, and under the Russells'

watchful eyes, only kissed Lili's hand lightly in farewell. The
pressure of the hand holding hers told her how much more he
desired, however, and she blushed as she smiled at him.

Halpern tried not to look too satisfied as he walked to Park
Lane. The first thing he did when he reached it was to write a
fervent love letter and order a huge bouquet of roses to accompany it.

He found it difficult in the days that followed to watch Lili
with other men. That silly Cary Warfield, for example. He had
never considered the young man to have much sense; to have
to see him fawning over Lili was almost more than he could
bear. He was so intent on her himself, he did not notice that
the men who pursued her tended to be those on the fringes of
society, the young and inexperienced, rather than those of the
inner circle which he himself adorned.

Wooed by the elegant Lord Halpern with his gifts of flowers, perfume, books, and candy, Lili basked in her power. She
ceased to notice the snubs she was receiving more and more
regularly as well. The viscount was not allowed to dance with
her more than twice an evening, or remain endlessly by her
side; sometimes he was not in time to secure the supper dance.
But there were moments in the various gardens of the houses
where they all attended evening parties for him to press his
suit with fervent words of love and kisses that left Lili breathless.

One warm evening, after he had taken her down the garden
paths of a mansion on the outskirts of town, he took more lib-
erties than he had attempted before. Lili knew she should stop
him, but she found she could not.

"Marry me, love," he whispered in her ear. One hand
cupped her breast and his warm breath made her shiver. "Say
you will marry me before I go insane with wanting you."

When she made no reply, he put her from him so he could
look in her eyes. "Lili?" he asked, his voice husky. "I won't be
able to go on this way much longer, you know. I am only
human."

"I am only human, too," she managed to say.

She thought he would pull her close again, now she had as much as admitted she wanted him, but he did not.

"Say you will marry me, girl," he ordered. "Say it, for there'll be no more lovemaking until I have your promise."

Lili tipped her head to one side to consider him. He did look intent, almost grim, she thought, wondering if she should continue to tease him. Something told her it would be most unwise. "Of course I will marry you. I have been waiting for you to ask me formally for a week . . ."

She was allowed to say no more, but instead of kissing her and murmuring of his love, Halpern hurried her from the garden in search of the Russells in order to tell them the news and press for an earlier wedding date. He was not successful then nor the next morning when he called at the Square with a lovely sapphire and diamond betrothal ring, but he did win Alastair's permission to announce the engagement in the newspapers. Lili was a little bewildered when he rushed off to do so, and not that pleased to be deserted so quickly. Nor was she happy when he wrote to tell her he was leaving town for a few days in order to apprise his parents of his great good fortune and would call on her immediately he returned. Still, as soon as the announcement was public knowledge, she got caught up accepting compliments and best wishes from some of her acquaintances and unbelieving stares from others. She saw 'Nelia begin to look confused and uneasy and she wished Graeme would hurry back to town. Something was wrong. She did not know what it could be, but she needed him to set things right.

Chapter Fifteen

It was a beautiful spring day when Halpern cantered up the long drive of Braybourne Hall in Hampshire. He was so intent he did not notice the soft air or the explosion of pink and white blossoms in the orchards he passed. He did not even remark the occasional hint of brine from the sea a few miles away, or the sharper smell of manure spread on the newly plowed fields. All his concentration was on his errand and his desire to return to Lili as soon as he possibly could.

At least she will not have that fool Warfield dancing attendance, not after the announcement is made tomorrow, he told himself as he clattered into the cobblestoned stable yard and called for a groom. As he removed his saddlebags, he reminded himself he must have a bath before he saw his parents. Walking up to the Hall he felt a tinge of uneasiness in spite of what he had told Russell. He did not need his father's permission to marry. Still, it would have been more courteous to discuss Lili with the man before he had her promise. He had not dared. She was like the moon, he thought, not only capricious but sometimes ellusive, hiding itself behind the clouds. For just when he had thought she was his at last, her delight in dancing with another or joining a group of young people in gay conversation, was only too obvious. Still, in spite of the fact she had almost driven him mad with her antics, he did not think she had done it on purpose. Lili would not tease. It was one of the things he loved about her, her directness.

He was not sorry that his parents were here at Braybourne. True, he had expected their arrival in Park Lane for some time, but when his mother had written his father did not care to spend the spring in town, he had accepted it, for it had happened once or twice in the past.

An hour later, he sought his father in the library and found him dozing in a deep chair near a window. Why, he looks so old, he thought, startled by the sparse white hair, the face so wrinkled even in repose, the thin white hands clasped over an ample stomach. He reminded himself the man was almost sixty-seven, an age heavy with years. As he took a seat opposite, prepared to wait for his father to awaken, the marquis opened his eyes and smiled.

"I dreamt of you last night, Graeme," he said as easily as if they had been speaking only moments before. "I should have taken that for the omen it was."

"I hope it was a pleasant dream, sir," Halpern said, rising to take his father's hand and kiss it in obeisance.

"I cannot remember a jot of it," Braybourne admitted. "My memory serves me ill these days. Some things that happened as recently as a week ago are gone, and in their place comes some silly thing from the distant past. Would you believe this morning I suddenly recalled how my sister Bess hated brussels sprouts and the stratagems she employed to avoid eating them?" He sighed. "Bess has been dead for twenty years. Died in childbirth, she did. Ha! Being a duchess did her little good. I never liked Kilstone. Bess was wasted on him, duke or not."

"Was that why you allowed Anne to choose her own husband?" Halpern asked idly.

"Indeed. Of course I made sure he was a man I could approve."

"How did you manage that, sir?"

His father's faded blue eyes twinkled. "There are ways to make sure the only men your daughter meets would make a suitable connection. Anne was ripe to fall in love; your mother and I placed Greyfound in her way.

"What are you doing at Braybourne, my son, in the middle of what I am sure people are saying is a brilliant Season? Don't they always?"

Startled for a moment by the sudden change of subject, Halpern hesitated to gather his thoughts. At last he said, "I have come to tell you you may stop fretting over me, sir. I am to marry next January and I wished you to be the first to know."

"That is excellent news indeed. Not that I have fretted over you exactly, Graeme. Not for the last few years, at least. Who is the fortunate girl? Do I know her, her family?"

"You have met her, sir," Halpern said, never taking his eyes from his father's face. "She is the young lady who fell in the stream here. Do you recall Lili Martingale?"

He watched his father's face darken into a frown and steeled himself.

"Martingale. Do we know any Martingales, Graeme?"

"No, sir. Lili is an orphan. Her mother was an Edson, a most respectable name. Martingale was an artist; they lived abroad. When Thora Martingale died in childbirth, her husband gave Lili to the nuns at Blamont to raise."

"That is all you know of the family?"

Halpern nodded

"I see. Does this Lili cling to Catholicism?"

"I don't believe so, sir. She asked to be removed from the convent. She has been living with friends of Alastair Russell's on an estate near Oxford. Mrs. Russell is a second cousin of hers, or something like that. I'm sure you recall she is the daughter of Sir Reginald Wakefield of Berks."

The marquis raised a tired hand. "Enough distant geneology. The girl is not suitable to be your marchioness. But since you have asked her and she, not at all surprisingly, has accepted, the marriage is as good as accomplished. I told you she would have you, Graeme. However, I did hope that at your age you would not be taken in by a little girl, or fall for her oh-so-innocent wiles . . ."

"Lili employs no wiles, sir. I had the devil of a time convincing her to marry me," Halpern said, striving to keep the anger he felt hidden.

"Clever as well, I see," his father murmured. "Pour me a glass of port. I need it.

"Your mother will be distraught, of course. She had so set her heart on an exalted match for you. Oh, it would be most unwise to mention the girl's father was an artist. Artists are not suitable people for the Wilders to know. Your mother only became one after her marriage. She was very strictly raised; that will come as no surprise if you recall your grandmother.

"Thank you," he said as he took the glass of port he was handed and swallowed it. "Is this man Martingale dead, by the way? It would be helpful if he were."

"He may be. No one seems to know where he is. He left the area right after Lili was born and has not been heard from for years."

"Pity, that. You will always have the danger of him popping up someday, demanding money or recognition or a part in your lives you would rather not have him play. It is obvious he has not become famous; not since he is unknown. Although your mother will probably find that more acceptable, come to think of it."

He fell silent then and turned away to stare out the window at the sloping green lawns of the Hall, the ornamental water at their foot, and the deep woods beyond. Halpern admired the view as well. Braybourne was a noble place, and beautiful, he thought.

He was recalled to his father when he heard him sigh, and turned to see him wiping his eyes. He was shocked. He had never known his father to cry. He found it hard to believe he was seeing him do so now.

"Well, there's nothing to be done," the marquis said weakly. "Best you let me relay the news to your mother. She is out somewhere, sketching views of Braybourne. We'll not have her company or her attention until the light fails.

"Leave me now, Graeme. I would prefer to be alone."

His son rose and bowed. His throat was tight with emotions he could not voice. He was aware he had disappointed his father and he was sorry for that. But nothing was going to keep him from marrying Lili, not even his father's tears or his mother's expected disappointment. He would have insisted on it even if Lili had not agreed to marry him as yet. Because he did not want to live his life without her. Because he needed her the way he needed air or food and water to survive. How quickly this has all happened, he thought. How much I have changed. I never knew love would strike like this.

Halpern remained at Braybourne Hall for three very long days. He hoped that by doing so he might bring his parents to a more agreeable state of mind where his future wife was concerned. But while he thought he might be succeeding with his father, his mother was another story. She had been appalled by his announcement, and no matter what he said, she only grew more bitter. Of course she did not make any accusations or even mention the duty he owed his ancestors and his name. Neither did she retreat into disapproving silence. Such methods were not worthy of the Marchioness of Braybourne. But her cool conversation on every subject but her son's betrothal, her carefully composed face, were reproaches in themselves.

Early on the last morning, his father came out to wait with him on the front steps for his horse to be brought from the stables. It was a raw day, more like March than early May. Halpern saw his father was shivering in the fresh breeze blowing straight from the Channel, and suggested he seek refuge inside.

"No, not yet. I've something to say to you, Graeme."

The viscount schooled his expression into what he hoped showed filial interest and no more.

"I wanted to tell you that although I cannot like this unsuitable match of yours, I believe in the long run it will be better for you to marry a woman you love."

Halpern turned to him, amazed.

"I know. I know," the marquis went on. "A completely foreign thought for me, and one your mother would say was ridiculous. But I myself married for the title and estate, and just see where it has brought us."

"You—you did not love my mother, sir?" Halpern dared to ask.

"No, nor she, me. It was an arranged marriage to which we both agreed, bound and determined to 'do our duty.' Now that's a sorry thing to take to the marriage bed with you, is it not?"

"I don't know what to say. I always thought you were, well, at least content."

"Content? Perhaps. Happy? No. And to compensate for her lack of happiness, your mother began to study painting professionally. Art made her happy as I could not. And I? I went from one mistress to another, always searching for something I discovered I could not have and probably did not deserve anyway.

"I think this is the reason your mother is so inconsolable. For after giving her life to Braybourne, she has to resent you and this marriage you are so intent on. To her, you are all but crying out to the world that her sacrifice was only a petty thing not worthy of her devotion. I believe you can understand why such a thing would not sit well with her."

He looked at his son then and seemed to see something very like awe on his face, for he shook his head and added, "I have surprised you with my understanding of the situation, eh? How sad it is it takes us human beings so many years to finally come to wisdom.

"Enough. Let us hope when the Russells return to Wyckend in a month or so, we will have a chance to get to know Miss Martingale better and come to approve her."

Halpern did not think he sounded at all optimistic, but he replied, "I hope so, sir. She is such a wonderful girl, she—"

"Spare me your paeans of praise, Graeme," his father said, grasping his shoulder for a moment before he turned away. "I shall go in now. The wind is cold. Safe journey to you."

Halpern pondered the things his father had said as he cantered along, but the closer he drew to London, the less he found his thoughts on Braybourne and his surprising parents. Lili, he thought as the first signs of London began to appear.

He would be with her soon. He could hardly wait. He felt as eager as he might have when he was only eighteen and he laughed at his foolishness.

He was disappointed later when he called in Grosvenor Square to discover Lili and the Russells had gone out driving. Accordingly he went to Hyde Park in search of them, but they were not there.

He had no way of knowing the three had not gone out for a drive at all. The rumors that had been circulating about Lili and Cornelia had become common knowledge. That afternoon Lili had returned home in tears. When taxed for the reason, she had confessed a confrontation with the Rowleys had upset her.

"We will not be receiving visitors this afternoon, Marks," Alastair had told the butler as he ushered his ladies into the drawing room. "If Viscount Halpern should return to town and call, tell him we have gone out driving.

"Now then Lili, tell me exactly what these Rowleys had the temerity to say to you."

"I was just returning from shopping when I saw the two girls in the park in the center of the Square," Lili said, her face still pale from her tears. "Their brother Arthur was with them.

"I sent the maid on ahead and waited for them to come around to the gate. I could not enter. Miss Rowley had locked it behind her and I did not have our key."

Alastair snorted. "Typical," he said in disgust. "Yes, they are the type who would set great store on having the park kept private, and would do their best to keep out the hordes of commoners who clamor to gain admittance. Provincial nodcocks!"

His voice was rich with sarcasm but neither his wife nor Lili was amused.

"Go on," he said, waving his hand.

"I should have guessed Miss Rowley had no intention of speaking to me," Lili confessed. "She has ignored me in the past, and when they came around the last curve and I waved, she looked the other way. But I was not clever enough, and as they drew abreast, I asked them to open the gate so I might join them."

She paused then to stare down at her clasped hands. Her face was set and she was biting her lower lip. Cornelia would have spoken, but a signal from her husband kept her silent.

"Mr. Rowley spoke to his sisters then, saying what a shame it was that the Square had become the home of people without a decent background and no morals. He added he was astounded a future marquis would even consider such a person as a suitable wife. I—I lost my temper at that, I am afraid."

"Lashed out at him did you? Good for you!" Alastair encouraged her. "What did you say to the insufferable prig?"

"I told him I had no idea what he was talking about but that I found him rude beyond belief. His sister spoke up to defend him, for Mr. Rowley had gone very red and was coughing uncontrollably.

"She said it was well known all over town that I was nothing but a love-child of yours, 'Nelia, and she was horrified that such as I had had the gall to approach decent young women.

"I did not wait to hear any more, I'm afraid. Instead I turned my back on them and ran home."

"And I found her sobbing in her room moments later," Cornelia managed to say. Lili looked at her gratefully, but she could not help wondering why 'Nelia seemed so upset. Surely she would not be so affected if what she had just been told was only a baseless rumor. Could it be true then? she wondered. Could 'Nelia be her *mother*?

"Of course there is not a grain of truth to any of it," Alastair said sternly. "And we all know who started the rumor, do we not? Who has been busy spreading it throughout the *ton*?"

"The dowager," Cornelia said sadly.

"The very same. This is too much. Sarah must be punished."

"Will you banish her to the dower house, my dear?"

"No. That is nowhere near a severe enough punishment. And when you think that her own son was . . ."

"Alastair!"

"I beg your pardon, 'Nelia. I am angry. I did not think. No, I shall give her the house on Upper Brook, but that is all she shall have from us. With the competence her husband left her, she will not want, but she will not live at Wyckend ever again."

"It seems so harsh," Cornelia murmured, still looking troubled. "You know how she loves the place."

"And now she has forfeited it by her arrogance. She should have believed me when I threatened her. No more. I shall call on her tomorrow.

"Has there been any other unpleasantness, Lili?" he asked, turning to her again.

She hesitated, but now she thought of it, all the whispers and snubs, all those horrid looks made sense if the dowager had been parading her pet theory around the *ton,* aided by her bosom bow, Mrs. Parmeter. "Yes, there has been," she admitted and told them everything.

"You should have come to me, dear," Cornelia scolded. "You should not have had to bear this alone."

"Especially when not a word of it is true," Alastair added. "You are the perfectly legitimate daughter of good English folk, with nobility on your mother's side that makes you as eligible as anyone to grace the *ton.* Well, we shall see. Our ball takes place next Friday. By then I will see this fairy tale has been scotched once and for all. Until that time, you will hold your head high and treat any detractors to the famous Russell 'look.' You do remember it, do you not, Lili?"

Lili felt better, now that she was not bearing everything alone, but still she had trouble looking as arrogant and disbelieving as Alastair expected.

That evening, the three of them found Halpern waiting for them when they left their carriage at the first party they were pledged to attend. He knew how eagerly they were being watched, and he bowed deeply and gave Lili his most adoring smile, holding her hand tightly as he did so.

"Excellent," Russell remarked. Lili had thought both he and

his wife still looked grim, and she wondered at it. "I trust you found your parents in good health, sir?"

"As you say. Cornelia, how charming you look this evening. Shall we try and find a quiet nook and hope we may all be able to converse?"

"There's not a chance of it," Russell told him as they inched their way past the servants who had taken their wraps, and began the long tedious wait to climb the stairs to be announced. "Come and call tomorrow—not too early, mind. Or better yet, plan to meet Lili and 'Nelia in the park for a morning ride.

"Beckworth, dear fellow, do take my advice and allow your valet to tie your cravat from now on," he said to the gentleman standing directly behind them.

"But it is your own design, sir," Mr. Beckworth sputtered. " 'Pon my honor, your very own."

"Then I *dis*own it," Russell told him.

As they continued to converse, Lili forgot them, She was trying to look her fill of Halpern without appearing obvious.

"Is my cravat also unsightly?" he asked her quietly. When she shook her head, he grinned at her as if he knew only too well why she was staring. "Do you think we will be able to wait till tomorrow?" he went on. "Or shall I see about finding that private nook just for the two of us?"

"Do so, if you please, sir," she said, waving her fan gently to and fro before her face. At the look in his eyes, she increased its pace, saying, "How warm it has grown this evening. Don't you find it so, my lord?"

"Not as warm as it will be," he told her and chuckled at the blush that rose in her cheeks.

He turned to speak to Cornelia then and Lili knew he had not heard any of the gossip. She wondered how long it would be before he did, and how he would react when that happened. Would he beg her to cry off? Or would he believe the Russells that it was not true? Would he be as angry as Alastair had been, or would he wonder if there might not be a grain of salt to the story, and begin to feel trapped?

Chapter Sixteen

Halpern had not heard anything of the gossip. His close friends, mostly unmarried gentlemen his own age, had not been made privy to the rumors. Others, who had heard it, did not dare tell him. The viscount was known not only for a noteworthy temper, but for his expertise with his fists, a pistol, and the foil. And of course, it was not until his betrothal to Miss Martingale had been announced that the gossip had flourished, at a time when he was away from town in Hampshire.

But the next day, as he was eating breakfast before collecting Lili for their ride in the park, he was visited by his cronies, Percy Ridgeway and Cecil Kenyon, Lord Gore.

"My word, chaps, what can be the matter?" he asked as his butler admitted them. "This is hardly the hour to be making calls. Has there been some dire national disaster? Never mind. Sit down and let me pour you some coffee. Unless you prefer home-brewed?"

Both men took a seat on either side of him where he sat at the head of the table. Halpern looked from one to the other before he carefully lowered the silver coffeepot. "Out with it," he ordered. "And no hemming and hawing either."

Percy Ridgeway cleared his throat. The more articulate of the two, he had been chosen to deliver the bad news. "We had to come," he said. "We are your friends. Your good friends, Graeme."

"Yes, you are. And you were saying . . . ?"

"There is something you should know. Something everyone else knows and is talking about."

"And that is?"

"We do not believe it, do we, Gore? But it seems so dastardly, and so serious—well, we thought you should hear about it as soon as possible."

"Which I am having the devil of a time doing. Can you not stop explaining and just *tell* me?"

Mr. Ridgeway took a deep breath and said, all in a rush, "There is a rumor going around that your fiancée is the illegitimate daughter of Cornelia Russell."

There was nothing but silence in the room for a moment.

"What did you just say?" Halpern asked in a deceptively quiet voice.

"Now you just control yourself, man," Lord Gore spoke up. "Know it's damnable, but people are talkin'. Percy didn't make it up. It's not his fault. Beg you to stop lookin' so murderous at him."

Halpern nodded, but he still looked grim and Mr. Ridgeway kept his hands on the edge of the table just in case he had to push his chair away to beat a hasty retreat.

"The reason everyone believes it, is because there is such a strong resemblance between the two," Ridgeway continued. "You must admit that it is so, Graeme. That black curly hair and the way it grows from such a distinctive peak at the forehead. Their blue eyes, even the shape of their faces."

"A family likeness, no more," Halpern protested.

"Of course," Ridgeway was quick to say. "But you know how people will talk, old son. And the worst of it is, Cornelia Russell's own mother-in-law claims the relationship is real."

"What?" Halpern demanded.

His friends nodded solemnly. "She's the one who started the rumor. M'mother says that proves it, for it hardly puts the late earl in a good light. And it's common knowledge the dowager doted on her son."

"Wait a moment," Halpern said, raising his hand. "Mrs. Russell is only thirty, and Lili, seventeen. How would it be possible for her to have a baby at thirteen? She is Sir Reginald Wakefield's daughter, too."

"Well, there is that," Ridgeway said carefully. "Of course she could have lied about her age when she came to town, taken off two or three years. Wouldn't be the first time a woman did that."

"That is true," Gore chimed in. "Besides, my uncle was telling me just the other day of a case on his land where a girl of twelve delivered a healthy baby boy just last month."

"Cornelia Russell is not a farmer's daughter. She would have been carefully watched," Halpern said. "And unless it was rape, it cannot be true. She is too fine a person. I simply cannot believe any of this is true."

"Unfortunately there is more," Ridgeway said in a gloomy voice.

"Yes, and that is?"

"Well, we may not remember—don't know why we should—but the old ladies certainly do. Cornelia Wakefield never had a Season. She was kept in the country, almost as if she were in disgrace. And there's bad blood between her and her brother and her father. Don't know what that is. Just know it's there."

"She could have been in mourning," Lord Gore said, trying to be helpful to his friend in his distress, not that he believed any such thing.

"Tell me, if what you are saying is true, how did Lili end up in a convent in France?" Halpern asked, his voice deceptively mild now. "Surely it would have been dangerous, not to say unnecessary, to send an infant to a country with which we were at war."

"Who is to say she was ever even there? Besides the Russells, I mean," Ridgeway said. "Why, she could have been tucked away somewhere in England with no one the wiser. And we only have the Russells' word for it that they went to France to get her before going on to the Congress in Vienna. Might not have happened that way at all. They might have fetched her here in England and quietly taken her abroad, pretending she had been in France all this time."

"Why would they do that?" Gore asked. He was not noted for his needle wits.

"To make the story of this Martingale more believable, of course," Ridgeway said as patiently as he could.

Halpern shoved his chair back and rose. Just as quickly, his friends joined him on their feet.

"We had to tell you, Graeme, old son," Ridgeway said, careful to keep a heavy chair between him and the viscount. "We couldn't just let you go on not knowing what was being said after all."

"Didn't want to. Damnable thing to have to tell a friend," Gore chimed in.

"I appreciate your candor," Halpern told them, his taut face belying his words. "You must excuse me now. I am pledged to ride with Lili this morning."

"You are? Sure that's a good thing? Why . . ."

"Of course," Ridgeway said, interrupting the tactless Gore. "We must be on our way as well. You may be sure we will say nothing about this, Graeme. Trust us to be discreet."

The viscount thanked them as he ushered them from the room.

Behind them, in the house next door, Alva Potter lowered her spyglass reluctantly. Something was amiss over there, or she was not Alfred Potter's widow, she told herself as she poured another cup of tea. That Viscount Halpern had looked ready to do murder, and the other men had been frightened of him. She wished, not for the first time, she had mastered the art of reading people's lips. She did so long to know what it was all about, especially now that she had read in the paper of Lili Martingale's betrothal to Halpern.

Perhaps she should plan a visit to Grosvenor Square in the near future instead of waiting for Cornelia Russell to come to her again, she thought.

It only took one glance at Halpern's face when he arrived at Russell House for Lili to know that sometime between the time they had parted last night and this morning, he had heard the gossip. She was sorry for that. She had meant to tell him last evening as soon as they were alone, but lost listening to his murmured words of love and the kiss they shared, she had forgotten to do so. No, not forgotten, she admitted as he had a lively discussion with the groom about the necessity of Flynn's riding with them. It was a short discussion, for Flynn had taken the viscount's measure, too, and was more than happy to be dismissed.

Lili and Halpern walked their horses from the Square. They did not speak. Lili swallowed hard, determined she would not cry, no matter what came of this morning's meeting. Once on Park Lane, Halpern suggested they go out of town instead of riding in the park. Lili could only nod. She had not been able to read anything into his carefully modulated voice; she knew she would have to wait and see how desperate he was to escape this betrothal that bound him to marriage with a girl with a questionable past.

When they reached the open countryside at last, Halpern led her down a narrow lane to a meadow bordering the Thames. She watched him tie his horse to a branch before he came to lift her down.

"You have heard what people are saying, haven't you?" she asked, unable to put off the discussion another moment.

"Ridgeway and Gore came to tell me this morning. They did not want me to hear it first from other, more unsympathetic, persons," he said. Lili listened carefully but she could tell nothing from his voice, not if he was angry or just annoyed, or even disgusted.

"Why didn't you tell me about this?" he asked next. Lili had noticed how quickly he released her as soon as her feet touched the ground, and her heart sank.

"Did you know before I left London for Braybourne?" he demanded. "Well, never mind that. It doesn't matter. What matters is you knew last night, didn't you? Yet you said nothing to me—nothing."

"I was so glad to see you," she told him, her eyes never leaving his face. "I did not want anything to intrude, especially something as ugly as those rumors."

"How did they start?" he asked.

"The dowager countess maintains I am illegitimate. She has done so from the moment I arrived at Wyckend. And although she has been told over and over it is not so, she continues to believe it."

"I find that hard to accept. Surely it puts her own son in a bad light, hoodwinked into marrying a woman who had borne another man's child."

"Alastair says the dowager is so old she does not realize that. Perhaps she even thinks people will sympathize with him—and with her. Oh, I have never understood her. I do know she hates me."

"Well, she has made mice feet of your reputation, to say nothing of Cornelia Russell's," Halpern observed grimly. "I imagine Russell will have something to say about that."

"He is seeing her today to tell her she will never be welcome at Wyckend again. He has warned her before. She did not heed him. She is to have the house on Upper Brook Street. She has wealth. She will not want."

Halpern tipped up her chin with one hand and leaned closer so he could stare deep into her eyes. "Is it true, Lili?" he asked. "Tell me."

She hesitated, her face troubled. "Both Alastair and 'Nelia assure me it is not," she said at last. "They insist I am the daughter of Thomas Martingale and his wife Thora."

"Why do you frown? Don't you believe them?"

"You will never know how much I want to! But—but I have to wonder why 'Nelia is acting as she does. If it were I, I would be protesting my innocence to the world, but she just goes about with an absentminded air and keeps her own counsel.

"Then, too, I have to consider the Martingales. My 'mother' certainly died conveniently, did she not? And where is my father? Why did he put a newborn into a convent? Why didn't he see I was returned to England, especially since we were at war with France? And where is he? Why has no one heard from him all these years? And why has 'Nelia been so good to me? Surely what she has done, and continues to do, is unusual for a distant relative."

Lili drew a deep breath then, determined to be as honest as she could. "And I must admit, as must you, it could have happened. 'Nelia never will discuss her family with the exception of her sister, Phillipa. Why does she dislike her father and brother so? What happened to estrange them?"

"Yes, it could have happened," he mused, taking her arm and walking her toward the Thames. They did not speak, not even when they paused to watch a barge passing. Suddenly Halpern's expression brightened. "But it did not happen, and I know why," he said. He sounded so alive and excited, Lili held her breath, waiting for him to explain.

"There is no way Cornelia Russell would jeopardize her reputation and her marriage by introducing a bastard child into her household," he said. "Do not prate to me of motherly love. If she is your mother, that quality has been decidedly absent for sixteen long years. Yes, yes, I know she came to get you when you were thirteen, but did she keep you beside her? She did not. She left you with friends of her husband, deep in the country. If she had been your mother, would she have done that? And knowing how closely you resemble her, would she have brought you to town and sponsored you for a Season? She has lived in London a great deal. She knows society and its love of vicious gossip. She would know moreover comparisons were sure to be made, and theories proposed that would bring censure even without the dowager's assistance. No. I believe she brought you here in all innocence because you are truly only a distant relative."

"Do you really think so?" Lili dared to ask. "Really?"

He smiled at her. His face was still set but he did seem more at ease, and for a moment Lili allowed herself to believe that everything would be all right, that the gossip would end, and they would be married as they had planned.

"Yes, I believe it," he said, but he did not put his arm around her or make any move to kiss her. She wondered why.

"What is wrong then?" she asked. "Why are you still so grim?"

"I suppose it is because it bothers me you did not entrust me with the secret earlier. You must not keep things from me, Lili. And not just the important things, either. Can you imagine what a difficult situation it puts me in when I cannot help you because I do not know anything is amiss? You must tell me what is troubling you from now on. Will you promise to do so?"

She nodded, her eyes brimming with tears. Still, when they were riding back to town after a morning spent on the bank of the river, she could not still a tiny nagging doubt that plagued her. 'Nelia's handsome face topped with hair identical to her own came to mind. The same dark blue eyes. Even the same chin and nose—that damning, distinctive peak at their foreheads.

And she found it hard to believe a distant second cousin would have been as kind to her as 'Nelia had, showering her with gifts and clothes and affection, and seeing to it she had a London Season that other girls could only dream about.

Riding beside her, Halpern was left with his own doubts. Every time he remembered his parents at Braybourne, he shuddered just picturing their distress if the gossip should reach them. He could almost hear his father offering whatever amount of money it took to get Miss Martingale to cry off; hear him announcing that even the stigma of a broken engagement was preferable to marriage to a bastard. And wasn't it bad enough Miss Martingale was a nobody? his mother would ask. Would he let his children suffer as well as his parents? Was he willing to throw away their lives and his proud name because of love? Had he no pride?

He could almost hear her scorn, and he had to admit these were valid points he would do well to consider. The only way they could be resolved would be to prove Lili was not Cornelia Russell's daughter, and he had no idea how he might do that.

When they reached Grosvenor Square again, Halpern in-

sisted on coming in to have a word with the Russells. He was
not a military man but he knew a good offense far outweighed
a good defense. Plans would have to be made and coordinated,
and the sooner the better.

He found the Russells outside in the garden. For a moment,
he paused at the drawing room doors to watch them. Alastair
Russell had his arm around his wife, his blond head bent over
hers as he talked earnestly to her. Halpern was most interested
in Mrs. Russell's expression while she was off guard. To his
dismay, she looked distraught, more so than she should have
even contending with this ugly piece of gossip.

He must have moved, for Russell looked up then and saw
him. He nodded, his own handsome face grim. "Returned
from your ride, have you?" he inquired as they came forward.

Halpern met them halfway. The garden would be an ideal
place for any confidences. There was little chance they might
be overheard by the servants, he thought.

"Where is Lili?" Cornelia Russell inquired.

"I sent her up to change," Halpern said, falling in step with
them. "I wanted to see you alone. We must make plans, the
three of us, decide how to handle this damnable situation."

"You are not thinking of crying off, m'lord? You have not
suggested Lili do so?" Russell asked, not hesitating to throw
down the gauntlet.

The viscount stared at him. "No, I have not. Is there any
reason I should?" he asked, his own voice as challenging.

"Of course there is not," Cornelia Russell interrupted. "Oh,
do not brangle, if you please. Surely things are bad enough
without that, and I cannot bear it."

"You may be easy, my dear," her husband said. Then, indicating some chairs set on the small lawn, he added, "So, we
shall confer, m'lord. Perhaps you have some ideas about what
we should do?"

Halpern waited until they were all seated before he spoke.
"I think there is only one thing we can do and that is to act as
if this gossip is such a ridiculous falsehood we will not even
lower ourselves to dispute it. And we must not hide. If any-

thing, we must go to each and every entertainment we have invitations for, and with high spirits. I do hope you did not intend to cancel your ball, sir?"

"On no account. It never crossed my mind. I intend to fight this thing and I am happy you have a mind to do so as well, m'lord."

"Whatever will your parents think?" Cornelia asked, speaking up again. Halpern noticed there were dark circles under her eyes and she was paler than usual. He saw she was twisting a damp handkerchief between her hands. As he watched, her husband took it from her. She looked at him steadily for a moment. Then she took a deep breath and sat up straighter.

"They would be distressed, of course," Halpern told her. "I pray they will never learn of it, for they remain in Hampshire this spring."

"I shall pray for that as well," Cornelia told him. "I know Lili is not the wife they would have chosen for you, but she is a dear, good girl. And I do assure you, on my honor, sir, she is not my daughter. I have never had a child but Lili has become as dear to me as if she were my own."

The viscount smiled at her. It was the first sincere smile he had managed all morning. "I am sure that is so, ma'am. Lili is so easy to love, is she not?"

"Well, this is all very charming and April and May, but shall we return to the matter at hand?" Russell asked, sounding testy. "What are your plans for the next several days, sir? What parties do you attend?"

For half an hour the three sat with their heads together. When Lili joined them, washed and dressed in a pretty muslin, she discovered she would have little time to brood. Beginning with a stroll in Hyde Park that afternoon, the four of them would be constantly in each other's company. Alastair had suggested this, for he claimed if Cornelia and Lili were not seen together as was their wont, people would take it as an admission of guilt, done solely to prevent comparison.

Both Halpern and Alastair Russell managed to keep the cartoons that suddenly appeared in the print shops from reaching

Cornelia's and Lili's attention. The viscount would have liked to buy them up, but only a moment's reflection convinced him that would be useless. They would only print more.

He was a little surprised they were not snubbed, not even by the highest sticklers. But then he realized Beau Russell's reputation, to say nothing of the exalted name of Braybourne kept them safe from outright, public condemnation. There was also people's curiosity, their desire to see the culprits for themselves and judge accordingly, perhaps even catch one of them looking conscious or uttering a falsehood. The dowager had not been slow to reveal the punishment she had been given for her part in the debacle, nor was a smiling Mrs. Parmeter, busy moving households to be her friend's constant support, reticent. This had the opposite affect on the *ton,* however, and several of the more intelligent, thoughtful members remained sceptical of the old women's accounts. They took a wait and see attitude and remained friendly. You may be sure both Halpern and Beau Russell made a note of their names and counted them as friends.

All this was hardest on Cornelia Russell. The two men bluffed it out easily, their demeanor daring anyone to even question them about such a ridiculous rumor. And they all shielded Lili, so she was never alone with anyone who might shatter her precarious calm. But Cornelia bore the brunt of it. She heard the whispers, saw the intent, wondering looks, and heard the titters that were barely concealed.

When Alva Potter came to call late one morning and bullied her way past the butler, she found Cornelia in her sitting room, crying. The old lady was quick to put her arms around her and hug her, and she soon had the whole story.

"Well, that is a horrid thing to say about anyone," she said as Cornelia concluded. "I won't remind you how I told you in Vienna no good would come of your taking care of the gel; why, I even thought she was your child myself.

"Now, now, don't ruffle up! You do look so very much alike you can't blame people for thinking it, human nature being what it is. And as for the slights you are receiving, dear Cornelia, and the cuts women are giving you, that is only to be expected. There is no one quicker to spread gossip than a man, as we can both attest, but for just plain nastiness, women take the palm and always will."

In the hall, Lili was dismissing her maid and the footman who had accompanied her out that afternoon. As she did so, she saw the late post had arrived and been placed on the customary side table, and she went and examined it idly. She was surprised to see there was a letter for her, its cover addressed in an unknown hand, and for some reason she shivered. She realized she had been waiting for this letter ever since her betrothal had become common knowledge and as she went to her room she wished she did not have to open it and read it, for she was sure it was going to be unpleasant. Halfway up the flight, she had to pause and cling to the bannister, she was trembling so.

Chapter Seventeen

Lili Martingale disappeared the morning after the much-anticipated Russell Ball.

That had been a glittering affair and very few people had sent their regrets. The house itself had been decorated *en fête* under the careful supervision of Alastair Russell himself, its rooms cleaned and polished and filled with floral arrangements. Besides an orchestra playing for dancing in the ballroom, a string trio entertained in the drawing room a flight below, and a wandering troubadour with a guitar beguiled those who sought relief from the warm evening on the terrace and in the garden. The troubadour was soon the center of attention. Alastair had chosen him for his ability to make up songs about the guests, and he purposely told him not to forget he himself, his wife, or Lili either. Soon everyone who heard the songs was laughing and telling their friends, and many more people changed their minds about the Dowager Countess of Wyckend's accusations.

"For, my dear, Mr. Russell would not call attention to the unfortunate business if it had a grain of truth to it," Lady Croth said to her long-suffering husband. "I shall disregard any more rumors I hear; I suggest you do so as well. As you know, my love, I never liked the dowager, no, not at all."

Tall footmen, many hired for the occasion and dressed in full livery, carried trays of champagne and other drinks among the crowd. They were followed by an innovation in entertaining, more footmen bearing trays of various treats; delicate sweets, soft confections and tiny scones, as well as pastries filled with almond cream or jellies.

The guests were entranced and even those who came merely to see and condemn found themselves caught up in the good spirits and camaraderie. Both Cornelia and Lili looked very fine. Cornelia wore a gown of deep blue gossamer satin with matching sapphire and diamond jewelry. Lili, who at Halpern's wish was wearing her hair loose this evening, held it back with a narrow comb of pearls. She wore a spectacular set of pearls and diamonds at her throat and on her wrists, a gift, Cornelia was quick to point out, from the viscount. Lili's pure white gown was simple, as befit a girl her age, but it showed her excellent figure to advantage. One elderly gentleman was heard to announce he didn't care a fig whose daughter she was, she was a fine-looking young lady and he would have been happy to welcome her into his family, if only one of his scatter-brained sons had had the good sense to try and win her hand.

The evening had not only a lavish supper but a breakfast much later for those who were reluctant to see the entertainment end.

Throughout the evening, Halpern had remained beside Lili. Although there was no direct reference to it, it was assumed the occasion marked not only Lili's proper come-out, but her engagement to the viscount as well. Many guests spoke of how happy they were, and how well-suited. The difference in their ages was no longer remarked. Even Cornelia sighed when she observed them waltzing, Halpern's head bent close to Lili's, his eyes admiring, and the way she blushed at his murmured words.

At last it was over. When the last guest left, extending his compliments one more time, Russell sent the servants to bed, and dismissed the musicians. Time enough tomorrow to set the house to rights, he said as he put his arm around his wife and helped her up to bed. Halpern took Lili to the library for a private farewell.

"It went well, don't you think, love?" he asked when he could bear to stop kissing her. "I wouldn't be a bit surprised to discover the gossip has been thoroughly vanquished after tonight. Many people went out of their way to assure me they had never believed a word of it. Huh! Well, never mind how we get out of the fix, as long as we do. Perhaps you should always wear your hair down, and Cornelia wear hers, up. It does make you look less alike. What do you think?"

He did not give her time to answer. Instead, he said, "Do you know what I wish? I wish this had been our ball, in our own home, and right now I was carrying you up the stairs to bed. Mmmm, now that's a thought to take to my own lonely bed tonight."

Lili sighed. Later Halpern would recall he had not been able to see her face, for her head was resting on his shoulder. The only thing he could remember was her warm breath on his skin, and how it had made him feel.

He let her go at last, to the relief of the butler, who had been sitting up so he could usher Halpern out and lock the door behind him. In a very short time, Russell House was quiet.

Later that morning, no one thought to look for Lili. It was assumed she was sleeping late after the festivities. Cornelia herself did not wake until after ten.

The maid who crept into Lili's room to make up the fire had noticed nothing amiss, although when pressed, she could not say for sure Miss Martingale had been there—her one quick, envious glance at the bed had shown her only bunched up covers and the top of a lace nightcap. Early in the afternoon when Cornelia sent her maid to see why Lili was sleeping so late, it was discovered the pillows had been arranged to make it appear someone was sleeping there, the nightcap stuffed with a rolled up petticoat.

Cornelia dismissed her maid and sent a footman flying to Brooks Club, where her husband had repaired to accept congratulations on a brilliant affair, and more importantly, absent himself from a house being restored to order.

The footman had to avoid some workmen removing large urns of flowers and greenery, and dodge others on the steps, who had come for the hundred gilt chairs that had been hired for the occasion. In the park in the middle of the Square,

Arthur Rowley and his sisters looked on with disapproving eyes although they did not miss a thing. Needless to say, they had not been honored with an invitation to the ball.

By three that afternoon, the Russells and Viscount Halpern were closeted in the library, the door shut firmly and instructions given they were not to be disturbed for any reason.

"But where is she? Where can she have got to?" Alastair growled, for both he and his wife had thought Lili might have eloped with the viscount. Halpern's prompt arrival in response to their summons had scotched that hope.

No one answered. The silence in the room seemed a living presence.

"She left no message? I cannot believe Lili would just go off without a word," Halpern said finally.

Cornelia handed him the note she had found tucked under Lili's pillow only moments before his arrival. As he read it, Halpern looked so bewildered Cornelia had to look away. She knew the note by heart. It began by saying Lili was leaving because it would be the best for everyone if she did. She thanked the Russells for their love and all their many kindnesses, and she asked Cornelia to tell Graeme she would always love him. But she gave no reason for her sudden decision to leave, and no hint of any destination she might have had in mind.

Halpern stood staring at the note for a long time in an attempt to control his feelings. When he looked up at last, his eyes glittered. "What did she take with her? Anything?" he asked, glad his voice showed none of the emotion he was feeling.

"Very little," Cornelia told him. "I have been through her things with my maid and all we can discover missing are two summer muslins, a shawl, some shifts and hose, and her missal. She wore a plain navy gown and sturdy boots, clothes she brought with her from Oxfordshire."

"Is it possible she has returned to the Moorlands?"

"We could write and ask, of course, but I doubt she has gone there," Russell said with a shrug.

"Why not?" his wife demanded. Ever since Halpern had

come in, she had been praying that was Lili's destination, praying she would reach it safely. It was the best place she could go, and Ben Moorland's love for her was of little matter now.

"Because, my dear, she knows that is the first place we would look for her. It is obvious she does not want us to find her. That is why she stole out of the house as she did, without a word to any of us. She wanted to disappear. We will not find her in Oxfordshire."

"What about friends?" Halpern asked next.

"She has none," Cornelia admitted sadly. "She had so hoped to meet girls her own age, make friends. Of course that is because she has never had any. For her first thirteen years she was in the convent, then with us in Vienna, and finally at the farm."

"Wait a minute," Halpern said, sounding hopeful for the first time. "Is it possible she might seek sanctuary in a religious retreat?"

"But there are no convents in London, or the surrounding area that I know of," Alastair mused.

"You do not suppose she has been—been kidnapped, do you?" Cornelia asked, her clasped hands held tight to her lips.

"That is most unlikely," Alastair said kindly, for he could see she was too upset to think clearly. "A kidnapper would have had to force an entry, unless he arrived with the guests and hid somewhere until the house was quiet. And would a kidnapper take the time to assemble even the few clothes Lili took with her? He would not have bothered with her prayer book, and he certainly would not have allowed her to write that note."

"Of course. How stupid I am."

Alastair smiled at her and shook his head before he turned to Halpern and said, "You must forgive me for asking this, my lord, but I have no choice. Was everything well with you and Lili? She was not having second thoughts, was she? Did she say anything that might be construed as a desire to escape marriage?"

He was watching Halpern carefully. He saw the disbelief and then the anger cross his face, but it was quickly gone. Still he did not relax until Halpern held out his hands palms up, and shrugged. He knew of the viscount's temper and he had no desire to get involved in fisticuffs with him, but he had had to ask that question.

"What of the servants?" Cornelia asked, her voice despairing. "They will all know by now Lili has disappeared. What are we to tell them? And what are we to tell society?"

Now it was Alastair's turn to frown. The other two stared at him, waiting to hear his suggestions. "There is no sense in denying something is amiss," he said finally. "Servants are not stupid. They will not be taken in by some trumped-up story of a sudden visit to friends. At dawn? Sneaking from the house after a strenuous party that lasted for hours? No, I am afraid we must be honest with them and ask for their help."

"They will be loyal?" Halpern asked.

Russell looked grim. "As far as I know, they will. Most of them are Wyckend servants. We can rely on them. But several were added when we arrived in town for the Season. The butler is new to us, for example."

"I think we will need his help especially," Cornelia said. "And the housekeeper's, of course. The others, well, we can assemble them and explain, beg for their silence. Perhaps it will serve."

"But it will only work if we can find Lili without too much delay," Halpern added. "It is too rich a secret to keep for long. What shall you tell them? And what are we to tell our friends? We must have the same story and stick to it."

"Let us say Lili was called to the country because of a relative's illness," Alastair said slowly. "Let it be an Edson who is at death's door; that's the more reputable side of her family. Now why do you look so distressed at that, love?" he asked his wife.

"Because John Moorland is slowly dying," she said. "Nancy told me there is nothing anyone can do and it is only a matter of time. I pray using that excuse will not bring bad luck."

Russell rose and knelt by her chair. "We must hope so indeed, 'Nelia," he said.

She managed a weak smile and Halpern turned to look out the window so he would not intrude. He found he was envious of them, married and secure in their love for each other. And when there was trouble, like now, they did not have to cope alone. It was what he had hoped he and Lili might share. And now she was gone without a word to him. He did not understand and he found it hard to forgive her. Perhaps she had been regretting her decision to wed him, as Russell had implied? Perhaps, as young as she was, she knew no way to tell him she had made a mistake? But no, he told himself fiercely, it cannot be that! She kissed me last night and clung to me so tightly. And she did say she would always love me in her note.

"Has Lili received any unusual mail recently?" he asked, struck by a sudden thought. "I mean, it is possible someone wrote to her, mocking her and calling names. That would upset her. It might even make her think we would all be better off without her."

"Well, it is true she does love the dramatic gesture," Cornelia admitted. "Oh, I hate to point out any fault of hers, but disappearing would be something she might choose to do because it was so striking. She is, lest we forget, only seventeen."

"As for mail, she often received letters from Nancy Moorland, Ben used to write as well, but he has not done so lately. And once she had one from the Mother Superior of the convent at Blamont. I do not think there were any others, but of course she would not show me anything hateful."

"Dramatic gesture or no, she must have had a destination in mind," the viscount said. "She is not foolish. It has to be some safe place we would not be likely to consider. And there is something else. How much money would she be apt to have with her?"

Cornelia frowned. "Why, hardly any," she said. "Only a few shillings in fact. I asked her two days ago if she needed more pin money, for she had just purchased a book and some ribbons and I knew she was not plump in the pocket. Oh, to think she is without the price of a meal or a warm bed . . ."

"Now don't you begin to dramatize, too, 'Nelia," her fond husband scolded. "As Halpern reminded us, Lili is not a fool. And knowing that is a great help to us. For since she has so little money, she could not have been planning to travel far. I'll wager anything you like she is still in London."

"But London is enormous," his wife said sadly.

"Large, perhaps, but Mayfair is not. I say she is within a mile of us right now."

He saw that although his wife looked a little brighter, Halpern did not and he frowned at him to buy his silence. It could be Lili was near; he had no way of knowing. However, he vowed when he got his hands on her again, he would give her a setdown she would not forget, for worrying them all this way.

"Now then, shall we summon Marks and the housekeeper, 'Nelia?" he asked briskly. "Start with them and tell them what we have decided before we call in the rest?"

Halpern left the Russells to deal with their servants. He went immediately to his house on Park Lane, for he had no stomach for his clubs, indeed, anyplace where he might be accosted by friends. He knew he would have to lie eventually, but he preferred to delay that as long as possible. Accordingly, he told his butler he did not care to be disturbed.

Seated at his desk in the library, he idly inspected the post that had arrived in the early afternoon delivery. There was nothing unusual; some invitations, a note from a friend, a bill or two.

As usual, there was nothing from his mother although he looked for a letter. She had written only once since his visit to Braybourne, an impassioned plea for him to remember his name, his heritage, and his sacred obligations. The letter had not sounded at all like the marchioness he knew. Although she could be sarcastic on occasion, and was prone to irony, she was generally stiff and controlled in her demeanor. He had

written to her by return post, begging her pardon but restating
his determination to marry Lili. He had not heard from her
since.

Where could Lili have gone? he wondered, pushing the post
aside. What safe place had she discovered that neither he nor
the Russells could bring to mind?

Next door, and a flight above, Lili hid behind a heavy pur-
ple velvet drapery in Alva Potter's drawing room and peered
down into a window of the Braybourne library. She could just
see the back of Graeme's head bent over some papers on his
desk. As she watched, he dropped the sheet he was holding
and leaning forward, buried his face in his hands. It looked
very much as if her disappearance had been discovered.

"Has he returned home?" a sharp old voice asked behind
her and she turned to see Mrs. Potter entering the room. A
footman carrying a tray followed her.

"Come and sit down, girl," the old woman ordered. "There's
tea here for you. For myself, I prefer a glass of sherry."

She barely waited for the footman to close the drawing
room doors behind him before she said, "Now, tell me again
why I agreed to this madcap scheme of yours to house you all
unbeknownst to my dear friends, the Russells?"

"Oh, please, you must not give me up to them," Lili cried,
running to kneel at Mrs. Potter's feet, her face streaming tears.

"There now, stop that, girl," she was told sharply. "A regular
watering pot, ye be. I'll not empty the bag since I agreed to the
plan this morning. But still, it troubles me, it does."

"I know. It troubles me, too," Lili confessed, taking the cup
she was handed and retreating to her seat again. "But what I told
you was the truth. And I am not fit to be a marchioness. I have
no training for it, and I've no exalted family. Besides, I am no
Polly Peachum."

"And what, pray tell, does she have to say to anything?"

"You know her story?"

"Of course. All poor girls knew the tale and sighed over it,
even as old as it was. Lavinia Fenton was the toast of London,

adored by many titled men. And when she married the Duke of Bolton, there wasn't a girl in the country who didn't hope she might do the same. Fools! As a rule, dukes do not marry actresses, no matter how lovely and winsome they may be. However—"

"Nor do viscounts who will be marquises marry girls with suspect pasts."

"As I was saying, before I was interrupted, it can happen," the old lady said, shaking her finger at her guest. "Halpern wants ye, don't he? Loves ye? Well, then!"

"But what about when his love fades? What then?"

"Now who told you it would?" Mrs. Potter asked before she tossed off her sherry. "I suspect another's hand in this, and not Cornelia's or Alastair's, either."

Lili looked sad. "No, they agreed to the betrothal, however reluctantly. They did say Graeme was too old for me. I used to think he was, too, when I first met him. I as much as called him an old man more than once."

"*That* must have pleased him," Mrs. Potter muttered, grinning to herself.

Lili did not notice. "I soon realized he was not too old at all. And I do love him so very much . . ."

"I pray ye, no more tears! But if ye do love him, and he loves ye, where's the problem? And do not continue to prate of your horrid background. You agreed to the marriage, the betrothal has been announced and bandied about, and I understand ye have accepted valuable jewelry from the gentleman. Something had to have happened that forced you to change your mind. What was it? Or, as I suspect more likely, *who* was it?"

There was silence in the elaborate, stuffy drawing room. Lili stared helplessly at her hostess. After what seemed a long time, Mrs. Potter shrugged and rose. "Perhaps ye will find yerself able ter open yer budget at another time," she said stiffly. "Far be it for me to pry. That would be most unbecoming.

"It is time for my nap. I suggest ye lie down and rest as well, instead of peering into the windows next door all afternoon. Mr. High and Mighty is very apt ter look out and catch you at it, and then where would ye be?

"Ter say nothing of where *I* would be for aiding.you in this mad scheme," she added as she swept to the door and shut it with a snap behind her.

Chapter Eighteen

Left alone, Lili sat back in her chair, overcome with guilt. Of course she should confide in Alva Potter. The woman had been so good to her, taking her in and promising she might stay for as long as she wanted. Lili didn't have any idea what period of time might be required. She suspected 'Nelia and Alastair would continue to look for her, but surely Halpern would forget her, sooner or later. And when that happened, she would be free to write to the Russells and beg their pardon. And she would have to find a way to return the betrothal ring Graeme had given her, and the magnificent set of pearls and diamonds, all of which were hidden at the bottom of her reticule, wrapped in a linen handkerchief. She had not dared leave them in her room at Russell House lest one of the servants be tempted. Neither had she been able to put them in Alastair's strongbox, for that was always carefully locked and hidden away behind a window seat in the library. No matter how consuming her other troubles were, she was always conscious of the jewels, and frightened of what might happen to them while they were in her care.

Despite being nervous and tense, Lili yawned. She had not slept after the ball. Instead, she had sent the sleepy maid to bed, packed the few things she intended to take with her in a shawl, and dressed in her old navy gown and sturdy boots. Then she had written her note to the Russells, tucked it under her pillow, and arranged the bed to make it appear to a casual glance she was fast asleep there. That accomplished, she had sat up in a chair to wait for first light, afraid if she lay down, she would fall asleep and miss her chance.

Originally she had thought of going to Alva Potter before the ball to explain her predicament, but she had discarded that idea quickly. Mrs. Potter was 'Nelia's friend. When they had all been living together in Vienna, she had made no secret of her distaste for Lili Martingale. There was no reason she would take Lili's side instead of her friend's now. Instead, Lili decided she must go to Mrs. Potter's house early the morning after the ball, and throw herself on the old woman's mercy, begging her to help her and hide her. Indeed, when she crept from the house in Grosvenor Square at dawn, she told herself not to think of what might happen if Mrs. Potter refused to have anything to do with her. She had little money and no way of getting more. She would just have to pray the old lady's curious compulsion to be in on anything to do with society would stand her in good stead now.

She had set off in the opposite direction from Park Lane first though, her destination St. Patrick's Church in Soho Square, which she had discovered on one of her walks around Mayfair.

She was early for Mass, but she chose a seat toward the back of the church and began to pray. She felt comforted by the familiar surroundings; the faint smell of lingering incense, the flickering candles, the hard kneeler and pew. Soon the front pews began to fill with early worshippers; servants and tradespeople mostly. Lili did not think she would be remarked in her old navy gown with a shabby bonnet hiding her curls. She was the last to leave the church, for it was too early to go to Park Lane. Instead, she walked the streets, until at last she heard a church bell strike eight. Only then did she head for Alva Potter's mansion. This was the tricky part, of course. If Graeme's room was on the side of the house facing Mrs. Potter's and he happened to be looking out his window, all would be lost. She had toyed with the idea of using the servants' entrance, but she was afraid she would be turned away there. And so, taking a deep breath, she gave the knocker on the front door a mighty clang.

The butler she remembered from her earlier visit stared at

her when she asked for Mrs. Alva Potter. But such was her air
of assurance and educated tones, to say nothing of the famous
Russell "look," he let her in and went to seek guidance from
his mistress. Lili was glad he could not see how her knees
were quivering.

Told a young miss who would not give her name was even
then seated in the hall, Alva Potter abandoned her soft-boiled
eggs and freshly baked scones.

Lili rose and greeted her and before the lady could blurt out
her name, she took her arm and drew her back to the breakfast
room. Once there, she closed the door firmly in the butler's
face and it was only then she began her explanation and en-
treaty.

And now, safe for the moment, she went to the window
again. As far as she could see, the library was empty. She wondered where Graeme had gone and what he was doing. And
more importantly, what he was thinking.

Last night had been the most difficult night of her life. The
agony of smiling at him, dancing in his arms, kissing him
good night, all the while knowing it was for the last time, had
been excruciating. But although she had made her plans to
leave Russell House days before, she had not wanted to do so
before the ball. Not for herself, of course! She felt well past
anything so childish. But Alastair and 'Nelia had worked so
hard, she could not ruin their big evening by disappearing.

And no matter how painful this was, she knew she was
doing the right thing. She had known it long before the letter
from Graeme's mother, the Marchioness of Braybourne, had
arrived.

Strange, that. It was almost as if fate had arranged for her to
intercept it before anyone else saw it. She had just returned
from the lending library as the postman was leaving. Mr.
Marks, the butler, was not in the hall, and she had riffled
through the pile of mail, wondering if there was anything there
from the Moorlands for her.

She had not recognized the handwriting on the thick packet
addressed to her and sealed with a fat glob of red wax im-

printed with a crest. But it had made her uneasy, and she did not open it until she reached her room and was quite alone.

The letter was neither harsh nor accusatory. It only stated facts she already knew. Still, she had not been aware Graeme's family went back so many generations, nor that it had had so many illustrious members; statesmen and royal confidantes, learned scholars, explorers, an inventor, two generals, and an archbishop as well as the esteemed, well-born women who were their wives. And to this roster, the letter continued, was to be added the common name, Martingale? Was such as she to be wed to the heir of Braybourne, the future head of the family?

The marchioness asked her to reconsider this drastic step. And she asked what Lili would do when Graeme grew tired of her, as she was assured he would. Who could she count as friends then? Confidantes? All society would shun her because she was an impostor. She would be alone, despised by her servants and ignored by an indifferent husband who regretted every day a union made in lust with no common interests or background to sustain it.

Finally, the marchioness promised her money, a great deal of money if she would leave Graeme alone and promise never to reveal his mother had been instrumental in her abrupt change of heart.

Lili had no intention of ever telling Graeme what his mother had done. She could not inflict that kind of pain. And although she could understand why a mother might try this way to save her son from what she considered a terrible mistake, it did not make it any easier for her to still her resentment.

She remembered she had asked Graeme about his mother and father right after he returned to town, how she had thought his answer evasive. All he would say was that although his mother had run true to form, his father had truly surprised him. She had wondered in what way. His vehemence? His anger? His distress? She did not know. Graeme had not told her.

She had read his mother's letter over many times before she consigned it to the fire. Burning it had done nothing but keep it from other eyes, for even now she could recite it word for word. Of course she had no intention of taking any money from the marchioness. The very idea made her feel ill. Instead, she would ask Alva Potter to provide the means for her to return to the convent at Blamont. She knew she would never love another man, and since she could not marry Halpern, she would never marry anyone. But she also knew the marchioness was right. She had suspected it all along, ever since 'Nelia and Alastair had taken the trouble to point out her prospects, and warn her she must not expect anything grand. Graeme's mother's letter had merely reinforced their views, Polly Peachum notwithstanding. That was the stuff of fairy tales, "once upon a times" and "happily ever afters," not the warp and weft of the fabric of real life. And so she would leave England.

Just as soon as she could force herself to do so.

Graeme Wilder did not leave the house on Park Lane all that day and night. Instead, he thought of Lili, not only wondering where she had gone, but almost as importantly, why. She had promised him she would never keep anything from him again—he remembered how he had exacted that promise from her. What had happened to make her break it? It must have been something serious, for the nuns had to have taught Lili a vow was sacred.

He had to believe Lili must have heard something that upset her, in spite of the Russells' denials. All right. She had no close friends, but there had to be *someone*. He thought of the people she had spoken of most often. The Moorlands first, but why would they consider her marriage to him a disaster? Ben Moorland might, of course. Would she listen to him? He did not think so. Besides, she had agreed to marry him after Ben's London visit.

Then there were those Rowleys who were visiting in the Square. She had mentioned meeting them in the little park. Was it possible they had upset her? He recalled the family, the self-important brother of no distinction but what existed in his own mind, the invalid mother who saw no one, the elderly grandparents. Then there were the two sisters. The shy younger one could not be guilty but he could easily picture the prim, disapproving Miss Rowley taking pleasure in wounding Lili. How could he find out if it was her? How could he approach her?

He could think of nothing, especially not if he hoped to preserve the story that Lili had left London for a relative's deathbed.

Thinking of that, he stopped pacing his room. It was late. He had sent his valet to bed long ago, and unable to sleep himself, had continued to ponder the problem as he paced his room. A relative. Could it be possible that Lili's father had discovered her whereabouts and had approached her sometime when she was outside Russell House? He made a mental note to question the maid and footman who accompanied her whenever she left the house.

Suddenly it seemed so logical to him. For if her father were poor and ragged, and of low estate, it might make her think that made her unworthy as well. It was silly of course, but it would not seem so to an impressionable girl.

Halpern paused to throw the window open. His room seemed stuffy and he wanted a breath of fresh air. As he stood there, he noticed a light in a window across the way. Obviously someone else was sleepless tonight. As he watched, he saw a hand pull back the drapery and caught a quick, blurred glimpse of a pale face before it disappeared. As he shut the window, he hoped the old woman who lived there would be able to sleep soon. He seemed to remember hearing somewhere that the elderly often had trouble sleeping.

The next morning he went to Russell House early to see Lili's maid, only to find Alastair Russell had questioned her before him. According to the maid, Lili had never been out of her sight and no one had ever dared to approach her although she had attracted the usual close inspection from many a gentleman. It was Cornelia Russell who told him this, for Alastair had gone out.

"He feels it would be wrong for both of us to continue isolated. I am allowed to refuse guests because I have contracted an infectious cold." Here Cornelia shook her head. "It is because I have no head for dissembling, you see, my lord. Alastair says my face gives me away."

Silently, Halpern agreed with Russell. He had never seen anyone off the stage look more tragic. "I expect I had better have a look-see in at my clubs today," was all he said however. "And if I look depressed, surely the sudden departure of my fiancée to attend a family funeral will be ample excuse."

As Cornelia Russell nodded, a jeweled comb she wore in her hair twinkled in the light.

"But how could I have forgotten? Idiot!" Halpern exclaimed, hitting his forehead. "Tell me, ma'am, did your husband lock up Lili's jewelry after the party? I remember I kept her up after you both went off to bed."

His hostess stared at him. "Why no, he did not. And of course in the morning when we discovered Lili was missing, we were not thinking of jewelry."

"You did not notice them in her room?"

Cornelia shook her head, suddenly paler.

"Then she may be anywhere by now," Halpern said, rising to pace the room so she would not see his distress. "She could have sold the pearl and diamond set, her ring as well."

"No, no, she would not do that," Cornelia assured him. "She would keep them safe. And how on earth could she find a moneylender in any case? She knows nothing of such men."

"I shall make some inquiries to be sure."

Cornelia did not try to dissuade him. She suspected it would be better for the viscount to have something to do. It was why she had sent Alastair off to his tailor. She sighed. She had slept little the previous night and she didn't think Halpern looked in any better case.

And Lili had been missing now for over twenty-four hours. Marks had informed her the servants were still firm in their promise not to reveal the truth of her flight, but he didn't know how much longer they could expect such nobleness to con-

tinue. The story of the runaway fiancée was too delicious to be
kept secret. And there was the temptation of monetary reward
from one of the many newspapers as well, he had added, looking pained. Cornelia had begged him to do his best with them
before she fled the hall.

She listened now as Halpern told her his theory about a
hateful letter writer and she agreed it was possible, although
privately she did not believe a word of it. Who would do such
a thing? Lili had no enemies.

"Oh, my," she said in a stunned voice.

The viscount turned and strode toward her. "You have
thought of something, ma'am? Something that might help?
Tell me!"

"It just occurred to me that perhaps the dowager countess or
that truly repulsive crony of hers, Mrs. Parmeter, might have
had a hand in this. Alastair told me how Sarah carried on when
he exiled her from Wyckend. Might she not have decided to
make Lili pay for her own mistakes? She has never liked her
and . . ."

"I will go and call on her immediately," Halpern vowed.

It was only with the greatest effort that Cornelia was able to
persuade Halpern not to do any such thing. She said if the
dowager had any hint that Lili was missing it would be all
over London by nightfall. Furthermore, even if she had written
to Lili, she would not know where Lili had gone.

Halpern left her shortly thereafter and walked briskly toward St. James Street. He found Lord Gore at Boodles. He
was reading one of the morning papers and enjoying a glass of
claret.

Gore was delighted to fold the paper and call for another
glass for his friend, for he was not fond of reading and had
trouble even keeping up with the court news. "Marvelous
party Beau Russell gave the other evenin'," he began. "Your
lady looked a picture, indeed she did. Almost tempted me to
look about—well, at least *begin* to look about, that is. Mustn't
rush into anything so important, what?"

"Certainly not," Halpern agreed. "Haste makes waste, and

he who loves and runs away, lives to love another day, and all that.

"Tell me, Cecil, who would you suggest if a chap needed money?"

"What chap?" Gore asked, bending closer although he did not bother to lower his voice.

Halpern shrugged. "Never mind who. It is not important. I told him I'd not spread it about. He won't take money from me. Insists on getting it by selling some jewelry he has."

"Tell me it's not Ridgeway," Gore persisted. "I know how often he is up the River Tick, but I lent him a sum not a fortnight ago, and . . ."

"It is not Ridgeway. You may be easy on that head. Come now! I know you are often in dun territory yourself. Surely you can supply a name or two for the poor fellow who asked me?"

Lord Gore frowned, thought for a long moment, and finally gave him two names, one of whom did business in Seven Dials, that infamous section of London known to be a den of iniquity frequented by thieves and murderers. It made the viscount shiver just to think Lili might have gone anywhere near the place.

Still, when he investigated both moneylenders, neither showed the slightest sign they knew anything about a very young lady intent on pawning her jewelry.

"Tell ye in a flash, I would, gov," a Mr. Mulligan assured Halpern. The viscount was sure he was right, for he had offered to buy back the jewelry he described at an excellent price.

"Don't hold with young ladies sellin' their pretties, I don't. And she was very young, ye say? Wal then, I'd have nothin' ter do with her. 'Gainst the law 'tis, ter deal with minors."

If Halpern had been feeling more the thing, he would have laughed at the pious expression on the old Irishman's red face. Instead he nodded curtly and left abruptly, delighted to quit the vicinity.

In the hackney headed back to Park Lane, he tried not to

feel discouraged. Still, it did seem everywhere he turned he met failure. Assuming Lili had gone to ground in Mayfair, where could she be? And if she still had the jewelry, was there any chance she might try and return it to him? That might be something she would feel obligated to do with her convent upbringing. But there was little time left to wait for her to do that. Already a day and a half had passed with nary a sign of her.

He thought hard for a moment. Could it be possible she might have gone to the dowager countess? It sounded like the old lady's wits were addled. She might have taken Lili in to repay Beau Russell for her exile.

Halpern snorted then, shifting uneasily on the cracked old leather seat, for handsome new vehicles did not frequent Seven Dials. He knew he was grasping at straws because he was so desperate.

The hackney was not able to stop before Braybourne House because a large carriage with a crest on the door was already pulled up there. Halpern saw footmen and grooms running in and out as they unloaded the baggage. He stared at them, frowning. So, his parents had come to London after all, had they? He wished they had not done so, especially at this time. As he paid the cabbie, he saw the old lady next door—Mrs. Poltner? Porten?—standing on her front steps, quite blatantly watching the activity. She smiled at him and nodded, raising her hand as if to wave, and he glared at her.

How dare she busy herself about his family affairs, he thought as he strode to his own front door. He did not even bother to greet the servants from Braybourne, he was so exasperated.

Chapter Nineteen

He found his parents seated in the drawing room, drinking wine. He thought his father looked much the same as he had at Braybourne, his mother less so. She had lost weight and her face was pale with dark circles under the eyes, as if she had been having trouble sleeping. He was sorry for it, but her appearance did not change his mind about marrying Lili. When he found her, that is. And he would, he promised himself as he bowed and greeted them.

"A surprise for you, but not an unwelcome one, I trust, son," the marquis said. "Come, have a glass with us and tell us we may stay with you a week or so. Your mother has business at the Royal Academy. I came only to bear her company."

Halpern forced himself to smile and nod. The marquis had given him Braybourne House in London on his twenty-fifth birthday. But although it was nominally his, in reality, his father made use of it on his infrequent trips to town. He was always punctilious in asking permission to do so, however.

"You are welcome indeed," Halpern said as he poured himself a glass of claret. "All goes well at Braybourne?"

For a short time, they spoke of the estate and its problems. The marquis then begged to hear all the current scandals; news, he said, it was impossible to glean from the London papers. Halpern obliged. He wondered at his mother's silence. Generally she was not a woman who sat shy and quiet while men conversed. She never had been.

At last, during a lull in the conversation, she said, "Is everything well with you, Graeme? Somehow you seem tense, perturbed, to me."

"I have not noticed anything of the kind," the marquis murmured.

"Men never do, I believe," she retorted.

Halpern thought for a moment. It would only be a matter of time before his parents learned of Lili's absence. He could, of course, tell them the tale of a sudden deathbed visit, but somehow that lie stuck in his throat. So he put down his empty glass and said, "Yes, there is something amiss. Something terribly amiss that I pray you keep to yourselves. The story being told around town is that Lili—Miss Martingale—has left London to attend the deathbed of a family member. In reality, she has disappeared and no one knows where."

"I say," his father exclaimed, looking perturbed. "When did this happen?"

The particulars were soon explained, as well as all the futile steps being taken to locate her.

"She is very young," the marchioness said at last, for she had sat silently again while her husband and son discussed the problem. "Perhaps she felt marriage at her age too drastic a step?"

"No, I do not believe that," Halpern said quickly, rubbing his brow to try and rid it of the sudden headache he had acquired.

"Because she wanted so to be a marchioness someday?" his mother suggested.

As Halpern stared at her, he willed himself not to lose his temper. "You might find this hard to believe, ma'am, but she doesn't particularly care about being a marchioness. Or a viscountess either, for that matter."

His voice was soft and even. Still his mother's hand crept to her throat and she pressed against the back of her chair, never taking her eyes from his face.

"I know that she loves me, and it is only that love that has made her at all easy about her future situation. Think, ma'am! Lili was raised in a convent to regard worldly matters of rank and wealth of little importance. No, she has left for another reason entirely. I will find her. Somehow. I will not rest until I do.

"What I fear is that someone has spoken to her, made her uneasy about this unequal marriage, and mind you, I do not mean the difference in our ages. I wish I knew who that person was. I would happily throttle him or her for the mischief that has been done."

"I agree. It is too bad by half," his father said. "More wine, Graeme? Jean, my dear?"

The marchioness refused as she gathered her belongings. "No, I must see we are properly settled. And may I suggest it would be well for you to rest, my lord?" she added to her husband.

The marquis rose obediently and she went on. "Do you dine in, son? Your father and I plan an early night."

Although Halpern had intended to stay home, faced with the prospect of dining with the two of them made him say he was pledged to a friend.

He stood and watched them leave the drawing room arm in arm. As he did so, he remembered what his father had told him at Braybourne about the state of their marriage, and he found he pitied them both.

Halfway up the stairs, the marquis paused to catch his breath. He waited until a footman coming down was safely past before he said softly, "We must certainly hope that Graeme never discovers your hand in this debacle, my dear. He might not throttle you, but I do not think he would ever forgive you. He loves that girl in a way you and I have never known, more's the pity. I do hope it was not envy that made you try and stop this marriage."

"You are so sure I am at fault here?" she asked, but he noticed she did not appear indignant to be accused. "There is no proof," she added.

"Obviously you wrote to Lili Martingale. It was all you could do. If she has saved that letter, Graeme will have all the proof he needs. Even if she has discarded it and only tells him about it, who do you think he will believe? And he will cast you off, madam, never doubt it. You should not have meddled."

"I did it for Braybourne," she said slowly, her voice strained. "Everything I have ever done has been for Braybourne."

Her husband shrugged as he began to make his laborious way upward again. "But Braybourne is not worth such sacrifice," he said. "What is the place really but a few hundred acres, a handsome mansion, and a graveyard full of Wilders? It is not holy ground and neither are the Wilders so important the line must be preserved at all costs. Far from it. We are merely mortals, very like every other mortal on earth."

She stopped to stare at him. "You are not well, sir," she said. "You cannot be well to be spouting such heresy. Come, I will feel more comfortable when you are laid down on your bed. Next you will be telling me we are no better than a wandering tinker and a scullery maid. Shame on you."

The marquis said no more. He allowed himself to be shepherded to his room and tucked up in bed. He admitted he was weary. Traveling had become more and more exhausting for him. As he closed his eyes, he thought of that pretty little girl and he said a halting prayer for her safety, for his son's sake.

As soon as all activity ceased next door and the large traveling carriage was driven away to the mews, Alva Potter set off for Russell Square. Not for her a hackney cab for the short distance she had to go. The town's fine ladies might effect helplessness, as if they had no legs like every other human creature—for limbs she would not call them, no, not even if "legs" was ill-bred—too namby-pamby for words, some of them society ladies were.

Mrs. Potter had given the matter of Miss Martingale much thought, although she had not told Lili that. Neither had she mentioned her errand today, but she had to see for herself how Cornelia and Alastair were taking the girl's absence. Earlier she had promised Lili she would not reveal anything to them, but she thought she would be justified in breaking that promise if she felt the Russells were suffering. Cornelia, especially, she thought as she walked briskly along. She had been very good to her, unlike her husband, who patronized her sometimes. But she would see the lay of the land for herself.

Safely arrived at Russell House, she bullied the butler into admitting her. Vainly Marks tried to say his mistress was not receiving for she was laid down on her bed with an infectious cold. Mrs. Potter refused to be denied, and resigned, he led the way to Cornelia's small morning room.

Alva Potter thought she looked terrible, wan and tired, and her heart went out to her. "Now what's amiss?" she asked as she took the seat beside her friend and reached for her hand to pat it. "And don't bother to deny it, my girl, or prate to me of infectious colds. I'm more than two-and-ten and I know you have a problem. Out with it!"

Cornelia bit her lower lip hard. At last she nodded as she reached a sudden decision. "You are right, Alva, there is a problem. I wasn't going to tell you, but I must speak to someone or go mad! And Alastair is no comfort to me in this. He is so horridly cheerful for my sake, I cannot bear it.

"Lili has disappeared. She left the house very early the morning after our ball and we have no idea where she might be."

"I see. That viscount of hers? He don't know either?"

The two discussed the situation for some time, and when Alva Potter rose at last to go home, Cornelia was in a happier frame of mind. Perhaps it was the older woman's down-to-earth way of looking at the problem, her comforting words, that made the difference.

As she stood on the front steps, smoothing her gloves, Alva Potter wondered if she should have been more open. Something had prevented her from revealing the secret although she intended to ask Lili to release her from her promise.

Lili was horrified by her request and shook her head so hard, her curls came loose and fell down her back.

"No, no, no, ma'am," she cried. "You must *not* tell 'Nelia

and Alastair, you must *not*! You must not break your promise! If you do I will run away to—to France, I swear I will."

"And what will you use for money?" Alva Potter asked, ever practical. "Answer me that, my girl."

"I can sell my jewels," Lili declared, although the thought of selling Graeme's gifts made her want to cry. She knew she would do it, however, if she had to.

Alva Potter could tell by the girl's expression she would do just that, and it frightened her. London was not a city for a young, convent-bred miss to be wandering about in, especially with a fortune in jewelry in her reticule.

"Well, there now, all right," she said. "I was merely testing you to see how strongly you felt about avoiding this marriage. Now I am sure you are determined, you need not fear. I won't tell the Russells, and I will see you have the necessary money to reach the convent. It will take me a few days to hire a chaperon and a courier to escort you. I trust you will be able to contain your impatience until then?"

Lili declared she might have all the time she needed, for she was already dreading the finality of crossing the Channel and leaving England—and more importantly—Graeme Wilder behind.

"Did you notice the excitement next door earlier?" Mrs. Potter asked. "The toplofty Marchioness of Braybourne and her husband, the marquis, have arrived from the country. I do not think they make a long stay. They had little enough baggage, only three portmanteaus and a pair of trunks. Oh, and some vegetables and a brace of ducks and a basket of fresh eggs. I am sure if I was a marchioness, I wouldn't travel with dead birds and eggs, no matter how fresh they were. The very idea."

"I missed it," Lili confessed, diverted. "I must have been napping. I—I did not get much sleep last night."

"Hmmph! I'll be bound you spent most of the night trying to peek into his bedchamber, you saucy girl," Mrs. Potter said just as the footmen brought in the tea tray she had ordered. Since that was exactly what Lili had been doing, she blushed scarlet. She still remembered that moment when she came face-to-face with Graeme, leaning from his own window. She had moved back immediately, her heart pounding, and she had dropped the drapery as quickly as she would have dropped a hot coal. Since then she had lived in dread anticipation that he would come to the front door, demanding to see her. When that did not occur, she had to admit he had probably not recognized her. The houses were set many yards apart. It had been a dark night, with no moon, and what light there had been, had been behind her. Lili began to dream about what might have happened if he had chanced to see her.

Alva Potter eyed her shrewdly over the rim of her cup and when Lili excused herself, she sat on, surveying the littered tray and cake crumbs and wondering what she was to do. She could not let Lili travel to France. She knew that. She could of course go to Cornelia and tell her the truth. She owed no allegiance to Lili Martingale. If truth were told, she had never much liked the girl from the time she first met her in Vienna when she was only thirteen. She was too good, too saintly then. And now she thought her silly. She had never heard of anything so stupid in her entire life, to be passing up a chance to be a marchioness because she felt she wasn't good enough for Halpern.

Ha! She could have told the girl it was the other way around entirely. Men were not good enough for women, not a one of 'em. Why, only consider their nasty habits, their unsavory business deals, their lies and cheating and their lust and dissipation. And to think they held the ridiculous opinion they were set on earth to rule and dominate because they were stronger and smarter and better somehow. She would grant they were stronger, but that was all.

Much later that night, Mrs. Potter was still wrestling with the problem. The Russells deserved to know where Lili was, but there was that promise she had made. And she did not like to break a promise. Suddenly she sat straight up in bed when it occurred to her that she had not promised that she would not tell Viscount Halpern, simply because Lili had not thought to demand it of her. Why would she when none of the Wilders would recognize the likes of Alva Potter? But one of them at least would recognize her now, she thought as she slid down in bed and smiling, arranged her covers. She would write to Halpern first thing in the morning. She would tell him they must meet somewhere away from Park Lane so Lili would not see them. And she would mention Lili's name to make sure of his compliance. Oh, all sorts of good might come of this, she thought. She fell asleep dreaming of a grateful Halpern showering her with attentions and invitations.

It never was necessary for Alva Potter to write that note. Viscount Halpern was on her doorstep long before most people commenced morning calls. Mrs. Potter's butler, a very superior gentleman she had lured from a duke's employ, knew he should deny him. But the cachet of admitting a future marquis to a house that never saw the nobility was too much for him.

"The mistress is at breakfast, sir," he said. "If you would be so good as to wait here while I see if she is free to receive you?"

Halpern nodded curtly. He was listening as hard as he could for some sign Lili was in this house. His epiphany had, like Alva Potter's, come to him last night. He had been pacing his room when he remembered the scene he had witnessed the previous night—the face at the opposite window that disappeared in a blur, the hand that dropped the curtain so quickly, yes, that smooth, white hand! He had seen it plainly and he would swear it did not belong to an old woman. He had stopped pacing then and closed his eyes, the better to think. Was he grasping at straws to think that might have been Lili's hand? Think, man, think! he commanded himself. He seemed to recall Cornelia Russell once mentioning how kind this Alva Pointer?—Posner?—had been when they were all in Vienna for the Congress three years ago, and yes! he had seen Cornelia leaving the house only a while ago. Lili had been at the Congress, too. She must have stayed with the old lady in Vienna. And what better place to hide? No one would suspect she would flee to the much-ridiculed and ignored Mrs.—whatever her name was.

The butler returned in only a few moments to usher him to a drawing room. It was dark there; the draperies had not been drawn. Looking around in the dim light, Halpern could see the place had yet to receive the housemaids' attentions. His brows rose. He was hardly accustomed to this kind of reception. As he stared about, the little old lady he recognized as his neglected neighbor ran in. She was smiling, her hands outstretched in greeting.

"Do forgive me for receiving you here, milord," she said in a husky whisper as she dropped a curtsy. "What a strange coincidence this is! I was about to write to you, and here you are. Oh, please be seated, milord."

"There is no need, ma'am," Halpern said stiffly. It had just occurred to him that he might be about to make a fool of himself. "I do not stay. I have only come to ask if by any chance you have a guest staying here with you?"

"A guest?" she echoed, smiling and tapping her nose. "A *guest,* you say?"

Halpern wondered if she had all her wits. Surely his question could not have been clearer. "Yes. A young lady, ma'am."

She tittered. "You have lost one, milord? For shame."

Halpern felt his temper rising. "Shall we be plain, ma'am?" he said, his voice cold. "I am looking for a young lady. I believe she may be residing in your house."

"However did you find out?" she demanded, not at all intimidated by his temper and toplofty tone.

Halpern answered without thinking. "I saw a figure in a window over here late the night before last. It disappeared quickly, but I remember the hand holding the curtain back was young."

Alva Potter looked down at her gnarled, wrinkled hands with their prominent veins and age spots, and sighed. "How clever of you, milord,"

"Is Lili Martingale here?" he asked eagerly. "I beg you be straight with me, ma'am."

She paused for a long moment, relishing the moment. At last she nodded. "Yes, Lili is here. She came very early the day after the Russell ball and she has been here ever since."

His smile, even in the dim light, was blinding and she blinked.

"Thank you," he said. "Thank you for keeping her safe."

"I did it for Cornelia Russell, not you, milord," she told him. "Mrs. Russell used to be the Countess of Wyckend, y'know. She is a *particular* friend of mine, as is her husband, Beau Russell."

To her disgust, Halpern ignored these impressive credentials. "What is Lili planning to do?" he asked. "Surely she does not intend to stay here."

"Why not? What is wrong with my house?" Alva Potter demanded, bristling like a broody hen.

"Why, nothing. You mistake me, ma'am. I only meant that she cannot want to stay indoors, hiding for the rest of her life."

"No, nor do I want her to," his hostess said, eyeing him as if she still suspected his explanation. "I'm too old for all this carrying on, and tears, and . . ."

"She cries?"

"Of course she does. Most of yesterday in fact. And she has no appetite and less conversation. It has been . . . boring."

"I am sorry," he said, nobly swallowing a laugh.

"When do you plan to take her away?"

"I cannot say, just like that. I was not sure she was here, you see, and so I have made no plans."

"Best you do so," she told him, wagging a finger at him just as his nanny used to do when he misbehaved. Halpern felt about six as she went on. "She's all for haring off to France, of all places, back to that convent."

She looked her guest up and down and nodded. "Can't imagine why she would want to do that, not with the likes of you hot for her, I can't."

"Er, thank you, ma'am. I shall make my plans immediately. May I send you word of them by note? I think I should like to surprise Lili."

To his astonishment she came to him and began to push him in the direction of the door. "Heavens, that I could forget," she muttered. "You must be off at once, milord. Lili will be coming down to breakfast any minute and if she catches you in the house there'll be no surprise nor anything else neither."

"Perhaps it would be best for you to make sure she is not in the hall now, ma'am?" he suggested, amazed at how strong she was for a tiny old lady.

"Yes, I'll just have a peek," she said, darting to the door and opening it a crack. Halpern prayed Lili was nowhere around, for surely such behaviour from her hostess would tell her she had been found out. Not that it mattered, he told himself, but still, he preferred to compose the ending of this affair himself.

As Mrs. Potter beckoned to him, he said, "I am eternally grateful to you, ma'am. I will not forget what you have done."

"Yes, yes, but not now," she hissed, waving frantically. "Be off with you, man, before she comes down. Go!"

Under the stunned gaze of the butler, Halpern found himself hustled out to the front steps without further ado. He wanted to laugh badly. Laugh at the comical scene he had just been engaged in with his irrepressible conspirator. But mostly he wanted to laugh with joy. Because he had found Lili. Because they would be together again.

Chapter Twenty

He found his mother had gone out to the Academy and his father still kept to his bed when he returned to Braybourne House and he went to his rooms, leaving orders he was not to be disturbed.

His first thought was that he should let the Russells know Lili was safe. He knew how Cornelia was suffering. The beau, too, although he suspected he was angry at Lili for upsetting Cornelia as much as he was concerned for her safety.

As he handed the note to a footman to deliver, he knew he had not been honest when he wrote he would return Lili to them shortly. He knew he had no intention of capturing Lili and then calmly returning her to Grosvenor Square. No, and he did not intend to wait for her to reach her eighteenth birthday before marrying her, either. Much better to make her his viscountess at once, lest she keep on changing her mind about the wisdom of marrying him. The sudden exchange of vows could be explained away to the *ton* by her attendance at a relative's deathbed. Surely it was understandable he would not want to wait for her through whatever period of mourning was necessary. Indeed, now he thought it over, the whole situation had resolved itself admirably.

He made a note to himself about getting a special license today, and another to order a large bouquet of flowers for Mrs. Alva Potter.

Before he began to plan where they would be married, he considered the means he would employ to remove Lili from the Potter mansion, without raising an undue amount of noise.

It must be something dramatic, he thought. That would please her, and because it would mean she would not be able to argue, it certainly pleased him.

He got up and resumed pacing, his brow furrowed in thought. At last a grin spread across his face and he began to laugh. He had discovered the perfect plan. He was sure Lili would agree.

For the next hour he was kept busy writing notes and memos. He sent another one to Russell House, asking for Lili's clothes to be packed and delivered to the Braybourne stables in the mews behind the house. As he sent it on its way, he hoped Mrs. Russell would not kick up a dust over such unorthodox behaviour. He suspected she could be very strait-laced, could Cornelia Russell.

He would never have imagined how hard she laughed when she read it. She and Alastair had been eating breakfast when the first note arrived, to their great relief. And now, to be told Halpern was planning an elopement made them both smile as they sought to clasp each other's hand. It reminded them so much of their own elopement, that mad dash from Oxford to Doctor's Common in a blizzard. Alastair had wagered he could do it, and he made it—just. And as elopers themselves, they were hardly in a position to pretend horror at Halpern's plan.

"He does love her truly, my dear," Cornelia said, reaching up to cradle her husband's face between her hands. "We must let Lili go."

"I know," he said, bending to kiss the tip of her nose. "And I will confess, my love, I am not at all sorry to do so. Now we can live our lives to suit ourselves. Having Lili here with us was trying, and I admit it."

She told him he was very bad, but secretly Cornelia Russell agreed with him. She suspected they were both too young for the job of chaperons, and she would be happy to turn Lili's care over to an eager husband.

Back at Braybourne House, the staff was set abustle. Halpern's valet began to pack his clothes, and a likely looking maid was chosen for Lili's abigail. A groom was sent cantering off to alert the staff of a house on the coast near Bournemouth that his grandmother had left to him, of Halpern's imminent arrival. There was a message as well for the vicar of the Braybourne church. Halpern remembered his meeting with Lili outside the church. It seemed only fitting they exchange vows there.

Only once, as he was returning to Park Lane after procuring the special license did he feel the slightest doubt about what he was doing. It was true Lili had run away from him, and vowed never to marry him, but surely she had not *meant* it. Had she? And surely he would be able to change her mind if she had, wouldn't he? He vowed he would solve this problem as soon as he had her in his arms again. She loved him, she had said so in her last message. Whatever had happened to send her into hiding was of little importance and he could deal with it.

It was afternoon before he had everything in train, and he went to the library in search of his father. He found the marquis sitting in a deep wing chair reading the London papers. A pair of spectacles was perched on the end of his nose. When he saw his son, he snatched them off.

"There now, Graeme, if you didn't catch me," he complained as he tucked them in his pocket. "I hoped I wouldn't have to admit I need such things, but age has a way of creeping up on you, y'know. Tell me, anything of Miss Martingale?"

Halpern repeated his good news and what he intended to do, and his father began to laugh. Lady Braybourne found them that way a moment later.

She did not laugh when the situation was explained to her, but at a hard look from her husband, she managed a smile.

"It is to be tonight, you say?" the marquis asked after she had excused herself, pretending she had some letters to write.

"Yes, it would be easier in the daylight of course, but where's the romance there?" his son said with a grin. "As soon as it is dusk, I'll be off. We'll not reach Braybourne tonight, though, more's the pity."

"That hardly matters since you wed tomorrow," his father told him. "We shall hope none of the worst gossips spy you out, however. There has been enough talk about Lili Martingale and I'd have no more of it now she is to be your viscountess."

He stood up then a bit ponderously. Halpern hurried to help him and he was surprised beyond words when his father hugged him tight. He felt his eyes fill with tears and he had to blink them away and swallow hard. Not since he was a small boy had his father hugged him like this.

"Go safely, Graeme," the older man said, his voice husky. "Let us know how you do and when we may expect you at Braybourne. I am sure your mother will want to plan a gala house party there for you and your bride."

To Halpern, it seemed no day had ever been longer. He did manage to sleep a little, since he had been doing without it for two nights. When he rose and dressed, he called for some food. His valet and the maid had set out earlier for the house on the coast with his and Lili's belongings strapped on the large traveling coach. His curricle would be waiting for him in the mews.

He had written a long note to Alva Potter, making arrangements, his lips curling up as he did so. She was such an unlikely confederate. Her reply had been priceless. It was full of underlines and some bawdy suggestions for handling a new, and perhaps reluctant, bride. He had tucked it away to savor again in the future.

At last it was dark enough for his purpose and he donned the black velvet hooded cloak he had selected, and put on the mask his valet had provided. He stared at his image in the pier glass for a moment before he left his rooms. He did not want to frighten Lili and to his own eyes he looked a proper highwayman come to life. But as he put the mask in his pocket lest he frighten a maid here, he suspected Lili would guess his identity and his purpose in a very short time.

Seated in the drawing room of the mansion next door, Lili tried to at least appear interested in the lengthy monologue her hostess was engaged in. She had been asked to join her here before dinner to discuss some new decorating scheme Alva Potter had in mind. She could not understand it. The smell of paint applied only a short time ago could still be detected.

"I thought I would change that to ivory color," Mrs. Potter was saying now, pointing a gnarled finger at the offending woodwork. "And what do ye say to striped wallpaper? Perhaps gold and green, and none of yer narrow stripes, neither. I had somethin' broad in mind."

Lili could just imagine how broad and she hid a shudder. For all her money, Alva Potter had no taste. Still, she nodded as if she agreed.

"Then, instead of all this old stuff—I am sure I don't know what came over me to have chosen Queen Anne style when she's been dead almost a hundred years—I shall follow Prinny's example and order some of the new furniture that is all the crack now. Ye know, the settees with the crocodile legs? And the lacquered bamboo tables?"

"It should be very interesting," Lili said nobly. "Are you going to keep the window treatments? Those draperies and undercurtains look brand new."

Mrs. Potter stared at the heavy gold brocade. "No, they must go as well," she decided, turning to stare at the Cartel clock on the mantel. It was not the first time she had done so. Lili wondered if she was hungry for her dinner. She had been told Mrs. Potter preferred to dine at three in the afternoon as she had when her husband had been alive. It was only to conform to fashionable custom that dinner was now so late.

"You are thinking of changing that handsome clock, ma'am?" Lili asked. Mrs. Potter looked startled and Lili wondered why she seemed so tense this evening.

She did not have to wonder long. Suddenly the French doors at the end of the room were thrown open and a tall masked man clad all in black stood there, pistol in hand. Alarmed, Lili jumped to her feet and screamed.

"Well, it's about time," Mrs. Potter said tartly.

Her words, and the fact that no servants appeared to investigate the scream told Lili who the interloper was. Her heart, pounding furiously from the fright she had sustained, skipped a beat. Halpern! Dragging her eyes from what she could see of his face, she saw her hostess was wearing a satisfied smirk on her old, wrinkled face. Furious, she picked up her skirts and ran to the hall door, intent on escape. Halpern caught her easily and pulled her close to him with one arm.

"It will be no use to scream, Lili," he told her. "You are coming with me now."

"No, I am not," Lili cried. "I won't go with you! Oh, you have ruined everything, ma'am, telling him I was here!"

"I never told him. Figured it out for himself, he did," Alva Potter said, getting up to pour herself a glass of sherry. She gestured with the decanter, but to her regret, the viscount shook his head. She would have dearly liked the two to work out their differences in her drawing room, where she could listen in, but it was not to be. Really, she thought as she took her seat again, the young are so selfish.

"Will you come peacefully, or must I gag and carry you?" Halpern asked softly. Being held close against his side made Lili feel breathless.

"You would do that? Gag me?" she asked.

"I would like to think you would come willingly, as I assume Lochinvar's lady did, but you may believe I will do whatever I have to," he said.

She could tell by the light in his masked eyes he meant every word he said, and defeated, she nodded.

He smiled down at her and lifted her hand to kiss it. As he led her toward the French doors, Alva Potter spoke up.

"Aren't you forgettin' something, milord?" she asked as she went to the hall door. She took the articles a footman held ready; a scarlet cloak lined in gold satin with a matching bonnet, a pair of gloves, and Lili's reticule. When she saw that article, Lili cried out.

"Yes, of course you must not go without your jewels," Alva Potter told her. "The cloak will be too small, o' course, but 'twill serve. I believe it is a warm night, and I trust ye have not far to go?"

She began to chortle then, her eyes dancing. "No, looking at milord there, I am sure it won't be far at all."

Lili did not seem to understand what she found so amusing, but Halpern shook his head. At the sight of the red that stained his cheekbones, Alva Potter laughed even harder.

"Be off with ye," she said, making shooing motions. "Let me know the end of the story someday, if ye' please," she added.

"You shall have a detailed account, ma'am," Halpern told her as he wrapped the cloak around Lili and jammed the bonnet on her head. "My thanks again. Without your help, I doubt I would have been successful."

Lili found herself half carried across the grass to the mews. She saw the viscount's curricle was waiting for him, the groom holding the team, carefully looking the other way. Only a moment later they were off.

Where, she had no idea, nor did she inquire as Halpern expertly negotiated the busy streets. Instead, and in spite of her joy at seeing him again, she felt a wave of dark despair. Everything she had done for his sake was in vain; her disappearing from his life to no avail. She was not concerned that by going off with him, her reputation was ruined, for who cared what happened to a Lili Martingale. She was nobody. Girls like her were ruined every day. She would become Graeme's mistress eagerly, she knew. At least then she would have some memories to sustain her. But marry him she would not, no, no matter what he said or did. She was sure she would be able to convince him such a move was unnecessary. Why wouldn't he take what she was offering without the marriage tie? It would be entirely to his advantage to do so. And he would be saved. Saved to marry some noble well-born woman who would make him a marchioness he could take pride in.

She stifled a sob and then clutched the side of the seat as the traffic thinned and Halpern dropped his hands. Obediently, the team settled into a canter, heading down the road that led to the coast and the Channel ports.

"You are very quiet, my love," Halpern observed. He had removed his mask and put the pistol away and he did not look like a highwayman anymore. "I wonder if Lochinvar's lady was as reticent as you? But no doubt it was more difficult to converse galloping away on horseback."

Still Lili said nothing. She sat staring straight ahead, for she did not dare to look at him. Just the sound of his deep, teasing voice set her senses reeling. And to her surprise, she discovered she felt a growing anger as well. How dare he just whisk her away and expect her to be all melting compliance to whatever plan he had in mind? Had it even occurred to him that she might have run away from the engagement because she had had a change of heart? And how dare he subject her to this—this kidnapping and expect her to be full of happy conversation? His arrogance was unbelievable! Well, he was certainly in for a surprise.

"Very well, we will not converse," he said so cheerfully she wanted to hit him. "We do not travel far. I knew we could not reach Braybourne with this late start and have arranged for us to spend the night at an inn along the way. You are warm enough?"

When she did not answer, he said in a different tone, "You will tell me, Lili, or I will stop the curricle and wait until you do."

"Yes," she said, and with that he had to be content.

"I see you are angry," he went on, his voice cheerful again. "I suppose it is because I kidnapped you. And yet I seem to remember you saying once you would like to be kidnapped. My, there is no understanding women, at least not for a mere man. Very well. We will be silent. It will give you the opportunity to admire this soft spring evening, the night before your wedding day."

Lili started, but she did not give him the satisfaction of exclaiming, or even crying out there would be no wedding tomorrow or any other day. Time enough for that when they reached the inn he had mentioned.

Chapter Twenty-one

Halpern turned into an inn yard an hour later. It was a small place, set well back from the road. Still, flambeaux burned on either side of the door, and when an ostler came to hold the team, Lili saw they were expected.

She wondered why the viscount's lips twitched as he lifted her down and bustled her past the owner of the inn. But when she caught a glimpse of herself in the glass in the private parlor he had engaged, she knew why. Alva Potter's bonnet was pulled well down on her head. She had not noticed what a garish hat it was, complete with a high crown, two curled ostrich plumes dyed gold, and a large bunch of artificial grapes. The cloak as well was more suited to an equestrienne at Astley's Royal Amphitheater than a lady of fashion. Since it ended several inches above her ankles, her old navy muslin, now much crushed, looked very out of place. Quickly, Lili removed the hat and cloak while Halpern leaned against the door and never took his eyes from her.

"That is much better," he said. "The old dear has terrible taste, does she not?"

Pushing his shoulders away from the door, he came toward Lili and she retreated until the table was between them.

"There are things we must talk about, m'lord," she said.

He leaned his hands on the table and bent toward her, and she forced herself to stand still. "There are indeed," he said softly. "May I suggest we wait to discuss them later? Dinner is about to be served. No doubt you would like to freshen up. You will find everything you need in the bedchamber next door. Do you promise you will not try to escape the inn, or must I come with you to guard you?"

She nodded her agreement and he held the door for her. Lili went by him carefully so as not to brush against even a piece of his clothing. She had no thought of escape. There was no place to go, here in the countryside, and she was too tired to run in any case.

The meal provided was excellent, so excellent Lili was sure Halpern must have had it sent down from London earlier. She knew most inns were not noted for their fine cuisine. Still, she had little appetite, and she was angry when she saw with what gusto the viscount attacked his food, unaware of how little he had eaten these past two days.

At last the dishes were removed, a decanter of port and two glasses placed on the table, as well as a dish of confits, and the host ushered the maids out, bowing deeply before he left them alone. Now they were private, Lili could feel herself tensing for what was sure to come.

Halpern poured two glasses of wine. As he set one of them before her, he said, "Why did you run away, Lili? What happened to make you decide you did not want to marry me after all?"

He did not sound angry, she noted, only confused. She shrugged and looking down at the deep red wine, she began to move the glass that held it in careful little circles. She did not see Halpern's hand until it shot out and grasped her wrist to keep it still. Startled, she could not help a cry.

"Answer me," he ordered. "I think you owe me that courtesy at least."

"Very well," she said stiffly. "If you insist, m'lord.

"I came to see any marriage between us would not be at all suitable. You should be thanking me for saving you from it, not ranting at me."

"I am not ranting. Not yet," he said, sounding grimmer. "Now, who put that ridiculous notion in your head? You gave no sign of your intentions the night of the ball, yet I have to assume you had planned your disappearance some time be-

fore. Did you wait until after the gala so the evening would not
be ruined for the Russells?"

"Yes, that is exactly what I did," she told him.

"How kind of you. Do you remember promising me you
would always tell me what was troubling you and not just
keep it to yourself? Let me help you? Why did you break that
promise?"

"This was not at all the same thing," she said. He stared at
her and she realized how inadequate that statement was, and
added, "I couldn't tell you. I knew you wouldn't understand."

"I suspect, no, I am sure, you did not decide this on your
own initiative. There had to be someone else. Who was it,
Lili? I would have the name."

She hesitated but she knew he would insist she identify the
culprit. She had no intention of doing that.

"Oh, it was not just one person," she said finally, making
sure she did not look away or appear uneasy. "I received three
letters about it, all of them unsigned. Still, I could tell they had
been written by well-meaning members of the *ton*. And they
were not mean letters. They were not written to hurt me. One
of them sounded almost pained that it was necessary to call
my attention to the inequality of the match."

She paused, quite proud of her powers of invention. At least
she was until he said flatly, "You are lying. Lying and spewing
out a fountain of words to try and confuse me and cover up
that lie."

She stared at him, wondering how he could tell. To her own
ears she had sounded perfectly reasonable. "I am sorry you
think so, m'lord," she said. "But whatever you think, I have no
intention of marrying you. Not now."

She reached into her reticule and took out the linen handkerchief. Holding it out to him, she said, "Here are the jewels
you gave me. They are not mine anymore."

To her surprise, he tucked the package away in a pocket,
then sipped his port. "Does it matter at all what *I* feel about
this?" he asked. "What *I* want to happen? Or isn't that impor-

tant compared to the opinion of this unknown dictator? Don't you care?"

"I care. Believe me, I care. So much so I am even willing to be your mistress, Graeme," she told him, her cheeks flushing at her boldness. "That way you will have everything you want without having to contract an unsuitable marriage."

He did not speak. Instead he stared at her, his dark eyes intent on her face. She watched him carefully, but she could see no change of expression. Perhaps one brow twitched slightly; she could not be sure.

"Well," he drawled, never taking his eyes from hers, "that is a tempting offer indeed. How unfortunate I must refuse it."

"Why?" she said before she thought.

"Because frankly, my dear—I may speak frankly? Thank you—because frankly I do not think you would be very good at it. The profession calls for a great deal of expertise, expertise that in your case I fear is nonexistent. No, no," he added, raising one hand although she was too stunned to speak and only sat there with her mouth open, "do not tell me you would be willing to *learn*. I have never taken mistresses who need instruction."

Lili stared at him, horrified. She could see nothing in his face but boredom. He appeared to have changed back before her eyes into the handsome good-for-nothing she had first met on the road to Wyckend. But was it possible he was mocking her? she wondered, staring at him even harder. She thought she detected a light deep in his eyes and she said stiffly, "I am glad you find this so amusing, sir. I can assure you, I do not. And I meant what I said. I am serious about my offer."

"I do not find this at all amusing either, Lili," he said as he poured himself another glass of port. "And I also meant what I said. You will never play the whore for me and that's the end of it."

"Then we appear to be at an impasse," she said swiftly, although she was shocked at his language. "I won't marry you; you won't have me for mistress. What are we to do but part, in that case?"

As she watched, he rose and stretched. "Why, what I originally planned, of course," he said. "We will be married tomorrow at the Braybourne village church. It is all arranged."

"Is it indeed? I wonder you can want a bride so sadly in
need of instruction," she could not resist saying sarcastically.

He grinned at her. "Oh, well, brides are a different matter
entirely. They are not expected to be experienced, you see. Far
from it."

"Never mind that," she snapped. "I am not going to be one
and there is nothing you can do about it. You cannot force me
to marry you, no, not even in the Braybourne church, where I
am sure the vicar stands ready to do anything you say. But
even he cannot perform a service with a bride so reluctant she
will not say her vows."

"This bride will not be reluctant," he said as he came
around the table toward her.

Lili rose so quickly, her chair fell to the floor. But there was
to be no escape. Halpern had her in his arms before she could
take a single step.

"You would try and entice me to it?" she cried as she tried
to twist away. "Where is your pride, sir? Let me go! I don't
want to marry you and spend the rest of my life knowing the
ton disapproves of me and is whispering behind my back, and
so you might as well take me back to . . ."

She could say no more, for Halpern's lips came down on
hers and he began to kiss her. She fought against his seduction,
keeping her lips tightly closed and standing primly still. But he
did not try and hold her close to him, and his hands on her
back, while warm and possessive, only caressed her softly. His
kiss as well was not the passionate, deep consuming one she
remembered. Lili found she did not want this gentle, reverent
kiss. Neither did she care to stand an inch away while he held
her. It was as if she were kissing her brother, she thought, and
Graeme had never been like that to her. Without thinking, she
moved closer, molding her body to his and putting her arms
around his neck to bury her hands in his hair. Her mouth

opened under his and it was then he caught her to him so tightly she gasped.

"There, you see?" he said when he raised his head much, much later. "You do love me, Lili. I was sure of it."

"I never said I did not love you," she protested into the fresh-smelling linen of his shirt.

He picked her up and carried her over to a chair near the fire. Lili sighed and closed her eyes as she put her head on his shoulder. She was so tired, she thought. Tired and weak. She did not think she could fight him anymore. He seemed to have all the weapons in his arsenal while she had none. It hardly seemed fair, when you came to think of it.

"Listen to me," he said and she shivered at the rumble his voice made in his chest. "I have let you have your say, and now it is my turn. I do not know who spoke or wrote to you, whether it was one or a dozen people. It really does not matter. Because, you see, we are not going to pay any attention to society's opinions.

"Think back now, if you will, love. Remember the night of the Russell ball. Did anyone cut you? Sneer at you? Whisper to their friends about you, then laugh?"

He waited until she shook her head before he went on. "No, and they never will. Tomorrow you become Viscountess Halpern, and later—many years later, I pray—Marchioness of Braybourne. Those titles are all the credentials you will ever need to be accepted and revered. But you will see."

"Still, I fear I will always feel like Polly Peachum," Lili said sadly, still trying to make her point. Of course she wanted to marry Graeme. But did she dare in the face of his mother's opposition and dislike?

"You are not an actress. You are a respectable young lady who was most strictly raised in a convent and therefore have every credential for the posts you are about to fill," he told her. He sounded so serious, Lili sat up to look at him.

"Including the most important one, the love and adoration of your husband. What everyone—anyone—else thinks is of no importance at all."

His voice changed then, became huskier. "Say you will marry me, Lili. Say it now."

She hesitated, but only briefly. Then throwing all caution to the wind, she nodded.

"No, you must say it aloud so there can be no mistake," he ordered.

"Will you always be so demanding?" she asked. "Always insist on getting your own way?"

"Yes," he told her. "I will. Are you going to marry me anyway?"

She made him wait for a long moment while she pretended to examine the hands she had clasped in her lap. Then, peeking up at him from under her lashes, she said, "I suppose so, although I do worry that the extensive instruction you are about to undertake might be too wearying for you, m'lord."

Halpern's shout of delighted laughter was soon cut off as Lili began to kiss him.

Epilogue

Some fifty guests came to Braybourne late in the summer of 1817 to celebrate the wedding of Viscount and Viscountess Halpern only recently returned from their extended sojourn on the southeast coast. The gala house party was to continue for a few weeks so the bride could meet all the relatives and friends of the Wilders.

The first time Cornelia Russell saw her young cousin she exclaimed at her happy, glowing face. The viscount looked pleased with himself, she thought. He stood close to his wife, his arm around her waist, and when he looked down at her, his love for her was evident.

"I am sure I don't know why Lili chose that insipid pale blue silk," Alva Potter grumbled beside her. At the groom's request, she had come to stay at Wyckend during the festivities. "Needs a train and some satin ribands, and many more jewels, is what I say," she added, ignoring Alastair Russell, who stood on her other side. She was not speaking to Mr. Russell. He had insisted she remove her very best diamond tiara, saying he could not allow her to leave the house looking such a picture of fun.

The guests were all enjoying the warm afternoon on the broad terrace of Braybourne that overlooked the ornamental water. This evening there was to be a festive dinner and a soiree to which many local notables had been invited as well. Tomorrow there was a riding expedition planned for the gentlemen, and a trip to a ruined castle for the ladies. That evening there was to be a masquerade. The guests had been asked to come as famous historical bridal couples. Alva Potter wondered if anyone would dare impersonate Adam and Eve, but she did not say so. She was on her very best behaviour. There were to be other trips, as well as archery and tennis tournaments, fabulous picnics, even a treasure hunt. The marchioness had worked ceaselessly to be sure the event was a rousing success.

She stood now beside her husband at the balustrade of the terrace, watching Graeme and Lili in the garden below. He had just picked her a white rose, and then a red one. Idly she wondered what they found so amusing about that, for they both laughed.

"You have done wonders, m'dear," the marquis told her. "I can't remember a more notable house party. Surely ours will be remembered for a long time."

Jean Wilder did not look at him. She had only arranged things because he had ordered her to do so. Still, she was honest enough to say, "Yes, it has worked out for the best. Graeme seems happy enough and now there can be no gossip about the match.

"Excuse me. Lady Jersey is beckoning to me, tiresome woman that she is. Perhaps you might talk to the Somerset Wilders? They look quite bewildered over there by the door."

The two separated. Sometime later, the marquis found himself beside his new daughter-in-law. "You are enjoying yourself, Lili?" he asked, admiring her glowing face. "No, that's a silly thing to say. I can see you are. I am glad you are not intimidated by all these crowds. Most of them are relatives. You won't have to see 'em again until the next wedding or funeral.

"Something to say to you," he added. He paused then and stared out at the dark woods beyond the lake. "I know the marchioness wrote to you, trying to get you to cry off. I just wanted to say I am glad you did not heed her. And I cannot tell you how I admire you for not telling Graeme about her plea."

Lili stared at him for a moment. "I would never do that, sir," she said quietly. "Graeme is her son and I know how dearly she loves him. He loves her, too. If I told him it might destroy his love, and that would be a sin."

The marquis picked up her hand and kissed it, to Lili's great surprise. "I didn't like you either, at first," he told her. "As if that matters when Graeme loves you so! But I am happy to admit I was very wrong in my assessment of you. Very wrong, indeed.

"And here comes Graeme now to recapture you. Just as well. I was about to become maudlin, and that would never do. Run along, my dear, run along."

Lili curtsied and went to join her husband. Not at a run, of course. Viscountesses did not run. Then she smiled, remembering all the things this particular viscountess did do, now she had had some proper instruction.

"That smile of yours looks positively wicked," Halpern told her as he tucked her hand in his arm and led her down the terrace steps to the rose garden. "Now what are you about, love?"

Lili's eyes danced although her voice was demure as she told him it would be much better if he did not know.

Halpern nodded, a little absently. He was remembering the letter Cornelia Russell had pressed into his hand earlier this afternoon. It had come under cover from her older sister, she told him after making sure Lili was not in earshot. When he read it a short time later, he discovered that Lili's father, Thomas Martingale, had died this past winter in Italy. According to the letter writer, a Father Maglioni, Martingale had lived in Rome for almost seventeen years. He had achieved considerable success as an artist, completing several commissions for Pope Pius the Seventh. He had not remarried, and he had left all his money to the Church.

Mrs. Russell's sister had written in her cover letter that it could now be revealed that Thomas Martingale had been the son of a talented furniture maker. He had accompanied his father to the Edson home in Yorkshire, to help make a dining table and chairs for the family. There he and Thora Edson had fallen in love. Forbidden to marry a tradesman by her irate parent, Thora had eloped with him and run away to France.

As Halpern tucked the letters away in his coat, he wondered what had been so dreadful about the match that it had to be kept secret all these years. True, the man was not of noble birth, but he was hardly despicable. Families and their secrets, he thought, deciding he would not show Lili the letters until later tonight when they would be alone and he could comfort her when she cried.

For as tender-hearted as she was, Lili was sure to cry. She had told him how she missed the father she had never known. When she learned of his death she would need comforting, especially when she realized how quickly and completely the man had forgotten her in the new life he had forged for himself.

"How serious you look, Graeme," she complained, tugging on his arm now. "Several guests are watching us. I beg you smile, sir, lest they think you are not satisfied with your bride."

He bent his head and whispered in her ear, and Lili had to put both hands over her mouth to contain her delighted laughter.

Up on the terrace, the Marquis of Braybourne smiled as he watched them. But when he looked back, after turning away for a moment to answer another's question, the handsome couple he had been admiring was nowhere to be seen. He smiled again as he raised his glass in a silent salute.